Hemingway's Island

Hemingway's Island

by Eleanor Johnston & Wayne Fraser

Hemingway's Island is primarily a work of fictionalized history. Some characters, particularly Ernest and Mary Hemingway and their circle of friends and employees, along with many of the story's places, incidents and events, are historically real but used fictitiously. The authors have attempted, on the basis of their research, to tell the story of what these people might have said and done when placed in other, fictional, circumstances.

Issued also in electronic format.

Website for *Hemingway's Island* – wayneandeleanor.com

ISBN 978-0-9880716-0-5

Other Publications:

Eleanor Johnston
The Blessing Game - mystery novel in private school
Parent – Teacher Interviews - self-help for parents/teachers
Mr. McAvity's Opa- aid for pre-schoolers dealing with grandparent's death

Wayne Fraser
The Dominion of Women - academic study of Canadian women's literature

We dedicate this book to the God of life and love, to our children, their spouses and children, to all our relatives and friends, and to each other, with love for our lives.

E. J. and W. F.

Early in the new year [1960], Pappy and Tillie Arnold invited us for roast beef at their Ketchum, Idaho house and, since Ernest hesitated to drive at night on the slippery roads, came out to pick us up. Snow was drifting down without wind, huge quarter-sized flakes, and in the eave lights outside their big dining room window it was a fairy-tale spectacle. But looking out Ernest noticed lights in our local bank down the hill a couple of blocks away.

"They're checking our accounts," said Ernest.

"What nonsense. Who?" said I.

"R.G. works late sometimes," Lloyd said. R.G. Price was the bank manager and a genial friend of all of his clients.

"That's just the usual cleaning women," Tillie said.

"They're trying to catch us," said Ernest. "They want to get something on us."

"Who's they?" I asked.

"The FBI," said Ernest flatly.

"Maybe you're tired, honey," said I. I had never seen my husband so disturbed about an imagined, illusory threat.

Mary Hemingway, *How It Was*, 1976

Tuesday, July 19, 1960

And if you ask how I regret that parting?
It is like the flowers falling at Spring's end,
confused, whirled in a tangle.
What is the use of talking! And there is no end of talking--
There is no end of things in the heart.

Ezra Pound, "The Exile's Letter," 1915

"Wife pinch-hits for Ernest Hemingway!" Or imagine this
headline: "Ghost writer for Nobel Laureate pens memoir!"
I realize, of course, that the editor and the readers are interested in me only as Wife of Ernest Hemingway. I can,
nevertheless, bear witness to our last week in Cuba. I can, in
fact, attest that we are being booted out.

Here's the situation. *Life* Magazine has contacted my husband, the publicity magnet, to write his impressions of the
Cuban Revolution while he is still living here. The editor is
fishing for dirt. Has Ernest gone Commie? Is Castro backed
by the Russians? What happened under Batista?

Ernest is too anxious, and usually too drunk, to think
straight, let alone write a coherent sentence.

His Royal Hemorrhoids has asked me to write the piece
for him and actually announced our departure date as next
Monday. This gives me the structure for my article: "Letters
from the Island," seven letters, to the readers of *Life*, one
per day.

I was just getting started this morning in the writing room
of the Finca tower when Ernest came stomping up the three
flights of stairs. I remembered the time he criticized my
writing and smashed my typewriter.

Today he began to give me instructions about how and what
to write, and I told him firmly, despite my fears, that I am

writing in my own style about how we are being tormented and forced to leave this otherwise gorgeous life we have here in Cuba. What more does any reader want than conspiracy theories and glamorous lifestyles? A mix of spies, sex and sun? Well, I can still do that.

Ernest said he wants to use my notes for this magazine assignment as fodder for his next memoir. I told him, "I don't like the role of research assistant, thank you very much!" Fodder, indeed! My goal is to provide compelling material about Cuba and our life here, using events of the coming week before our forced departure on Monday.

But Ernest kept bellyaching. I snarled, "If you want to get started on yet another book, start writing." Sometimes I have to force him to see the obvious.

I reminded him that he'd said he'd paint some black magic symbols on my cover page. He sat down at the paints I had prepared and made a few strokes, and abruptly the images appeared. Nothing like a little voodoo to scare off spooks and baggage handlers.

I told him of my plan to carry my articles to Key West and mail them to New York from there. I certainly wouldn't mail them from Havana. Why? Think spies. He asked me how I thought Key West would be any better. Briefly it felt that we were working as a team, and I was glad he had come up.

Ernest was right: getting these letters to the publisher may be tricky. He said that our major challenge is figuring out how to spirit my manuscript past the spies and counterspies who will be watching us carefully as we go through both customs.

Probably no one in Washington, Havana or Key West has a clear idea of who's spying on whom, but we suspect that the people currently in power, if they get their hands on this document, will simply confiscate and burn it, black magic be damned.

Ernest stood up then and moved over to the window. Leaning against the frame, he looked down. His face went pale, and for a minute he didn't move. Whatever was engrossing him made him wince and turn abruptly towards the stairs. Still huffing and puffing, he stomped off past me as if I didn't exist. I went to the window and looked down to see what he'd been looking at. Nada.

Then I noticed two overweight men moving away from the fence of the property. Both were dressed oddly. By the time Ernest emerged from the base of the tower and looked around, they were out of his sight, hidden by the shrubs along the fence. He turned right and took the path to the back door of the kitchen.

In the still-early quiet I start clicking away on paper twinned with carbons. I will keep the copy on me until I set the top one on the *Life* editor's desk.

I'm using an extra portable Royal that I had bought for Ernest. It's on the mahogany desk I found for him and set up on the top floor of the tower I had built for him. This space has everything a writer needs, but he has lost the knack of writing and in the past year or so has only pecked away down in the main house, distracted by every person and thing that moves. After building the tower for him, I'm discovering its usefulness is primarily for me.

When I phoned the editor to inform him that I am doing the writing, he seemed quite surprised by our departure plans. "Why are you leaving Cuba?"

I gave him the dramatic pause, then said, "That is precisely the question your readers will want me to answer. They might also want to ask, 'Who is persecuting Ernest Hemingway?'" The phone line went silent, as I thought it might, our phones having been bugged off and on for at least a dozen years now. Waiting for our line to be reconnected might take awhile, but for now the editor is intrigued with me as his author.

We have only one week left in Cuba. No one ever notices me or what I do, so my plan is to come back to supervise packing after I get Ernest to Idaho in one piece. We have so much stuff here, starting with 8,000 books and hundreds of boxes of letters and pictures. I couldn't get packed up in a week if I tried, especially with hours of writing every morning and Ernest so distraught.

I know in my bones this will be our last time here together, and already I feel nostalgic for our Finca Vigía and for the time when Ernest still hoped he could write more great stories. For him to ask me to do his writing is totally out of character and, I fear, a sign of desperation.

He has watched the persecution of Arthur Miller after the production of *The Crucible*, the play that perfectly demonstrates how the American fear of Communists in their midst is destructive hysteria fostered by the authorities. No wonder Ernest is afraid to leave the Finca Vigía and return to the US of A. There you have it, Americans! You need to know that the Red Scare is simply your government's means of controlling you and that your freedom is best defended by your artists.

Why are Americans so obsessed with being all-American or un-American? America's most famous novelist chooses to write about a Cuban fisherman and about wars in southern Europe. Said writer hasn't been back in decades to his childhood home in Oak Park, Illinois, not even for his mother's funeral. Said writer has spied for his country. How does one define "American?"

Everyone thinks that it was the fault of Ernest's mother that he fled his mid-West background. He has always had a trapped look about him, and he talks about his mother as a monster. At times he has felt imprisoned by each of his four wives (including me) and his two serious lovers, the two that I know of.

The big monsters are his other prisons: alcohol and his bad-ass blues. Nowadays he blames the Federal Bureau of Investigation and the Internal Revenue Service. He is somewhat paranoid but mainly justified. These agencies are tormenting him. Then you can factor in all his physical aches and pains. He is not fooling about being suicidal. I've got to agree, his life warrants suicide.

Ezra Pound was Ernest's mentor, helping him get published when he first arrived in Paris. When Pound fell in love with fascism, Ernest was torn between belief in freedom of speech and frustration with Pound's radio broadcasts for Mussolini. Ernest saw Pound jailed in an American psychiatric hospital, and since then he must have worried that his own sensitive mind might lead him to suffer at the hands of American authorities.

So here I am, writing. "Just the facts, Ma'am." That's what an editor actually told me once. "Just the facts," indeed! As if I didn't know how to write a feature article. As if he didn't know that I am an educated reader and a successful reporter in my own right.

At least I was before I became Mrs. Hemingway. Since then I have been at his side. Hunting, laughing, drinking, seducing, right there in all the pictures. No other women in sight, since I manage things so well. He is my full-time project, and he has left everything to me in his will. I expect his sons to sue, and they just might win. That's why I need a large influx of cash from *Life*. The editor is offering a good rate and promising more assignments.

"Reader, I married him." I've always admired Jane Eyre's stoical triumph. Isn't that what you want, too, but with a whole lot more bodice ripping?

Sorry, but I'm writing about an unhappy marriage that is likely to end all too soon in . . . . I have scribbled out the next two lines. There isn't time to type the page again. I feel like whispering what I've just erased and begging you to promise never to repeat it, but "you" are thousands.

Perhaps he'd be better off without me. I don't need all his money, let alone the aggravation of taking care of him, and since the incident with the ceiba tree, he looks at me with hatred and I look at him with anger and disgust.

What incident? Well, a massive root of the old tree at the front of the house was breaking the floor tiles inside. One afternoon, when Ernest was off drinking downtown, I called in a gardener who lifted away the broken tiles and sawed off a chunk of the root. I knew perfectly well that Ernest forbade anyone to trim any tree on our property, especially the sacred ceiba. But I had to do something about the floor.

Ernest appeared and started yelling. The carpenter took off, and he was lucky that he escaped being killed since Ernest was shooting at him from the doorstep. I distracted Ernest by grabbing my rifle and shooting out the open window. He swung around and I turned to face him. For a second that stretched into many, we both froze, our loaded guns pointed at each other. Then he turned and took aim at the trunk of another tree, but he didn't shoot.

I won't leave him. We have grown together through all these years, especially these last months in Cuba. Of all the women he's flirted with, I'm the only one who has seen the worst of his illnesses, his temper and his drinking. I am the one who has stuck with him.

Rumors whispered become facts.

Tuesday, July 20, 2010

"It will be wonderful, Tatie," my wife said. . . . "When should we leave?"
"Whenever you want."
"Oh, I want to right away. Didn't you know?"

Ernest Hemingway, *A Moveable Feast*, 1964

Morning

Some vacations are as laid back as a voodoo curse. Take my week in Cuba. What were my plans? To have a romantic time proposing to my girlfriend, Beth. And to find Mary Hemingway's unpublished article. The reality?

I remember funny and sexy moments, for sure. The overall impression is of danger, of Beth and me in flight. On that trip I learned that Ernest and Mary Hemingway's last week in Cuba was painfully sad. Cuba, where Hemingway realized he couldn't hide. Cuba, where I learned I was a thief.

We had arrived late Monday night. That next morning in Havana we had to wait at the hotel reception desk. I felt cool, imagining myself newly married and in Paris. To be honest, I was fretting that Alicia, our Cuban tour guide, was late.

Now Hadley, Hemingway's first wife, was every man's dream of an obliging young lady. I loved the way they spoke so formally, so kindly to each other in *A Moveable Feast*. That was Hemingway's nostalgic-for-the-glory-days-in-Paris memoir. And Hadley was the one he blamed for losing the manuscripts of his early stories.

A young lady approached, wearing a nametag: Alicia, a chick with one glamorous smile and two--I blurted, "Where's the taxi?"

I don't do transitions when I'm tense. She looked me up and down, slowly, and glared into my eyes. I ground my teeth and took a deep breath as Beth has instructed. As every woman since kindergarten has instructed.

What I like best about Hemingway is his short sentences. Strange that no one has written a paper about the odds of his having Attention Deficit Disorder (ADD). Or Attention Deficit Hyperactivity Disorder (ADHD) for that matter. He had every other 20th century disease!

Alicia, the private guide I had hired from the Travel Company of La Vieja Habana specifically for her advertised expertise in Hemingway, was meeting us in the foyer of our downtown hotel. The Meson de la Flota on Calle Mercaderes had once been a family business at street level and a home on levels two and three. The central courtyard featured a spectacular skylight pouring morning sunshine down to the lush tropical plants on the second floor mezzanine. Outside the elegantly tall doors of the bedrooms was a perfect view from the hallway lounge to the flamenco band and dancers on the small stage in the middle of the ground floor café. Their show played every night but Monday for two hours after sundown. Beth wasn't sure that this free flamenco show was a plus.

I entertain myself by practicing using long sentences and long paragraphs because my thesis advisor told me to grow up.

Alicia had turned her back on us, handing a parcel to the man at the reception desk. Aware that we were in the land of duplicity, where every other adult was said to be a spy, I took note of the name on his hand-written nametag: Federico. He did look suspicious. What was in that package?

Beth, my girlfriend, is at heart just like Hadley, way too good for me, as her intimidating father once muttered at me. Well, that story can wait. The thing about Beth was that she was suffering from morning sickness, and she was not a happy camper. I was agonizing, meanwhile, wondering when I would succeed in transferring the ring from its box in my pocket to her finger.

We had hired Alicia's expertise for three hours, and she began to give us a sleepy Grade 10 introduction to "the great writer." I didn't want to embarrass her, but I did not have time to be excessively polite.

I was the search party for a minority faction of the Hemingway list serve, a quixotic group consisting of my dad, my thesis advisor and myself. I had a specific but challenging goal: despite assurances from the Cuban government that the great Hemingway library was being restored and protected, we suspected that his beloved collection was steadily deteriorating because of the black market sale of his books and the humid Caribbean climate. I had to discover what was going on and what could be done to improve the situation.

I occasionally have trouble with subjunctive and conditional verbs. And I'm better with thoughts than actions. Like Hamlet. Alf O'Malley, University of Toronto undergrad at Vic College and now a perpetual grad student, I am easily riled by lesser mortals. Just kidding. I had finished all my courses and given myself one more year to finish my doctorate and land a real job. The pernicious pressure of the past perfect! My past was never perfect. My present, however, is fantastic.

My second quest was to determine if Mary, Hemingway's fourth and last wife, had actually written an article for *Life* Magazine about Hemingway's last week in Cuba. And if this article had once existed, why had it not been published? Had it survived the subsequent half century? If it had survived, where was it and was it readable? If all these qualifiers answered positive, what message was Mary trying to convey?

Most particularly, would it provide the substantial proof I needed for my doctoral dissertation? I had reason to suspect that Ernest Hemingway had been harassed by the FBI operating in Cuba as part of its campaign against post-WWII Communism. Would Mary's diary of their last week here record such abuse?

I hoped so. I had started writing my thesis at least partially relying on this document, assuming I would find it. I had to find it.

I was hoping, as well, to find some people who actually knew Ernest and Mary Hemingway, people who could verify what Mary had written about Ernest's interactions with the FBI.

On the Hemingway list serve, scholars had speculated that this rumored document, somewhat bluntly and totally unofficially entitled "The Woes of Mary," had been written by one of Hemingway's sons, using a voice that vaguely imitated Mary's, to demonstrate to his therapist how completely messed up his home life had been.

Another theory made Valerie Hemingway the real author. She was Hemingway's secretary in their last months in Cuba, and she later married his youngest son, Gregory. She may well have had reason to control what Mary might write about her.

Another, well, okay, my theory was that Mary was the author, just as she claimed, and that her description of her last week in Cuba with Hemingway was the draft for an article commissioned by the popular *Life* Magazine as a portrait of their last week in Cuba before they were forced out, in July, 1960.

I had contacted *Life* to inquire about Mary's commission for this article. They had no record of it. Perhaps that was true. Perhaps they were hiding something.

"Can we take a taxi out to the Finca for the morning?" I'm not exactly an expert, but finca, for those who don't know Spanish, means farm. Vigía is lookout. Hence the name of Hemingway's 1940's and 1950's home in Cuba is Finca Vigía. There was not much of a farm, as in crops and livestock, mostly living quarters and jungle. Hemingway claimed to have been the first person to import cattle to the island. He introduced four cows to Cuba as a means of supporting Fidel Castro's program of supplying milk to all children in order to improve their health. Somehow I couldn't picture Hemingway in farmer mode. Someone else would have had to do the milking. I could, however, certainly picture him taking the initiative to help out the poor.

Another feature of the Finca that fascinated me was the lookout tower that Mary had built for Hemingway, hoping he'd use the desk, chair and portable typewriter on its top floor as a place to get away to and write beautifully, as he once had. That didn't happen. As far as he was concerned, the lookout was only good for his spying operations. During their last week living in Cuba, however, Mary used this office to write her diary of that crucial week. That was the rumor, anyway. Ironic, eh?

"Sí, señor, but do you not want to see Papa's room in the Ambos Mundos Hotel and have a mojito at la Bodeguita del Medio, then take a taxi out to the Cojimar harbor after we see the Finca? Usually with tourists we do all these places and return to el Floridita for a Papa Doble before I leave them for their lunch." I could see Beth was impressed by Alicia's knowledge.

I wasn't. "Was Hemingway your Papa?"

"You do not use that name?" Alicia was beginning to look irritated with me, but really, I can't stand that nickname.

"No, do you?" I said. She rewarded me with another disdainful glance.

Alicia informed me, "When I do, I pronounce it properly, as he and his friends did, with emphasis on the first syllable. Also, it's pronounced Po Paw, not Paw Paw. Also, in Spanish Papa is Pope, not Daddy. He thought he was that important."

"How do you know all that?" I demanded.

Beth, my better half, and I mean way better, looked at me, perhaps annoyed by both our guide and me. She is a patient sweetheart, but this trip was my show. She was along for the sunshine and some fun with me. If she found time to learn something about her current majors, frogs and world religions, great.

I'm still wondering if she considers frogs and world religions juxtaposed, synonymous, or what. We've been together for almost a year and the longer I don't ask, the harder it is. It being the question about her thesis topic.

Then there's the engagement question hovering on my tongue, especially now she's preggers.

Speaking of whom, I had seen Beth talking to me but hadn't listened. And I had to work out plans with Alicia. "I figure we can find all the Havana places you've mentioned when we're touristing about on our own this afternoon." Alicia was looking puzzled, but I didn't want to spend all my sparse American cash buying her drinks. "I want to go to the Finca and spend the morning there, exploring it and asking you questions. Is that alright with you?"

"Tourist is a verb now?" Alicia was a feisty chick, challenging an academic in his own area of expertise.

Technically she was right, but I was a long way from capitulation. "It was an ironic misuse of slang."

Beth's head was swinging back and forth between us, apparently enjoying the verbal jousting. She definitely did not want alcohol in the morning. She hadn't had even one drink since she pulled the goalie. I think that metaphor is hilarious, but I can't quite bring myself to think much about the next step of her biological life. I wondered what she had been trying to say just then. She needed to speak up.

Front Desk Guy, the concierge/waiter/custodian, was hoisting the last of the three nighttime walls up and out of sight, like giant garage doors, to open the hotel's reception area and flamenco café to the street for the day. The air was already muggy although the sun would not reach over the buildings and down to the street for another hour. I bet Hemingway would have described the scene in just the same way.

Alicia stopped her slow and graceful movement towards the street. She did remind me of Hadley! "Would you like a coffee?" Alicia was thin, as were all the Cubans I'd seen so far.

Beth showed a flash of enthusiasm for the first time that day. "Coffee? That would be lovely, Alicia. I'll order three café dobles." She wasn't just being nice to Alicia. We'd slept in. Still, I thought Beth had put an embargo on caffeine. Guess not. Front Desk Guy went to work at a giant espresso machine.

"Suppose they'd have a toasted everything bagel with salmon cream cheese?" I knew she missed her Timmies. She grinned back, like a puppy unexpectedly petted. I wondered if Hemingway had ever heard of take-out food.

Hemingway had killed himself in 1961, so probably he'd never driven through a fast-food place. He was more the hire-a-chauffeur and fine-dining kind of guy. Well, too bad, eh?

Alicia looked quizzically at Beth and asked, "So, can he stop talking?"

Beth looked at me and saw me make a face at Alicia from behind her back. "He's great, just excited this morning." A loyalist lie, appreciated. We smiled at each other. Imagine: I could be a daddy soon.

Alicia pointed to some sweets that looked close enough to donuts that we nodded. She used tongs to lift three into a brown paper bag that she put gently into her backpack. In its side pouches were three bottles of water. The North American backlash against the use of plastic hadn't yet reached Cuba. Front Desk Guy lined the three espressos up on the bar. Alicia tossed one back and gestured to us to do the same. "Señor, señorita, keep with the tour!"

Our hits for the day started with caffeine. Not that we were into drugs, as the customs police had seemed to think. When our plane had landed on Hemingway's island the night before, we had stepped into a fragrant, warm tureen of Caribbean climate as we deplaned. The steward's use of this linguistic travesty spoiled my appreciation of the climate. Damn, I sound just like my Old English prof.

Our welcome to Cuba, however, had definitely lacked warmth. The Cuban customs men fixated on our suitcases and insisted on pawing through our belongings, including Beth's under-wear.

I'd been about ready to make the delay an international inci-dent. Beth wasn't trying to restrain me since she was, typi-

cally, asleep. She knocks out promptly at 10, no matter what
the party. Fortunately, two more customs police came into
the sweat-stinking room. They'd called us a taxi since we'd
missed the last bus into town. What a scam, I thought, as I
shook Beth who was sprawled over the end of a row of chairs.

She slept during the ride as well, not feeling the huge pot-
holes or seeing the palm trees or the old billboards weathered
by time. One even looked like Dr. T.J. Eckleburg. All winter
she'd been going on that she'd never seen a palm tree before.
Neither had I, but I did on that silent ride into the city.

This morning Alicia was leading us out into the heat. She was
wearing an attractive red scarf with the logo of her travel company. Somehow she made a scarf over a tee shirt and a short
skirt look elegant. I felt decidedly old-fashioned in my light-
weight sun-protection travel outfit that looked just like Beth's.
We put on our plaid fedoras that were promptly trimmed with
sweat mixed with sunscreen draining off our skin still untouched by this year's sun.

Alicia was watching us, looking a little puzzled, as she flagged
down a taxi and we headed out of the downtown into the
bright, hot morning countryside. Like I said, I don't do transitions. I'm talking now in terms of linking paragraphs.

In the back seat of the rickety old taxi, Beth and I reached for
the non-existent seatbelts as we swung around a corner past a
dusty construction scaffold. We hit a deep pothole and nearly
stayed there, then lunged at and almost sideswiped a young
family, two parents and two children, no helmets, on a small
motorcycle. What's with Cuban safety standards?

Alicia turned to speak to us from the front seat. "Luis here is a
good driver and San Cristobal is with us." Alicia pointed at the
tiny statue of the patron saint of travelers dangling from the
rear-view mirror and continued. "Are you an American profes-

sor?" She didn't give me a chance to answer, but chattered on as we drove along the Malecon and away from La Vieja Habana. "After the Finca we will visit Cojimar where Papa was inspired to write *The Old Man and the Sea*. There we will find the monument erected by the fishermen and the long bar of La Terraza where they all drank and told their stories."

She was about to tell us that Santiago had died only recently when I interrupted, "Most Hemingway scholars maintain that the tourists' Santiago is just after tips, that the real Old Man died in the 1930's."

"How can a fictional character die?"

She had me there, but I persisted. Beth says I can't quit an argument until I win it. "I mean the fisherman that Hemingway befriended and used as the inspiration for the fictional Santiago." Beth was reluctant to argue, considering it a waste of energy, and she detested the intricate formalities of what she called my wise guy undergraduate debating techniques. But boy, when she lost her temper, I was toast. Basically, she won by knowing she was right. Even when she wasn't.

Alicia, that morning, was game for dispute. "I know what you mean. Hemingway used the old guy whose family did not appreciate his being befriended."

Did Alicia want to alienate her morning's customers or what? At least she cared enough to argue with me, and I decided to pay attention to her on the off-chance that I might learn something. She then explained some remarkable family relationships, claiming that her great grandfather was Carlos Gutierrez, one of the two models for Santiago. "I guess you don't know about the connection between José's family and mine?"

"No, but tell me," I blurted. "Who's José?"

"Please?" Beth was sounding like the mother of a two-year old. What was her problem?

"When Gutierrez left Hemingway's employment as first mate and cook on the *Pilar*, Grigorio Fuentes took over the job and, after Hemingway left Cuba in 1960, Fuentes began to believe that he was Santiago. He'd sit on the dock and tell stories about the good old days with Papa. The tourists loved him and were honored to buy a couple of Cuban cigars that they would smoke together with him as they talked on the dock. The men in the following generations were Tomás, Manu and José. Manu was the model for the boy in *The Old Man and the Sea*, and his son, in real life, is José, my husband."

"So does that mean you are related to your husband?" I couldn't have asked this more stupidly if I'd tried. Which was what Beth, from her expression, seemed to think.

Alicia was more relaxed. "No, but we both have great grandfathers who worked as first mates on the *Pilar*; and Hemingway asked both of them about how traditional fishermen worked and thought and talked. Now Tomás pretends to be Santiago to make money from the tourists."

I was about to say, "Like you do, eh?" but something stopped me. Perhaps it was Beth's vice grip hold on my wrist.

My eyes were drawn to the tropical landscape on either side of the road, a lush green of many shades broken by flashes of brilliantly bright sea. Finally we pulled into a driveway that wound through more dense woods and stopped in front of a big, once-white stucco house.

Wow! The Finca!

I turned to Beth who was quite calmly pushing open her creaking back door. I started to follow her, then told myself to chill and get out my own side of the car.

To the right was the Guest House, a large shed where Hemingway's guests and hangers-on had camped. Its second storey contained bedrooms for his sons when they visited. Tense times. Movie stars in residence got along better with him than his sons did. Hemingway had been endlessly fascinated by fame and popularity, especially his own. His sons were, for the great author, at best a project. They were probably terrified of him.

I bounded up the wide steps to the entrance of the Finca. The house itself was one storey, elegant, with the front wall practically full of windows. I knew that to the left, around back, were the tower and the path past the swimming pool, where Ava Gardner had swum nude, to the wall-less shed, a wooden tent where the *Pilar*, Hemingway's beloved fishing boat, was in dry dock.

I gulped and swung around to Beth. She was still at the bottom of the stairs, smiling, almost laughing. The sunlight filtering through the leaves of the jungle all around us splattered over her. I knew she had caught my excitement.

After all these months of listening to me natter on, she probably knew more about Hemingway than any other Canadian grad student's significant other, to use an ironic cliché! What I had gone on about was not particularly useful for her. Still, over the long nights of the past winter I had appreciated her interest.

I certainly had tried to respond with comparable questions about the mortality rates of one species of frog. These croakers were found only in the wetlands around the Great Lakes of North America. I found this difficult. For three weeks a year they croaked. Made their croaking noise. I don't mean croaked as in died. Although I wished at times they would.

Beth, however, worried endlessly about the possibility of their croaking totally, as in extinction. And she was likewise passionate and nonsensical when she talked about the assignments for her comparative religions course or the lecture series on the Greek etymology of documents contemporary to the early books of the New Testament. Weird and weirder.

"Look," Beth said, still at the bottom of the steps, pointing at the big tree right beside her, "the ceiba!"

A moment's sheer exhilaration washed over me. Here I was, in a beautiful land with my beautiful partner. We had time to sort out the tensions that, if not addressed, could sour our love. I wanted desperately for her to want me for our lifetime.

I was probably wound up even more than usual because I was at the Finca Vigía. This is Hemingway Nut Heaven, Ground Zero. Here would begin the research discoveries of Hemingway's life in Cuba that would grow into a body of respected critical books and biographies, texts that would deliver tenure at UofT and establish my credentials as a Hemingway scholar.

After all, I already knew about one whole aspect of Hemingway's life in Cuba that no other aficionado even dreamed of, thanks to my dad's work as a translator in the espionage business.

My fantasy, despite interruptions, lasted about as long as it took for Alicia to turn suddenly and look towards the Guest House, her face intent. I followed her gaze and saw nothing new except the descent of the blind at one window. Why would she care who was in there?

Beth asked her, "Are you okay? You're pale."

Alicia turned back to us and smiled, "I am fine, gracias. I will speak to our driver." She instructed Luis to meet us at the front steps in two hours. Immediately he pulled over to a shady spot up the driveway.

She saw that we were looking doubtful, still staring at Luis. "If he left us here, he would take your tip money and go fishing or drinking for the day. If he stays here and has a nap he'll be ready when we are ready, and he will hopefully go straight home with your tip. I was a student with him in elementary school. Also, I am friends with his wife, Rosalía, who is curator here at the Finca."

Oh, so he'll need a tip. What's with women these days labeling men as immature? Beth opened her mouth to ask what I knew would lead to Alicia telling a story about this Rosalía's aches and pains and their friendship's up's and down's so I interrupted. "Have you heard of the early Hemingway stories lost by his first wife?" Alicia looked puzzled. "On the railway platform," I continued. "Early Hemingway means Hemingway when he was young, living with his first wife, Hadley, in Paris. In the Twenties."

As I spoke, Alicia's expression relaxed. "Señora Hadley. She did not come here."

"But have you heard about the stories she lost?" I could make conversation too. I hoped Beth was noticing.

Alicia looked puzzled as she peered over my shoulder at the Guest House. "Señora Hadley did not lose the stories."

"What?" I was astounded. "What do you know about Hadley?"

"Hemingway told his fishing friends that he had been torn between Hadley and Pauline who insisted that he blame Hadley, and he had done so." She paused to make sure we understood what she meant. "Pauline had enough money that he could spend more time writing. So he left Hadley and their baby and blamed her for losing the suitcase full of his early writings. Later he realized Pauline was not as attractive or as, how do you say, congenial, as he had thought, and he wished he had stayed with Hadley."

"Do you know where the lost papers are?" I had to ask. She couldn't possibly.

"Sí." Alicia laughed when I whipped my head around to stare at her.

"Where?" I repeated.

"I may someday tell you. Perhaps."

Here I was, at Hemingway's Cuba home, talking to a young woman who seemed to know more about him than I did. And she had opinions. And she claimed to know the whereabouts of the long-lost early manuscripts! I swallowed repeatedly.

Beth had wandered back down the driveway a little and stood at a pathway opening into the wall of green brush.

"Come on," I said to Alicia. "Let's catch up with her. Where's she going, anyway?" I reached for Alicia's elbow, and she haughtily pulled it tight against her ribs. Oops. She actually sniffed to indicate indignation. Okay, lighten up.

"Señorita, please, wait for us," she called, and hurried ahead of me along the road and into the opening.

There we found my wife (well, technically not yet), seated at a round stone table with two chairs in the middle of what was an enchanted, solitary glade. Glade is my all-time favorite Victorian word. It almost makes Tennyson and his ilk tolerable. Beth waved to draw my attention to various unfamiliar song-birds. I gestured to Alicia to take the other chair. She did so, and I perched on a large rock behind Beth. We sat in what I felt was a friendly silence, drinking from our water bottles, hats off, the breeze cooling our sweat.

"Hemingway and Mary had their lunches here," Alicia said. "She had a gazebo built in this clearing but it's now rotted away almost without a trace."

I waved at her backpack. "Let's break out the pastries. Seems like a good time."

Alicia held up her own water bottle. "This is water not from a tap. This is the only kind you will drink. Correct?"

"Hemingway would have had beer out here by this point in the day, right? Must have been restless to leave this place and go into town to the pubs so much."

"When we reach the Floridita bar, I will tell you the story of Hemingway's statue in the corner and show you the pictures of him sitting there with Spencer Tracy."

"Don't you like to drink?" I asked, diving off-topic. I'd already told her we would do the pubs on our own, later. And everyone knows the Tracy-at-the-Floridita story.

"Let us do the math. I used to be paid $10 American per month as a teacher. Each double daiquiri costs $8 plus tip. I can buy a week's food for less than one dollar. The value of the currencies we use is disordered."

I persisted. "Hemingway was looking for stories with local color. And after he'd watched the sophisticated Europeans try to exterminate each other for two generations, he began to think that the primitive Cuban fishermen were better people than the educated Americans, more dignified than the self-destructive Europeans."

"The noble savage as racist myth." Beth sometimes talked in article titles. As well as being a theolog, she wrote for *The Garlic*, a satirical Toronto zine into scorn for political correctness. I was waiting for that craze to pass. I sometimes thought that the frog craze was a joke.

Alicia took a long swig from her water bottle. "Are you saying that Cubans are primitive?"

"No, no, no! Sorry!" Beth leaned forward and smiled.

Maybe it was the heat, I thought. A crashing noise from the garage ended our awkward conversation.

Seconds later, Alicia was sprinting out of the glade towards the open yard in front of the steps leading to the deck of the house.

I grabbed Beth's arm as she started to follow. "Stay here, out of sight!" I pulled her into the bushes on the inside of the circle. We kept down, and she huddled under my arm as we heard shots, more shouting, silence. We waited, shivering and sweating, fumbling for our phones.

Beth asked, "What are you doing?"

"Turning off the volume. It's now on vibrate." Maybe my hands were on vibrate.

"Call 911?"

"No! This is Cuba. I don't know how to call for help! We've got to get away from all of them. Last night, I told you that the army and police are all fighting each other for control of the black market."

Someone's footsteps were at the table. "Beth, Alf, where are you?" It was Alicia's voice. "The fighting has stopped."

"Here!" Beth whispered.

"Keep quiet," I urged.

She persisted. "We can trust Alicia, for heaven's sake!"

Alicia called, "It is safe now. Come out!"

Beth gingerly picked up her bag, and I picked up my own. Alicia held back some branches as we emerged with dirt on our jeans, twigs and leaves in our hair. I handed Beth her hat from the table and pulled mine on.

By speaking sarcastically I was, I hoped, able to sound calm. "Oh, hi there, Alicia. We were just looking for some poison ivy."

Beth cut through the crap. "Was that gunfire we heard?"

Alicia looked like she too was faking calm. "Ready? Let us find Luis and leave here." But neither Luis nor his taxi was where he'd parked. In all the noise I hadn't noticed a car engine.

"Let's move it," I said, pulling Beth's hand and heading out the driveway. "Are you sure it's safe?" I shot at Alicia.

Struggling along in her high heels, Alicia barely kept up with us. "We can find a taxi outside the gates, in San Francisco de Paula, and it will take us to Cojimar."

That shut me up. I concentrated on helping both women make a speedy retreat. Hemingway would have sent them on ahead and returned with a glistening rifle or a high-powered shotgun and cleared the place of bad guys. Yeah, well, it was his place.

Afternoon

Once we reached Cojimar, the fishing town made famous by *The Old Man and the Sea*, Alicia put some effort into making our time together a more or less touristic experience. She led us along the main drag, pointing out historical and geographical landmarks. Still, since we'd run from gunshots at the Finca Vigía, the Mecca of our trip, Beth's enthusiasm for another Hemingway site was weak. And this village was crowded.

Alicia tried another tactic. "Would you like to meet José, as well as his mother, Francesca, and his grandparents? José's father, Manu, died some years ago, but as a boy he played every day one summer at the Finca Vigía with Hemingway's sons and he was the model for the boy in *The Old Man and the Sea*." She was starting to repeat herself.

"Your husband's father? You can't be serious!" Definitely too good to be true, I said to myself, grinning at Beth's chagrined can-you-not-be-so-childish look.

"Well, of course I am serious. We were nearly involved in a gunfight at the Finca that I was contracted to show you. This is the alternate tour."

Beth stopped abruptly, and we were almost separated by the crush of people swirling around us. "Do you mean that you always take your guided tours to an alternate destination when shots are fired?"

"No, please, do not misunderstand. You are the first people I have taken to meet my Fuentes family. I always like to visit them, and you who are Hemingway aficionados, you will have questions about him."

Would I ever! In my sudden excitement I took a short run at Beth and tackled and lifted her over my shoulder like a sack of potatoes. I kept twirling her around while she tried to get me to stop, and stop I did after just a few turns because I was dizzy.

"Gracias! Gracias! Por favor, step away." It was Alicia, shoving the crowd back and, I noticed, protecting our belongings from this sudden pickpocket's dream scenario.

When we stopped, we both staggered and would have fallen had we not been caught by passers-by. I love the plural on the first words of compound nouns. The Canadian favorite is "Governors General."

"What the hell do you think you're doing?" Beth was so angry with me that she was actually spitting. I'd never made her so upset before, and here we were, on a street in a town whose name I'd forgotten, surrounded by strangers laughing at me in Spanish.

I sank to all fours on the sidewalk, my headache pulsing. In those few seconds I figured out what I had to do. I looked up into the still-moving crowd. It was growing more tightly packed between building and street by the minute.

Turning around to where Beth's voice had come from, I lifted my hands and grabbed hers. "I'm sorry, sweetheart! I'm sorry!" Then I stood up and made another turn to face Alicia. "Please, forgive me, Señora!" My dizziness was gone and my contrition was awarded the applause of the crowd.

I turned one more time, slowly, and Beth squeezed my hands and smiled. She held out my backpack to me. Hers was between her elbow and her ribs. "We're okay?" I asked. She smiled.

"Beth," Alicia was shouting over the buzz around us. "Is he always like this?" Beth nodded. "Can you not do anything about him?" Beth shook her head. They were both laughing, with the crowd. I had no idea what all the fuss was about.

"Let's go see Santiago," I said to Alicia.

"Fine," she replied, "except his name is Tomás, son of Grigorio Fuentes who Ernesto used as a model for Santiago. But before we proceed, just check you have everything. Okay? Let us go."

The crowd had thinned in less than a minute, and we continued walking once more down the sidewalk towards the sea.

"But you called him Santiago earlier, not Grigorio or Tomás." I couldn't stand myself but I had to ask.

Alicia sighed. "It is the nickname of Tomás. Can you not understand?"

I answered, "So, let me get this straight. The first model for the Old Man, Carlos Gutierrez, was your great grandfather. He worked for Hemingway but was lured away to work for Jane Mason, Hemingway's mistress, an unstable woman who intrigued Hemingway in the last few months of his second marriage. This was before he bought the Finca."

She nodded. "You are full of information. Most people just assume that the model was Grigorio Fuentes who liked to play the role after *The Old Man and the Sea* came out. Carlos Gutierrez first told Hemingway the story of the old man and the big fish. No one knows if this Old Man was a real local fisherman or a myth or a mix of several people. In any case, Hemingway and American tourists since then have loved it, this story."

I had to be certain I had all this right. "After Carlos died, and Hemingway died, the role of story teller was taken by Grigorio Fuentes. His grandson is your husband's father. He played with Hemingway's sons when he was little. He was the model for Manuel. His name is really Manolito but his nickname is Manu. Right?" I hoped so. I needed another shot of espresso.

"Almost," she sighed. "You'll get us straightened out when you meet the men of the family."

"Whose last name is not Fuentes?"

"Whose last name is Fuentes."

"So your name is really Alicia Fuentes?"

"Yes, by marriage. Few women keep their father's name."

"Okay, it's fantastic! You could be, like, Hemingway royalty in Hemingway circles."

"What is a Hemingway circle?"

"All the professors, scholars, experts and grad students who meet each other every other spring at a big conference and every morning on their list serve."

Beth added, "An online chat group."

Alicia prompted, clearly intrigued. "What do you mean, royalty?"

I stopped, flummoxed for once in my life.

Beth, again, summed up a complex fact neatly. "Hemingway aficionados are most impressed by contact with people who knew him and might provide insight into his life and/or his writing." I just kept walking, grinning, nodding.

"Señor y señora." Alicia stopped walking and gestured to a two-storey shack made of tin.

Beth interrupted her. "We're not married."

Alicia, to my surprise, swung around and gave me a wink. "Not yet."

I casually asked, "Shall we continue?"

"You two are surprising me." Alicia looked from Beth to me and back again. "Come with me. Maybe we will find Hadley's suitcase."

There we were, standing in front of Santiago's house, and I was doing a double take, speechless for once in my life, then full of questions. "Have you seen Hadley's suitcase?"

Another wink while I agonized, then gathered my courage to ask, "Did its contents go for a high price?" What a travesty!

"Keep with the tour, Señor! One secret at a time."

Her knock was answered by a swarm of chattering kids who all tackled her at once. Behind them came a man who looked like a walking chick magnet. She introduced her husband, José, to us and then, as they emerged from the house, us to his very short grandparents, Tomás and Isabel.

"Welcome," said Tomás, after Alicia had explained who we were.

"Thank you, sir, for welcoming us into your home." Well, I can speak formally when the occasion warrants. Beth was looking at me with new interest, I sensed.

But my eloquence was lost on Tomás who responded, "Perdón?" Maybe he had less English than I had Spanish.

Alicia turned to me and smiled. "Just you wait, my friend. José will show you something no American has seen in years." She searched for the right words and didn't find them.

"We're Canadian," I reminded her and shook my head exaggeratedly at Tomás, "No American." He nodded politely.

Beth elbowed me. "You don't have to shout."

"Okay, okay. So what are they talking about?"

"How should I know?" That was about as rude as Beth ever got. José, I noticed, was carefully holding a medal in one hand, its faded blue ribbon in the other.

"What's that?" I blurted.

José silently held it, first, in front of Beth who leaned in for a closer look, then straightened up, obviously perplexed. He brought it to me, and I realized precisely what it was. "Hemingway's Nobel Prize for Literature, 1954!" This was an even greater shock than the gunshots earlier in the morning. Well, not really, but kind of.

"Of course, this is only a copy," Alicia said.

"Perhaps," José responded.

"Señor Ernesto." I turned to see what Tomás was saying. He was still sitting, but now with an ancient, obviously heavy book in both his hands. "*Vaticano Medico*."

What? A Vatican medical book? I reached out and he handed it to me.

Alicia said, "Here, sit down and be very careful. This book is from the time of Columbus."

"What's it doing here?" I demanded.

"Grandpa should not have shown it to you. He is mixed up and thinks you are Hemingway. This was your book, I mean, Hemingway's book, and Grandpa liberated it after he died."

I pushed aside the implication that Grandpa thought I was a ghost. "Do you have any idea what this is worth?" I had no idea myself but I just knew it should be in a humidity-controlled display case under the nose of the Pope's chief librarian and not here. A moment's doubt blew through.

I held the book carefully on my lap. It smelled old. I opened it only a crack so I wouldn't damage the spine. Peering in, I saw a script that looked like Leonardo's, spindly and perhaps mirror-image, with intricate sketches.

"Good God!" breathed Beth. "That looks genuine!"

"What should I do?" I stared at her.

"Memorize the title, author, and city and date of publication."

Alicia grabbed the book from me and carried it into the back room.

"Alf and Beth." It was José. "We must celebrate you in our house with the favorite morning drink of our friend Ernesto!" He gallantly held a tray with several glasses on it, first to Beth, then to me, and then to his grandparents.

Alicia re-entered the living room. "Mojitos, mis amigos. José, this is bottled water, yes?" José held out the tray for her to take a glass and then offered the last one to his grandmother who shook her head. He lifted it.

"Of course. And I washed the mint with bottled water as well. And the rum is our best."

Alicia smiled at us. "José has been a barman at the Hotel Nacional for years so you do not need to worry about bacteria. Grandfather, can you propose a toast to our Hemingway friends?"

The old man lifted his glass slowly and spoke softly, his voice quavering and tears glassing his eyes. "Salud!"

Alicia and José looked at us, glasses held up. I raised mine. "Bung-o!" They laughed as I turned to Beth and clinked her glass. "A toi, Amie!"

She smiled at me. "A toi, Cheri!" For the first time since we had left Toronto, I felt calm. Even calmer when, after a small sip, Beth handed her drink to me.

Minutes later we were snuggled in the back seat of a taxi that Alicia had put us in, probably hustling us off because she wanted to return to the ongoing issues in her family. I pushed out of my mind the questions that had surfaced that morning. Beth suggested, "How about we put off talking about Hemingway until dinner time?"

"Right! What about talking about Alicia's family?"

"No, that's talking about Hemingway. Let's talk about us."

I pulled her closer to me and resumed kissing her, then realized that the taxi's stop had been longer than a red light. With one eye I peered out the back window. Damn! Our hotel! Our driver was watching us in his mirror, silently laughing, and the meter was running. With red faces, we hustled into the hotel, picked up our key from Front Desk Guy, and scurried up to our room, and our bed.

Evening

When we woke up, it was early evening and our stomachs were growling. We quickly showered and dressed up for dinner.

Front Desk Guy greeted us, with a gallant bow to Beth. "Are you dining out this evening? May I remind you that the best flamenco dance show in town will be here, on our stage, beginning at sundown?"

"Gracias, Fede," said Beth.

He gestured towards the stage between the café's tables and the kitchen area. Three men were setting up drums, amps, and cables. Two women in impossibly tight red dresses and improbably high black stilettos were eating with determination what looked like rice and beans. One of the men was in costume as well. He looked like an old-fashioned matador minus the cape.

"Hey, there, Alfred and Beth! How are you?"

I stopped in my tracks, focusing on the older couple right in front of us. Good Lord, relatives!

"Hi!" Beth was sounding more enthusiastic than I was feeling. "We didn't know you were here."

My dad's sister, the tiny Aunt Sylvia, and her husband, Uncle Edmond, tall and fat, stood before us. Short, skinny and quiet, my aunt tended to be overlooked.

Ed, however, invariably drew all the energy of the room to himself. He stuck out his right hand for what I knew would be a manly shake. "We heard you were coming here, and we needed a break from the Varadero resort. We asked your father for the name of your hotel in Havana. We're in town for dinner. May we treat you?"

I turned to Beth who was not looking embarrassed. I was, but I managed to splutter, "Well, how about we have a drink here and work out the evening plans?"

Beth ordered a beer and I did the same, along with a plate of tapas. My relatives, after days of their all-inclusive, watched us vacuum up the munchies. Uncle Edmond ordered another plate and had it placed in front of us. The way he practically drooled on it showed that the temptation to eat was enormous. So why the hell did he choose an all-inclusive? No sympathy. I slowed down on the second plate.

What was Uncle Edmond saying? That he'd heard we were looking for Hemingway memorabilia, and that he might be able to help, but we should be careful, that Cuba wasn't Canada. I had trouble making out what he was saying because he was leaning forward, whispering, his hands covering his mouth so no one but I could read his lips. Our table might be bugged. Beth and Aunt Sylvia were laughing, apparently over a joke.

Had my dad talked to him about our trip? Both were in Ottawa diplomatic circles, somewhat hush hush. I told him, briefly, that we had heard gunshots at the Finca and seen some valuable Hemingway belongings being hidden from the black market by the son of the model of the Old Man, Santiago. I had a very irritated feeling that Uncle Edmond had been asked by his ailing brother-in-law, my dad, to keep an eye on us. They both obviously thought Beth and I didn't know how to take care of ourselves.

Uncle Edmond looked me straight in the eye. "What are you doing, for heaven's sake, mixing with criminals?"

I shrugged, trying not to look intimidated. "Our tour guide and her family are not criminals! They are hiding this old book, along with Hemingway's Nobel Prize medal, from criminals. The Finca Vigía is so isolated and there are so many valuable old books, a lot is going missing."

My uncle was practically spitting. "Haven't you heard that tourists can buy books from Hemingway's library? There are dangerous crooks there, selling books for $200. You should have known better than to even go near that place!"

"Luis is not a criminal," Beth added. "He was our taxi driver, to the Finca anyway. And his wife Rosalía, curator at the Finca, is Alicia's friend."

"Luis Ventura?" Uncle Ed's face was purple. "Luis Ventura was one of the crooks involved this morning. He was in the process of stealing a stuffed head from the Hemingway property. You were in a taxi driven by Luis Ventura!"

Suddenly Beth was crying! Aunt Sylvia was groping through her huge purse and emerging with a small package of tissues. She held one in front of Beth and looked accusingly at me. Or maybe her look was just bewildered. Maybe she didn't blame me. I was feeling guilty enough on my own initiative.

"What's the matter, honey?" I whispered quietly into Beth's ear, wishing passionately that my relatives would evaporate.

Beth's response was to sob so loudly that Front Desk rushed over, solicitous of the ambience of his entertainment space. I hated him as he schmoozed the relatives. He had a good effect, though, because Uncle Ed stood up suddenly, looked at his watch as if he'd never seen one before, and announced that they had to go, that their taxi was waiting. He assured us that Beth would feel fine once she acclimatized, and he was still talking to us and then to poor Aunt Sylvia as they disappeared out onto the street.

The instant they were out of sight, leaving me to worry that I'd be alone to care for Beth's case of whatever, she stopped crying, sat up straight and smiled a smile I could only interpret as conspiratorial. She reached across the second plate to tap my jaw closed, then helped herself to the food. "Pretty good fake, eh?" she asked. "I was getting tired of watching your uncle whisper at you."

I didn't say a word. I took one deep breath. "You're okay, then?" I finally got out.

"Of course, you nit. I was just getting rid of them. They don't know how to leave. They didn't really want to stay talking with us." She lifted her right eyebrow. "Are you upset?"

"No." I looked at her, seething. "Of course not."

"Right, then, I'll get you another beer." Beth's face went from one expression to the next to the next in slow motion. I had to get out of this. This was a familiar feeling. I'd run away before, but where this time?

She now sounded exasperated. "What's your problem?"

"Uncle Edmond was giving me important information and advice."

"What kind of advice? We are adults."

"I know, but he said that Luis and his wife Rosalía are criminals involved in stealing stuff from Hemingway's estate. Doesn't that mean Alicia and José are involved as well?"

"Maybe he's wrong."

"Big Eddy has been with CSIS for decades." She just stared at me. "Canadian Security Intelligence Service, you know, Canada's spies."

"Really?" Her inflection was mostly question, part acknowledgement. "Sorry to interfere, Alf."

I was impressed at how easily she could come around to a new perspective and apologize sincerely. "So what kind of beer are you offering?"

"What kind do you like?"

"Wet, with alcoholic content." We grinned at each other. I blurted, "That was kinda mean." I have no idea why I said that.

"You're right," she muttered.

"Probably not. I'm usually wrong."

There was a long pause while I wanted to touch her cheek. Instead, I looked around and there was Front Desk. "A beer and a soda water, por favor."

"Are you alright?" I asked her.

She nodded.

"So we're okay now?"

"I guess," Beth sighed. "I hate feeling guilty."

"They were totally boring."

"I am sorry."

"Don't say sorry. I love that you're smarter than me."

"I'm not smarter. We're the same. Okay?"

"Are you quoting Catherine in *A Farewell to Arms*?"

"Not on purpose."

The drinks arrived, and we raised our glasses and clinked. Front Desk was happy, and Beth was probably okay. For myself, I felt relieved.

In fact, I was actually cheerful. We decided to eat in since we were already established at a table right beside the flamenco stage. The evening promised a beautiful partner, a promising floorshow, an exciting city to explore! All this and we were still only on the first full day of our week together. Beth had never looked lovelier.

"Let's order," she said as Front Desk swooped down on us, now in evening attire, complete with a worn tuxedo and white serviette over his arm. Helluva long shift. The menu was entirely in Spanish. Within a minute Beth had ordered what sounded like fish, rice and vegetables. I gestured that I wanted the same. Sounded bland and probably tasted watery, but that was fine. Anything to recover from our sugar lows.

"So what's his name again?" I gestured towards Front Desk. "It sounds like Fed Day when you say it."

"Fred in English, short for Federico. You heard right, Fed Day, but spelled F.e.d.e. That's one Spanish name I know thanks to a kid on an exchange program in my high school."

By this time we were on the same wavelength again, laughing about all the people we had met that day.

Eventually, Beth turned serious. "Wasn't that scary when Alicia disappeared at the Finca and we heard gunshots?"

"Yeah, and downtown's scary with police carrying major-size guns at every intersection."

"But the people look so happy. Okay, I know. That's what tourists always say."

"Hemingway was into guns. No wonder he liked it here."

"What's with those treasures old Grandpa Tomás has? That book must be worth a small fortune."

"All I could see of the title, before Alicia snatched the book from me, was *Relatione della Corte di Roma*. I don't think it's a Vatican medical book as the Old Man seemed to think. But it certainly could be one of Hemingway's treasures that sweet old Grigorio or Carlos or Tomás or Manu boy ripped off from the Finca after 1960."

"1960, that's when Hemingway and his wife left town? Why did they?"

"He needed American medical care, and the Cold War was heating up between Khrushchev and Kennedy. Castro was growing nasty and threatening to confiscate all private property, which he eventually did, and that included the Finca. Bad scene."

"Red Scare and all? And the Cuban Missile Crisis?"

"Well, the Missile Crisis was October, 1962. Hemingway left Cuba in July, 1960 and died in July, 1961. For sure, he had a knack for finding himself in the middle of crises. The more guns being fired, the better."

"I never knew that."

"What part?"

"Anything about Hemingway after *For Whom the Bell Tolls*."

"That's a novel. I'm talking about his life."

"But what about Grigorio, Tomás' father? Was he the Old Man in *The Old Man and the Sea*? Surely Tomás is teasing."

"Yeah, remember that the first model for Santiago was Alicia's Great Grandfather, Carlos Gutieriez."

"So how did whichever pretend Santiago get this old book?"

"Probably just casually walked in, said hi to René, the Majordomo, if he or anyone else was there, looked around and took what he wanted. When Hemingway pulled out, he left thousands of books there. They planned to return, after all, but didn't."

"Who's they?"

"Mary, Wife #4, with Hemingway."

"Lucky woman, married to Mr. Chaos."

"She inherited his whole, rather impressive, fortune. A month after he died, in 1961, she came back and Castro himself led her around the Finca that he'd confiscated as the property of the people of Cuba. He treated her cordially and said she could take whatever was specifically hers. She'd point at one of the paintings and say on such and such a date Ernest had forgotten her birthday or their anniversary and in a state of drunken generosity said she could have her choice of the paintings. She'd choose a Klee, then a Masson and so on. After presenting each painting to her, Hemingway hung it back where he had just removed it. Smart lady. She was on the last boat leaving Cuba before the Americans started their embargo."

"So Cold War politics waited for our Lady of Perpetual Scheming to get her little hands on the best goodies?"

"Well, it's been said that JFK held back implementing the embargo until his specially large order of cigars was delivered. That sounds less convincing."

"What about his kids? Hemingway's."

"They got nothing, so they sued. It was a mess. Money messes people up." We sat in silence for a minute during which I thought about what I needed to do in Cuba. "We are pretty sure that Mary wrote an article, or at least a first draft, for *Life* Magazine, about their last week in Cuba."

"You've told me all this," interrupted Beth. "Mary decided not to submit it for publication. It's apparently hidden at the Finca. And we've got to find it this week."

I was glad to see she had a clear sense of my plans and seemed to want to be involved.

Beth continued. "How do you propose to find it this week? Legally?" That's the problem with Beth: excessive legality.

I attempted to regain control. "I am very hopeful, as of this afternoon, that Alicia and José will lead me to it. I expect I can do them a favor in return."

"Do you think it's legal that Tomás has that book?"

"I really don't know. But I would like to verify its provenance."

"Will you stop talking at me as if I'm your student?" She was certainly regaining her spunk. "And wouldn't the book be on the Internet anyway? I mean, it was a printed book, not a one-of-a-kind medieval handwritten manuscript, or a more recent book covered by copyright."

"Yeah, but such an old document is always valuable. It should be at Finca Vigía or, better still, in the José Marti Library. It's not, by the way, from the time of Columbus or Leonardo. The date of publication on the title page said 1640, I think. Roman numerals are hard to figure out."

"I've got three questions: where is the Marti Library, isn't going on Hemingway tours work for you, and how did Hemingway get this book?"

"In Havana, no, well, yes, and I've no idea. But he was living in Cuba and southern Europe for most of his adult life."

"That must have bugged the Red Scare patriots: 'Great American novelist at home in Commieland.'"

"*The Walrus*?" This is as far as I go in my efforts to draw Beth's attention to her somewhat irritating habit of passing off magazine titles as opinions. Perhaps she finds my responses indicative of admiration. As if *The Walrus* were around in 1960! Cool subjunctive, eh?

"Great American novelist wins Nobel Prize for Literature?" Beth ventured. "Too easy. Just name any newspaper in the US of A in 1954. Was that the real medal or a copy?"

"I don't know. They just flashed it by our eyes. Hemingway gave it to the people of Cuba."

Beth nodded. "Well, those two families qualify as 'people of Cuba.'"

"Ha, ha. He presented it to a church at the other end of the island, called el Cobre. It's like the superstitious thing to dedicate something valuable to this statue of Mary."

"Perhaps we saw a copy, and the original is around a statue's neck."

"I don't know."

Beth had really perked up, but I was starting to fade, thanks in part to the beer. It was also growing increasingly hard to communicate because the flamenco band was warming up.

Actually, by the time we had ordered the house specialty dessert with tea, since there was no decaf coffee, the MC was shouting into his mike that was up at full volume for the benefit of everyone in the small room and out the doors into the streets. He could probably be heard at the Finca Vigía, I grumbled to myself, since Beth couldn't hear clearly, even when I shouted in her ear. I was tempted to rip the corner of my serviette off and crumple it into two ear plugs. I would have if I had long hair like hers.

But the dancers were amazing! This flamenco was like a hot stew of vigorous tap dancing, Irish line dancing, Spanish castanets and Argentine tango.

Beth said being pregnant isn't so bad and I made a joke about being pacté. I had no idea how to spell that word but my Nova Scotian Francophone friends said it was Maritime joual for both drunk and pregnant.

Another pause in the conversation. I made a joke about "Hills like White Elephants" but she didn't get it so it didn't matter. I stupidly tried again. "I'm perfectly willing to go through with it if it means anything to you."

She still didn't know what I meant, didn't know that I would marry her if she wanted, and she could have the baby. I just hadn't really thought through these options when she told me back home that she was going off the Pill. When my next beer arrived she reached for my glass and drank from it eagerly.

"Hey, preggers, no beer for you! I'll get pacté for both of us. All of us."

"Do the French-speaking Maritime women drink when pregnant or perhaps pregnant?"

I could feel myself both exhausted and exhilarated. The flamenco dancers were doing a slow, soft, sexy dance, two women and one man. I wanted to dance with Beth but the flamenco moves were so much smoother, and the tourists wanted to watch the professionals, not us. It felt good to hold Beth's hand and watch her smile as she watched them, then applaud as they finished and bowed.

As we climbed the stairs behind the bar/reception desk, we could see the dancers through the rails of the staircase. On the second floor we sat down in the big chairs, something like Muskoka chairs back home, and we could see the small band and the three dancers doing their next number.

Then we were exhausted. I pulled the huge key for the huge door out of my pocket, and a few minutes later Beth fell into sleep, her lullaby the music, now gentle, below.

I sat awake. I needed to text what I had learned about Mary's article to my email account and cc it to my dad's dropbox. If

I could do this every night, I wouldn't have to worry about smuggling papers through customs on the way back. Using my iPhone, I briefly noted only the facts, and left my conjectures until the next day.

When I had finished, I realized that texting in that quantity was too slow. In future I'd type faster in my email message and send it to my dad's email account as well as his dropbox and my university email.

From our visit to Tomás's home I had learned that Hemingway's friends in Cuba knew very little about whatever Mary had written for *Life* Magazine. I strongly suspected, however, that her unread draft was in the possession of the family of one old man.

Or it might well be at the Finca Vigía, if my source of information were reliable. That source was one Fidel Castro, and I had to break into Hemingway's house.

Wednesday, July 20, 1960

What but design of darkness to appall?
If design govern in a thing so small.

Robert Frost, "Design," 1936

I've just read my Tuesday draft and it's bang-on the word length stipulated in the contract. I'm convinced that the editor will find my account of our last days in Cuba more coherent than the recent meanderings of the great writer. I sense, however, that my writing is too emotional, which is what uptight men say about uppity women who display anger. Ernest, the writer, was, in his prime, the genius of suggested rage. Not my league. Nor can I hope to write a classic essay for *Life*, and I'm aware they don't really want objective structures with emotions bled white into neat lies. What counts is that I can see what's going on here, and name it.

The loss of Ernest's skills is a tragedy to this world.

I am not about to give the editor much of what I suspect he really wants from this B-team writer: gossip about my husband's worsening depression and his growing preoccupation with suicide. I will downplay our squabbles that have sometimes, publicly, ended with my face dripping from the wine he has thrown at me or stinging from his slap. Like at the Ritz! Bastard. Newspapers have always sold copies by scandal-mongering, and Ernest's Hollywood friends play that game. I don't. I'm trying to write to my conscience, to take aim at the big issues, but I live in the everyday.

Ernest has been up for hours, and I suspect he's making plans to go to Spain without me. We had decided to return to our Idaho home to seek medical advice and nurture his peace of mind. If he goes to Spain to do more research for that bloody bullfight article, he will drink way too much again with the Consula crowd outside Malaga. I guess he knows this is his last visit to Spain. We both know he's losing his will to live. I want to tell him not to go, but he'll go anyway. I might just as well pretend to support his decisions.

It's hot and humid again. Already sweat is blurring and stinging my eyes. Maybe the top of the tower is not the ideal writing place.

But first a swim. I approach the huge, deep pool where the Hollywood types used to cool themselves while flirting and wearing off their hangovers. Ernest is there, talking with his friend from before the Spanish Civil War, Dr. José Luis Herrera. He is the most reliable of our friends, a godsend given Ernest's dislike of hospitals and of being treated by strangers.

The good doctor shakes Ernest's hands, bows quickly to Valerie, and scurries off. I had been hoping for a solitary swim. I have always hated watching my husband flirt. Poor me, the big man moans to the star-struck ingénue, reaching along the armrest of her chair so that his hand almost touches hers. The sex of fame. Kitten, Kittner, Pickle, he calls me. He's the pickle, helplessly attracted to any woman who will listen to his stories. I'm grateful to Valerie for doing that. The progress of his marriages, it has been said, is that each wife is more beautiful, rich, and/or famous than the one before. As Wife #4, I take this as a compliment.

The most frequently repeated gossip about our Cuban paradise, apparently, is that Ava Gardner swam naked in the pool. Big deal, we all swam naked. I am naked under a huge towel now, and Ernest, similarly attired, is on a lounge chair, and I can tell by his slow movements that he is in pain. He used to pontificate about all manner of subjects with his hangers-on as they splashed and laughed, some in bathing suits, others not. This morning he doesn't notice me as he drones on at Valerie.

I remember when every male turned and noticed me as I walked by. I was stacked, still am. I've never worn a bra and there was a time men couldn't keep their eyes off my blouse when I'd not done up the top buttons. My first memory of the great Ernest Hemingway was when we met in London and he stared down, wordless. Now he just talks and doesn't look. At me.

I walk along the brilliantly green pathway that leads back past our little gazebo to the house. I am conscious of my need to tour the property, memorizing it for the future. I had this glade near the driveway cut out of the dense jungle-like undergrowth and the whole gazebo, from roof to flooring, covered by mosquito netting. For years it was like a best friend, and Ernest loved it, too, our talking place. Now it is dusty, with ripped netting.

Gossip? I've got some spy gossip, since our world is swirling in it, and sex gossip is a tired whore.

In 1954, Ernest wrote an article for *Life* describing his two plane crashes in Africa. (Imagine living with a man who has survived two plane crashes. Let me put it this way: you can't.) I couldn't believe it when the full text of what he'd written was published. Guess he is so famous that the copy editor didn't dare stop the presses and say, "Oh, Senior Editor, this bit is off the contracted topic and, ah, libelous. And this bit. Actually, the whole thing, you need to read it."

What bit in particular? Ernest mocked Senator Joseph McCarthy by musing about putting a slug in him to cure him of his right wing verbal attacks on innocent Americans.

When I asked Ernest why he did such a stupid thing, he said it was just a joke. Why? Because McCarthy was a joke and his gopher Hoover was a joke. When I said his joke wasn't funny, Ernest said he had to fight back, and words were his best weapon. Still, he had threatened, in print, to kill an elected official. I expected that he'd be thrown in jail, but nothing like that happened.

I figured, if Ernest could call a threat a joke, so could I. When we met Lauren oh-so-cool Bacall in Spain, not long ago, she hung around him, laughing at every dumb thing he said. I came up beside her, my two hands closed, about boob level. I told her, "Which hand? Your choice will be your fortune." She chose the left, and I opened it, sinister, in her face, then held it up for everyone hanging around the celebrities to see--a bullet. "Keep with your own man," I said. If she'd chosen the right hand, she'd have got the same message. She made a prodigious fuss, but stopped her flirting.

If he wasn't a faithful husband, Ernest did hold to a few ideals when everyone else was fudging. If he wasn't a hero in battle, my husband did write of a heroic Spanish woman, a heroic Cuban man, and the sea. He has always been less impressed by Americans. With their nation's great wealth it's too easy for them to go to war again and again or to call their own citizens enemy.

The bull is always charging.

Wednesday, July 21, 2010

Never be daunted. Secret of my success. Never been daunted.
Never been daunted in public.

Ernest Hemingway, *The Sun Also Rises*, 1926

Morning

"Happy Birthday, Dear Ernie!" Somehow I suspect that most
of Hemingway's birthdays in Cuba were not particularly
happy unless, of course, he got out fishing and drinking with
his buddies. No one ever called him "Ernie."

I lay still in bed, letting Beth sleep in until it was time to get
up for another tour with Alicia and José. Beth moved like a
beautiful ghost for the first hour of the morning, I had discovered. She squinted, unwilling to turn on lights, open blinds
or put on glasses. I loved her messy long blonde hair and her
crisp, lacy white nightgown.

When Alicia and José joined us at our small, street-side table,
we were both awake enough to discuss what we wanted to
do for the day. I'd woken up early, worrying about Beth, and
she had quietly thrown up a couple of times in the bathroom.
So far her breakfast was untouched, the bacon fat coagulating
around the egg. I had gobbled my meal when it was hot; now I
felt nauseated.

"Why are you sighing?" Alicia demanded. "You both look
sick. Did you drink some untreated water?"

"No." I paused and repeated, "No." Couldn't she see that Beth
was pregnant?

José reached for Beth's plate and cutlery, asking her, "Okay?" She nodded gratefully and, as Beth continued staring at her hands, I saw, for the first time, the reality of their hunger. There wasn't an obesity problem in Cuba, except among the tourists.

"Can I order two more breakfasts?" I asked Alicia. This was really expensive for a grad student, but once I'd said it, I couldn't take it back.

"Yes, thank you. And I'll ask for toast and clear tea for Beth."

While José concentrated on his meal and the three of us watched Fede put in our order for more breakfasts, Alicia undertook to explain that there was no danger at the Finca so we could return.

Beth came to life for the first time this morning, interrupting Alicia. "Luis was killed yesterday." Apparently, while I was in the shower, Beth had read the morning paper in Spanish. Well, one article anyway.

"Luis Ventura died in the south Habana Hospital last night, as a result of gunshot wounds received at the Finca Vigía, formerly the home of Americano writer, Ernesto Hemingway." Beth can quote like no-one else I've ever met.

"Are you sure?" Dumb question. I sounded panicked, even to myself.

"But no," Alicia said to Beth, "you are mistaken. Our friend, Luis, has left Havana to help his brother at his tobacco farm. Yesterday at the Finca he was just chasing a thief off the place."

"Por favor." José paused, and I could see Alicia glaring at him.

He continued, "The guard at the Finca saw Luis Ventura, our friend Luis, and took a shot to scare him off." We sat, momentarily, in silence. José's voice was basically a whine. He seemed to see himself as the victim of authorities, a wannabe hero with grand solutions but no power.

José looked regretfully at Alicia before continuing. "The guard obviously didn't realize that his boss, Rosalía, had taken the stuffed animal from the living room wall and left it where Luis could easily grab it. He happened to be just inside that door when Luis was stealing the head. His warning shot missed Luis, but scared the hell out of him."

We sat in stunned silence. If Alicia's best friend, Rosalía, was a curator setting up thefts from the Finca, why would José tell us? And why tell us that Luis had not been badly wounded? Was the newspaper report wrong? Uncle Ed had been right.

Alicia looked ready to cry. "No, José, you're wrong. It was Luis Pergolese who was the thief. Our friend is at his brother's tobacco farm." She crossed herself and looked down at her plate.

José didn't budge, just stared at Alicia with a mix of anger and sorrow on his face. "Your friends are not all saints, Alicia. Your friend's husband, Luis Ventura, is in jail. Your friend, Rosalía, the great curator, is also answering questions at the police station."

"I cannot believe it." Alicia was even more beautiful when she was crying.

I turned to José. "Can you tell me who are all the players I need to know?" Their breakfasts had arrived and I wanted to clear up the confusion before trying to eat. "I want to know everyone who is involved."

"Why do you need to know everything?" He was almost belligerent, almost threatening.

"That's what scholars do, find information and develop ideas."

"That sounds like fun." He paused. "For players." Even I knew enough to recognize his irony.

"Humor: that which elicits laughter. The Forceful Fate of Hemingway's Finca." Beth was spreading jam on her toast and looked well on her way to another couple of pseudo-titles that would either defuse the tension or further insult and confuse our new friends.

I tried another tack. "Can you tell me if Tomás has ever talked about an article Mary Hemingway wrote for *Life* Magazine? She apparently has said this unpublished diary never left the island."

Alicia looked straight at me. "Why do you ask?"

"My dad was the translator for our Prime Minister, Pierre Trudeau, on his visit with Castro here in 1976, and they, Castro and Dad, met again at Trudeau's funeral in 2000. Castro had met with Mary several times by then. Even years after Hemingway's death, Mary was still upset at how he had been treated in his last year or two in Cuba."

"Treated by the Cubans? Hemingway had all kinds of friends in Cuba." Alicia was aghast.

"No, not by the Cubans, by the Americans in Cuba," I protested.

"This is incredible!" José sputtered.

"If you will be patient, I'll explain." For once I was dealing with people who jumped to conclusions faster than I did. Deep breath. Smile at Beth who looked somewhat detached from our pileup of suppositions. I tried again. "Mary told Castro how undercover Americans, the FBI to be precise, were operating in Cuba throughout the 1950's."

"That's not news! Surely he knew that," interposed Beth. "They were in all the Latin American countries, trying to destabilize them. They tried dozens of times to assassinate Castro, even using exploding cigars."

"That is just the sort of story that Americans fabricate to make Cubans look cute but dumb, like Desi Arnaz." José sounded furious.

I raised my voice to be heard over the other three all talking at once. "I'm referring to the Director of the FBI, J. Edgar Hoover himself, obsessing over Hemingway living in Commieland. The files have been on the Internet for several years. Every time I look through them I can't believe what I see."

They all stopped while the implications of what I had just said sank in. "You mean Mary wrote an article about these things but did not publish it?" asked José.

"But she told Castro about it?" asked Alicia.

"How do we know this really happened?" asked José.

"Now you see what I'm excited about." I was relieved to see their reactions. I'd been feeling like a precocious nerd hoarding my secret fascination. "Mary told Castro that the article which she lost described the last week she and her husband spent in Cuba." It crossed my mind that Alicia was easily the most beautiful woman I'd ever seen in real life, and that José didn't seem to notice her.

José grumbled. "What's so special about what she claimed happened that week?"

"Scholars have information on most of Hemingway's life except for some huge gaps in what happened after the War, during the Red Scare."

"Which War and what Red Scare?" asked Alicia.

"World War II and the 1950's panic in the United States about the spread of Communism in the Western Hemisphere. Perhaps Mary's article sheds some light on what was going on here."

"But what are you, a Canadian, doing here, looking for an American's article about the American government's war on an Americano in Cuba?" José didn't sound very impressed by me, Hemingway, or the American government.

"I'm trying to get at the truth of what happened because my dad is very ill, and I want to prove that he was right about Hemingway in Cuba before he dies."

I realized I was blurting out what I'd never even acknowledged to myself.

There was silence. Beth added, "Alf's father had a stroke earlier this year. His heart is quite weak, but we can hope."

I looked around the table. The three of them seemed to be waiting for me to do something. I could think of nothing but to continue my search. "I could use Mary's article as the basis for my dissertation. Can you tell me if you know anything about it or about Hemingway's last week in Cuba?"

Alicia nodded. "I know very little. The older people in our families have talked about many manuscripts and objects from the Finca that they don't want tourists to know about, or anybody, so they always talk when they think we are not listening."

As she spoke, my heart rate doubled. "Where are these manuscripts?" I tried to picture the inside of Tomás's house. Where would Mary's be? But first, what did Alicia know about its history?

José, meanwhile, was sneering. "Perhaps we can go and find it at the Finca."

I turned to him and forced myself not to be intimidated. "I thought it might be at your grandfather's place. Can you tell me what you know?"

Alicia looked at José who nodded. She said, "Si, I might know." She paused, "We have heard that a piece of writing was passed from René Villarreal, Hemingway's Majordomo, to José's great grandfather, Grigorio Fuentes. His son, Tomás, the old man you met, referred to it as a story. He claims to have seen part of it. Tomás might know where it is."

I began to grasp that a code of honor had held the valuables of Hemingway and the manuscript of Mary secure for half a century. Now, however, José and Alicia, who had likely never even met anyone by the name of Hemingway, felt the legitimacy of exploiting the financial possibilities of the American novelist's treasures.

José occasionally grimaced as he inhaled the second plate. Very soon he stood up. "Come on, Americano. Do you want a souvenir of your time in Cuba?" His voice, at this point, sounded confident and strong.

Alicia said, "What we will see this morning is the inside of the Finca. The renovations are taking place only in the afternoon.

While the books were kept in storage, rather haphazardly, no one without excellent credentials was allowed anywhere near the house. Somehow theft still goes on. One person was helping himself to boxes of letters. From the basement. For decades it had been totally ignored by humans, the territory of rot, rats and thieves."

"Do you mean you're taking us to the Finca to steal a book or something?" Beth demanded. I caught her eye to stop her talking.

José was explaining to Alicia that she was not to take Beth there that morning. Alicia almost yelled at him, "Do you mean all the books you said you bought for trade were really stolen? Do you mean our friend deserves to be in jail? And you, too?"

"This is not the time to be naïve, or so loud," José growled at her, then turned to me. "I have my bike so we can be there and back by noon. Are you coming or not?"

"Not," said Beth.

I swallowed hard. "Of course I am. Beth, can you stay in our room and rest while I go to the Finca? This is my chance to look around and find out a few things for my thesis." I was astounded to hear myself talking such patronizing drivel.

I switched to pleading. "Castro told my dad that Hemingway was revered in Cuba and certainly not kicked out by him. Castro wondered if Mary's picture of their life here would prove, to all Americans, how well treated Hemingway had been by the government and people of his island. Castro wanted to counter the negative propaganda controlling the West's understanding of his Revolution."

Beth looked at me as if I were out of my mind.

"Castro gave my dad several leads about where he might find the two parts. Dad wasn't able to follow them up."

Alicia sat stone-faced. Her tour had been upstaged, and her husband, well, the likelihood of his keeping out of trouble did not look good.

José, surprising me again, moved around the table to kneel beside Alicia and put his arm around her waist. He sounded sincere, and it struck me that Alicia, staring at his eyes, yearned to believe he was honest. Beth probably would say I have become cheesy in my old age if I shared such observations with her, so I didn't. Or maybe she'd want me to try sounding sweet or something else impossible for me. I should know.

"Just a minute," said Beth to José, then turned back to face me. She was always analytical, even in the midst of emotional chaos. "You've just mentioned two parts to the article. Before that you referred to the article, singular, that Mary wrote for *Life*."

I was so wound up I couldn't stop. "This isn't really important at this moment, but apparently Mary wrote at the Finca about the first five days of the last week and about the last two days in Key West, after they'd left Cuba."

"That makes sense. But, Alf, you told me that they didn't leave on the day they were supposed to. Were the extra days described in the second section or was there a third bit?"

"Whoa!" I exclaimed. "I love your sharp logic, but right now we don't need to look for complications."

"I'm just saying." She used this comment like "Checkmate." Our guides, I imagined, had seen me put in my place, but they had no idea how or why.

"Today, this morning, you'll stay here?" I was just as persistent.

"You're lucky. I could actually do with a snooze."

"Great. Now, Alicia, please excuse us from this morning's tour. Can we do it tomorrow instead? Beth will feel better then." I hoped.

Alicia reluctantly agreed, and I had the feeling that, once José and I had pulled out, the two women would have an interesting talk.

And I, for one, was ready to give José the benefit of the doubt. A man in an impoverished society, he had to interact with tourists interested not in his Cuba but in his father and grandfather's claims of friendship with the world-famous American. He had to pretend to remember scenes of great fishing triumphs and drinking prowess. With the Cuban economy chronically stalled, tourism and the black market were his best options.

I could relate to his having older generations involved in undercover activities. It's just that my family had the law on their side and his didn't. Or maybe it was just that my country was first world and his wasn't. José needed a chance to be a hero, and I decided that I needed to get in on the action.

First, I pulled Beth aside for a hug. "Is this okay with you, sweetie?"

"As long as you come back in one piece." I couldn't tell if she was speaking sarcastically or sincerely.

"If there is danger at the Finca, I'll get out right away."

"Okay, be careful."

I started to say something about bringing back a present for her, but stopped as I realized that she would not want anything stolen. What in the world had I been thinking?

I signed the bill for breakfast and turned to José. "Are you ready, amigo?" He gave me a high five, then led me out through the kitchen to his bike in the filthy, crowded back alley.

Why was I getting on a motorbike with a virtual stranger in an apparently lawless and helmet-free foreign land? That was easy: I would take pretty well any means, legal or otherwise, to get into the Finca Vigía.

Good thing I am a young man with balance! That 10-mile ride to the Finca was the scariest ride of my life. José must be a biker genius or something. He took every turn at full speed, leaning so low I could smell the hot pavement. Must admit I loved it.

He stopped, no Finca in sight. "We are walking now."

I got off, drenched in sweat. "Where are we?"

"Just outside the writer's place." José looked a bit disgusted by my lack of orientation as he pushed his bike through some underbrush. When he stepped back onto the road, brushing himself off, his bike had disappeared.

I followed him in silence until he stopped behind the *Pilar*. An armed guard, waiting for us, soundlessly received José's two Cuban bills and separated the barbed wire for us to slide through. The guard looked at his watch. "Ten minutes."

"Twenty!" growled José. "Come with me." José tied a cloth over his mouth and took his red tourist guide shirt off to cover my face.

I whispered, "What if some police or tourists see us? It's broad daylight."

The guard said, "Keep silent!"

"Shut up!" José growled at the guard, then turned to me. "There is no one in there. Let's go."

We left the guard and jogged along the path, past the empty pool, another checkpoint, another wave, then past the gazebo where we'd rested the day before. Now I was oriented.

I hissed. "Let's go up the tower first!"

"What for? There's nothing in there!"

"I'm going up to the top."

I heard José's warning, "There are broken boards in the stairs!" A rotten plank gave way. Luckily I was moving too fast to be hurt.

"C'mon!" I called down. As I entered the top floor office, I noticed the bright, clean, shine of the room. It had definitely not been neglected for half a century! From the north windows I could see the harbor and beyond that, the old jail and the ocean, no doubt the Gulf Stream. A powerful telescope was set for that direction. Here is where some surveillance might have been done, watching for U-boats approaching the harbor. But how did this telescope stay all that time without "walking" or "being liberated"?

Still, my interest was primarily on the contents of the fourth volume of a set of old Latin books: *Mappamondo Istorico* by Antonio Foresti (Foresti's *Historical Map of the World*) in 13 volumes, published in Venice, 1695. Not on the top shelf as I'd been told. There they were, bottom shelf, quite clearly old documents. I tossed José's shirt around my neck.

I could only hope the volumes were in numerical order. The fourth from the left came out in my hand, light as a paperback. It opened easily and there it was, the ragged hollowed-out centre, just as I'd been told. How could she have done that?

There was no manuscript, only the witness of Mary's selfish, thoughtless, rough cuts. I decided to take it. I had to take it, one part of the story corroborated but still, what use was the manuscript's hiding place without the manuscript? I tripped over the head of the bear rug in my haste to get out onto the landing and clatter down the exterior stairs. José was motioning me from inside the ground floor. As I sprinted in, he said, "We have less than ten minutes left. What is in your hand?"

"I'll tell you later," I said. Or not.

"Where's my shirt?" I tossed it at him.

José was not helping me much with getting into the main building. Having the key might have logically been part of the bribe, or did I have to toss in more?

I ran around the wide walls of the house, frantically. No door budged, but the window of Hemingway's bedroom slid open easily and I squeaked over the low sill, knocking my head on the frame.

I had to stop and gawk. There was his bed, his glasses lying on the bedside table. I heard José, no longer whispering, pleading softly, "Five minutes, no more!" It was pretty obvious, from his tone, that he was furious.

I was overwhelmed to see Hemingway's chair and desk in his office, all those books and trophies, his typewriter. Hemingway, everywhere. I resisted stepping into the bathroom to check if his weight was actually recorded on the wall. Just as Anne Frank's parents left the children's heights on the wall in their attic hideout. Just as anyone would.

There was no time to continue my search. We would have to return another day. Through the window of Hemingway's bedroom, I saw José outside, obviously waiting for me. I rushed out the door, said, "Let's go!" Once I knew how to make it into the house, I was the one worried about time.

José demanded, "Show me what you have." I hugged the treasure to my chest and shook my head.

Swearing softly to himself, José indicated that I should wrap it under my shirt. It was so awkward. The only way was to go shirtless and wrap the bundle under my arm.

He kept me out of sight as he waved to the guard that we were leaving. We raced out the back path, jumped on the motorcycle and were soon roaring down the road, laughing and shouting.

When we were on the outskirts of Havana, José pulled off the road in front of a bar. "We will have a mojito?" He was looking serious, tired. I began to feel the same.

"What about looking like a pair of thieves?" I gestured to my bare torso and to my shirt that was covering my theft. Good Lord, what had I done? "Canadian graduate student imprisoned, charged with theft from Hemingway's home." Not the best way to get a PhD. I missed Beth.

José parked the bike and hid it in the back yard. He told me to stay there, and he went into the bar and emerged a minute later with two mojitos in plastic glasses. Well, at least that was one time I didn't have to pay. Rum in the morning. What was it about Hemingway that called for a drink?

José handed me the drinks that I managed to hold in one hand while he pushed his bike into the underbrush and led me to the empty cabana behind the café.

We sat down and he demanded, "What did you take? What did you do that for? You could have had both of us killed or in jail!" He swore at me in Spanish.

"What's your problem?" I was angry, too. "Don't you steal stuff from the Finca all the time?"

He looked ready to punch me out. I looked past him to the distant sea, trying to cool down. I had to tell him. I explained, for the second time that morning, about Mary's manuscript and how I needed to find it to write my thesis.

José looked thoughtful but still sullen.

But he nodded when I said that Hemingway's last ten years had never been satisfactorily explained, that some scholars speculated that biographers of Hemingway's time in Cuba most likely underplayed his political involvement.

He shook his head and muttered to himself, "Tomás will be very interested in what you say." We sat there for a long time, in silence, both thinking.

We were startled by the sudden appearance of a cook who warned us that the police had arrived. He waved at a gate at the back of the yard.

We ran a few blocks and found an empty shed where we laid low for an hour beneath some oily sheets that had probably once protected a piece of pavement from a car tune-up. At first we were silent and motionless, oblivious to the heat and grime.

When no police found us, José started interrogating me about my interest in Mary's manuscript. "So you are studying the great Hemingway and his wife who lived at the Finca? You are a Canadian. Do you not have your own writers who were called Communists in the 1950's?"

"Yes, there was some pressure on some Canadian artists in the 1950's, but nothing like the anti-Communist hysteria in the States. My dad was in the diplomatic service stationed in Washington through that time, and he's always wondered why such intense hysteria was whipped up by the American government."

I was distinctly uncomfortable and way too hot to stay any longer under the tarp. "How about we find your bike and head back to the hotel?"

"I just hope that the guard I bribed didn't give the police our names."

"Well, if he did, we'll find them at our hotel. Let's not just waltz in the front door."

Afternoon

José was an accomplished back door user and we were soon sitting on the second floor landing of the hotel, with a good view of both front and back entrances and a hiding plan should the police come calling. Beth had insisted that we both shower and change; my clean shirt and pants hung loose on my new friend.

It seemed that Beth and Alicia had bonded as well over the course of the morning. They had gone out and bought the fixings for a simple but excellent lunch that they had spread out in the sun-filled, spacious mezzanine hallway.

As we relaxed, I pulled out, from my wrapped up shirt that
I had put carefully under my chair, the empty Volume IV of
Foresti's series.

Alicia turned white when she realized that on the table before
her was a book I had taken from the Finca Vigía. She touched
it gingerly. "Do you know what this is?"

I nodded. "Sort of. This old volume is where Mary told Castro
she had hidden the first part of her article." I opened the front
cover of the Foresti and looked regretfully. The desecrated
book looked like an empty box.

"Hey, Alf." Beth was shaking my knee under the table. "You'll
find the article. Don't worry."

"But you need to worry about this old book that you did not
need to steal," said José.

Alicia nodded. "Listen. I will get the old book back where it
belongs when we go for our tour that I have rescheduled. It
was at the top of the tower, right?"

"When's that?" José asked.

"Tomorrow morning."

"Good call, Alicia. Thanks." I was starting to imagine that I
might survive my recklessness after all.

José started to speak, then stopped. "Well," said Beth, "how
about Alf tells you what he knows about Mary's article?"

"Okay." I wondered where to start. "According to my dad's
conversations with Castro, Hemingway's Majordomo, René
Villarreal, and Julio Menendez, his groundskeeper, took the

manuscript from Hemingway on the day he and Mary were leaving Cuba for the last time. Hemingway, at a hysterical level of fear and illness, was convinced that the FBI agents had taken over the Cuban customs area and were planning to confiscate the document. Indeed, the FBI was very interested in what Mary had written. Their spy at *Life* Magazine had reported that she was writing an exposé of the harassment, by the FBI and IRS, of her husband."

"Why had she given it to Papa when he was so nervous?" Alicia asked.

"I think he still considered himself the big hero."

José said, "Keep going. What happened, according to your father? No, first tell us who told him this?"

"Castro. Castro likes talking at great length and the only person he could find to listen to him on the day of his long speech to the United Nations was my dad who had the gig as his translator. That was in 1960. They met again in 2000. That's when Castro was in Montreal for Trudeau's funeral."

I took a sip of my beer and continued, "Mary's description of their last week was valuable because it was an only copy, because *Life* Magazine had contracted to pay her well for it, and because it was rumored to be a criticism of the FBI. Two things, though. Hemingway was carrying only what Mary called Manuscript A. It covered Tuesday to Saturday. They were leaving on Monday, after all, and she hadn't had time to write down what had happened on Sunday. Or Monday, obviously."

"Did the FBI confiscate Manuscript A?"

"No. Papa managed to pass the chest pack it was in from under his shirt into Julio's backpack and Julio gave it to René who quietly walked out of the building and took it back to the Finca where he returned it to Mary's designated hiding place, inside this old book."

"Where is Manuscript A now?" asked Beth.

José answered, "I think we need to speak to my grandfather." The guy could be charming when he tried.

There was a long pause. Beth said to me, "You said you had two things to comment on, and you only mentioned one."

"Right. The other relevant detail is that Mary typed her story using carbon sheets so there was a copy of each page. She calmly carried this back-up in the bottom of her purse, and the customs guys didn't know about them, and they didn't find them."

Beth asked quickly, "Did Castro tell your dad this?" I nodded and she continued, "Did Mary make copies of the story of the last two days as well?" I nodded and Beth kept up the interrogation. "So where are these copies?" I shrugged. "You don't know?" I shook my head.

Beth continued. "What was Mary trying to do in writing this? You could figure out a lot about their marriage. Did she care about her husband, for example, or had she simply married for money, prestige and adventure?"

"I don't really know, but Castro told my dad that although Mary wasn't the most admirable person he'd ever met, she had an integrity about her that most Hemingway scholars have not recognized."

The realization that I had actually stolen such a valuable artifact was still sinking in. When news had surfaced in the 1960's that Hemingway had kept the Foresti set in the humid open tower, there was a huge uproar in scholarly circles, many blaming Hemingway for carelessness. What would they say when they heard about what Mary had done? Or when they learned about how I had taken Foresti for a wild motorcycle flight and hid it under an oily tarp and a sweaty shirt? I could see my doctorate fading away under the thesis committee's disapproving glares.

"Let's not ever tell anyone about what you did this morning. It's that simple," said Beth who obviously shared my grad student perspective. She turned, business-like, to José. "So, all these years, your grandfather kept Hemingway's treasures in his house and no one ever stole them?" It was José's turn to shrug. Beth persisted. "Did he expect Hemingway to turn up some day so he could restore them to him? Or, since he must have known Hemingway had died, was he keeping them for Mary or for Hemingway's sons?"

Alicia said, "Our great grandfathers did not speak often about the painful last years of their friend. They spent their time smoking on the dock at Cojimar, boasting about the glorious times they had spent with Hemingway out on the *Pilar* fishing, or spying during the war, or entertaining the Hollywood friends they saw in the movies. We could not bluntly ask such questions."

José crossed his arms and looked at me. "Our family has kept the secret of Mary's story safe until Mr. Hero turned up and started stealing. What I want to know is how a foreign student found out about our treasures?"

"Our treasures?" asked Beth. "Don't they belong to Mary's estate?"

José and Alicia seemed to have known very little about Mary's story. I challenged José. "You didn't even know that Manuscript A existed or that Mary had written about their two last days in Cuba, Sunday and Monday. Had you even heard about either manuscript?"

There was a long silence. We finished our meal and I was glad to see Beth consuming good quantities. Perhaps the trick was to distract her from her queasiness.

When the silence had grown uncomfortable, at least to me, I pulled the ancient Volume IV off the floor beside my feet. Empty. How could Mary have cut it like this? Where were the cut-out pages? Probably they had been strewn across the tower floor by the wind until René had swept them up and disposed of them.

I didn't want to let our Cuban friends know how profoundly important Mary's story was to me, or to my dad. We had invested so many years in talking about it and planning to find it that I had come to see it as the backbone of my thesis. In other words, it could determine my career.

Having evidence of its existence in hand was overwhelming. At another level, I simply couldn't believe it. I took several pictures of both the inside and outside of the ancient book with my iPhone and sent them to my dad. If I found nothing else on this trip, I had at least given him that.

I found myself pacing back and forth along the mezzanine that wound itself around the central staircase. In what looked like aquariums were intricate model ships, their history explained in Spanish and English on neat little signs. Focusing on a lovely sailboat, I calmed down.

The others, meanwhile, had sunk into an intense silence. I imagined that each of us had a grief, a fear and at least one hope entangled in this adventure. The fate of Alicia and José, of Beth and me, of the Finca library, all seemed at times hopeful, but at times tenuous.

"Okay," I said, since no one else seemed to be accomplishing anything, "here's something we can do. I brought with me a book that few people know about. It's called *Hemingway in Cuba*. The writer was a Russian diplomat, Yuri Paporov, who in the '60's apparently interviewed everyone who knew Hemingway when he lived in Cuba."

"What language is it in, Russian?" asked Alicia.

I shook my head and told her that this text had first been published in Russian as *hemingway na kube*, in 1979, then in Spanish, in 1993. Both editions were published by *Siglo veintiuno editores* which seems to be a well-respected publishing company with offices in Madrid and Mexico City.

"Hasn't this book been translated and published in English?" asked Beth.

"No. That's why I brought it here, hoping to get some Spanish-speaking person who knows something about Hemingway to read it and help me assess its usefulness."

"I can look at it for you," said Alicia.

"Would you?" I was so excited. "It's in our room." I couldn't help blurting out, "Can you look at it tonight?"

Before she could answer, I smelled grass, as in grass being smoked. José looked at the door to our room, and I saw smoke furling out from the crack under the door. I pointed, too scared to speak.

"Is our room on fire?" asked Beth, sounding puzzled, with an edge of panic.

"I think Fede's having his early afternoon joint," said José casually. "He and Paulo have been smoking for awhile now, and you have just now noticed."

"Paulo is Fede's friend," said Alicia, as if that explained everything.

"Paulo, your brother in jail, is in our room?" Beth exploded.

"Quiet!" hissed José, glaring at us until we hushed, then leading the way into our room.

"He can't be hiding and smoking at the same time," said Beth. She added, somewhat illogically, "Not in our room." Like me, she was grasping for something that made sense as we approached the door that, once José opened it, released a cloud of weed.

I remembered I'd left the old book sitting on the table in the hallway and rushed back to sweep it up. Swearing at myself as I joined the others at our hotel room door, I wanted just to evaporate for the afternoon, check out.

Alicia introduced us to her brother, Paulo, who was smoking with Fede on our bed. It seemed natural to greet them, shake hands, and join them. There we were, in a circle, cross-legged on the bed, passing around one joint, then another, as we heard Paulo's story.

Very early that morning José had busted him out of prison. Hearing this set Alicia, inexplicably, off giggling so Paulo tried again, using exaggerated pointing to ensure the references were explicit. José had busted Paulo out of prison.

Paulo went on to explain that they both, and we all pointed simultaneously at José, then Paulo, had to get off the island

and into sanctuary in the US or, even better, in Canada. Like immediately, that night. José said no one had seen him, so he would just get Paulo onto the boat to Florida, then be back with Alicia.

It occurred to me that Beth shouldn't be inhaling this, or any, smoke, but when I caught her eye, patted my belly and shook my head, she gave me a "don't get uptight" look. Jeez! Women! At least I hadn't said this out loud. Maybe being high was good for me. I entertained myself by measuring the relative size of my troubles compared to José's and then realized the others were all looking at me and howling with laughter.

Paulo whispered, "Be quiet!" The noise quieted down, and this was long enough for me to realize that I'd said all my thoughts out loud. They all, with gestures, repeated my muttered phrase, "long enough," threatening to light the laughter again.

To prevent this, Paulo stood up, balancing precariously on the edge of the bed. He said he wanted to thank us (now he led the pointing at Beth and me) for our understanding of third world dictatorships and our spiritual beneficence in offering holy sanctuary in Beth's church.

Everyone on the bed started to use big English words, or tried to, but I was the clear winner since Beth couldn't stop giggling. When there was a pause in the chatter I asked Beth, "When did we offer him sanctuary?"

"Paulo?" she asked. "I don't know."

I asked Alicia, "Where the hell did he get all those big English words?"

"Who?" she answered.

Everyone pointed at Paulo who said, "I do not know." He went on to explain that he had broken into our hotel room earlier in the day when Alicia was shopping and Beth was asleep. He did not want to startle her so he went back outside to wait for her to wake up or me to return.

"That was good of you!" I said. Pity that no one got my irony. Even when I gave it to them, dropped it right in their laps.

"Eh, mun, you gotta trust." Paulo did the Cuban equivalent of rolling his eyes.

I was starting to repeat to myself, "Her parents are going to kill me."

José turned to Beth and me. "Here is what I plan. My father and a friend have a boat and they will take Paulo to Florida tonight, and a cousin there will drive Paulo up to Maine tomorrow and the next day. On that night Paulo will walk across the border that a farmer calls his laneway. He will hitchhike to Ottawa and be there by Tuesday morning when you will meet him on the back steps of the Church of St. Columba at 9:00 am. You will arrange for Paulo to have sanctuary at your church, Beth, like you told Alicia about, and help him to have refugee status. In return, we will help your crazy boyfriend find Mary's full manuscript and our family members will give him interviews and totally cooperate with him so his thesis will be a clinch."

"Cinch," I said, coughing on a deep puff. Beth and I, holding hands as we stared at each other, absorbed what José had just said. "Where's Paulo?"

"Shush!" whispered Beth right in my ear, her breath so hot it tickled. "He's under the bed until the police move on. I think they're eating sweet fried buns downstairs."

"Timmies?" I blurted.

"Really, Alf, you are sometimes totally out of it!" Beth sounded impatient. I panicked and turned on our friends. "Can you let us alone, like right now?"

They didn't budge. Beth exaggeratedly explained to me. "The police here eat donuts, too!"

Still distraught and trying to get control of the situation, I whispered, "Where's Fede?"

They all looked at me in frustration. Alicia said, "Think about it."

"Oh, okay, feeding police to donuts. Donuts to police." I was embarrassed, as usual. "How about you guys all buzz off? Beth and I need some quality time."

"Remember, they're looking for Paulo."

"Then we'll have a siesta. Adios!"

José asked, "What about meeting Paulo in Ottawa?"

They wouldn't leave without an answer. "Okay with you?" I asked Beth. She nodded, I gave José the thumbs up, and he left with Alicia. Paulo was staying under our bed until the noise of the flamenco dancing and the darkness would cover his escape from his island home to begin a new life as a refugee in our care. Except for the fact that we were flying into Toronto. We'd left Ottawa for UofT years ago.

Beth lay down, reached for my hand, and placed it on her belly. What was she doing? I had no idea but I was fixated on naming the child. "Maybe we will call our baby Paul, or Paula." Then I felt something utterly new and wonderful. Beth was holding my hand still with two of hers, and I had the sense of there being a miniscule earthquake under my palm, of a butterfly fluttering, a bird gathering strength in its wings, creation.

"Is it the baby moving?"

"Upon the face of the waters."

"What?"

"It likes hearing you speak."

"Really?"

"Really."

"Hi, baby," I whispered.

"Eh, Beth, can I feel it, too?"

Beth and I were astounded. We'd forgotten about him. "Shut up!" I hissed at the man under our bed. "This is family time."

"But I am your family for as long as I am a refugee."

"Don't push your luck, amigo."

"I will be quiet now."

Silence settled in our room, and I think we all had a peaceful siesta.

Evening

When we woke, the heat of the day had passed, and Beth was hungry. The flamenco music was just cranking up as we discussed our options for dining out.

Back in Toronto we had spent one happy evening flipping through travel guidebooks and clicking around online websites until we had a short list of restaurants that would serve local dishes while catering to travelers' intestinal sensitivities. So far, everything had tasted the same: blander and more predictable than the pub fare in London, though considerably sweeter and much, much cheaper.

"Hey, Paulo," I nudged his arm under the bed, and Beth checked that our door was locked. When he emerged, he looked not just worried but also disheveled and exhausted and, well, dusty. "You okay?" I asked.

"Sí, I will say goodbye to you now, but not for long. We will meet in Ottawa at the St. Columba's church Tuesday morning, yes?"

"We'll be there with bells on," I said, not knowing what else to say. I suddenly felt weighted down by all the risks that lay ahead for him.

He shook our hands, paused and waved at the baby, then spoke seriously for the first time in our acquaintance. "When you go out to dinner, that will be the sign for Fede and José that I am ready to start off. Take your key. I will lock the door behind me."

I checked and saw Foresti's Volume IV was safe, under my clean shirts in the middle drawer of my dresser. I nodded silently at Paulo and left with Beth. How was it that we did what we were told by strangers? And trusted them with our belongings? And aided and abetted illegal dealings? I needed to figure this out.

Our #1 choice from the entertainment list was a block and a half east along our street. We strolled along the sidewalk, holding hands. "You know," said Beth, "we used to live in Ottawa."

She swung around to speak to me face to face. "I know that, but I don't know what's he going to do when we don't turn up."

I stared at Beth in the hope that a feasible answer might magically appear. "Your parents can meet him at St. Columba's. They know how to sign him up for the refugee process. We can visit him in a week or two."

"The least we can do." Beth looked chagrined. "I'll write my parents after dinner." We stepped off the sidewalk under a tree. I watched the people passing by. All shorter than us, and darker skinned. On we walked.

Beth and I finally found our restaurant. It promised conga, bolero and cha cha performed by a live band. And family food. That would be boiled potatoes, some mystery meat and a sugary dessert, eaten under the hungry eyes of a pair of once-sexy ballroom dancers. What we needed was time to puzzle out what we were getting into with Paulo, Alicia and José.

This restaurant provided, instead, distraction. We entered, took a table at the edge of the dance floor and ordered the day's special. Local color was immediately in our face.

The woman's outfit included high heels, a tight, skimpy blouse and a tight, short skirt, and the man's seemed to be a variation on the theme of matador, complete with slicked-back hair and deliberate moves, either sudden or slow.

This music was mellow and cheerful, lite (to use a horrid word) and familiar. For some pieces the leader played a Tijuana style trumpet. You could tell he was faking it, but then Herb Alpert's group sure looked as if they were lip synching at times. I looked around and spotted an old tape deck.

The second trumpet was also a mesmerizing dancer. After demonstrating his moves with the woman for one dramatic song, he led her to a chair and then turned around so he was staring at Beth. She stared back, then looked to me in embarrassment. "What is he doing?"

We watched and there was the evening's entertainment, mincing across the floor. He arrived close in front of Beth, his left hand held out, clearly indicating that he would teach her a dance or spin her off her feet, or both. She looked at me as if gauging my reaction, as if saying, "Why not? Could be fun."

I was as jealous as hell but nodded with what I hoped was cool sophistication. He bowed and offered Beth his right arm. When they reached the dance floor, the music began. He plastered her tight against his body. Beth, apparently as light as a feather and as agile as an Olympic diver, effortlessly kept up. The music sped faster. The other diners clapped and cheered. I tried to look happy.

The band was plainly enjoying the spectacle. It got worse. I became aware that the sexy woman dancer was eying me from her chair beside the band. Was she waiting for me to ask her to dance? My heart jumped in panic, and I looked down. Sandals. I couldn't possibly dance in sandals. I froze. As if anyone froze in Cuba.

Immense was my relief when the song ended. Beth was spun to a dramatic stop in front of her chair. Now what? The guy was hanging around beside me. Was I expected to tip him for dancing with my Beth? Not bloody likely! Beth read the situation and, looking not at all embarrassed, said to him, "We'll leave you something after our meal."

Our food arrived at the next moment. This place was bizarre! We shrugged and dug in. Not bad, we agreed, if you like lots of beans. Beth told me how, the night before, when I was cornered listening to Uncle Ed, Aunt Sylvia had told her that they had taken up tango classes back in Ottawa. We couldn't picture that but had fun trying.

My preoccupation with Mary Hemingway's papers seemed to fade as we chatted, walking along the sidewalk in the warm evening air, taking a large circle and ending up back at our hotel just as the darkness settled.

We entered, and I remembered Paulo. He must be so hungry, fleeing from his homeland. Here we were, forgetting all about him. For once Beth felt guilty at the same time as I did. She got over it faster, though, as Fede assured us that Paulo was by now well on his way.

We sat down near the flamenco stage. I picked up an *International Tribune* and noted that, as usual, the international (read: American and British) press found nothing of interest happening in Canada. I hoped Paulo wouldn't make the news. I hoped we wouldn't either.

"There's something to be said for holidays," I sighed, as Fede brought us each a decaf coffee. He must have gone shopping.

"We're not used to having more money than the people around us." Beth got straight to the main point. Then she wrote her parents a cheery postcard, asking them to take care of Paulo. "I hope they get my message to meet him."

"You'd better text this information, sweetheart!"

"I was planning to do that," Beth maintained. "The postcard is just a nicety. Actually, I realized my postcard might be problematic. There are better ways to ask them to help Paulo." She tore it up and dug in her pocket for her Blackberry. I raised an eyebrow and she winked. As much as possible, she chooses to protect her parents' illusion that everything is always light-hearted in her life as well as theirs.

I often thought that she liked to talk about the commonalities of the world's great religions because she was trying to persuade herself that Christianity is valuable and good, as are all religions. She persists despite her parents' propensity to cling to out-of-date notions that alienate even semi-intelligent non-believers.

I was almost positive that talk of frogs was a red herring in her academic progress. "Is your study of world religions about religions about the world or about the religions of the world? And my other question is: how does the world as a planet have religions?" Wow, that was deep thinking for me.

Beth loved theoretical questions, especially when they came out of nowhere. I could tell because she savored them. She slowly stirred her coffee. Religion, for her, meant social justice.

I remembered Richard, her boyfriend before me, who claimed to be into saving the third world, one NGO at a time. His current thing was going on builds in Haiti, living and working with the people who would, having lost their homes in the great earthquake, receive a new home and a fresh start. I would be more impressed if I weren't jealous. Beth had once been totally involved in such trips. When she left Richard for me, she was the dumper and he the dumpee. Still, I wasn't sure she was over him.

Nor did I yet know what her values really were, or if I shared them. Richard hadn't seemed to bother with doubts; he was simply convinced he was 110% right.

One thing I knew for sure that Beth did not like about him: his power of positive thinking clichés. And she and I were happy together. I wondered if that counted for more or less than shared values. I could tell she had once found him very attractive, but now was relieved to have landed on her feet with a more or less honest, if geeky, grad student.

The music, again, was loud and lively, precluding conversation. I needed some time to think.

It hit me that this would be a good time to propose. I wanted to, but just didn't know how to go about it. I wanted to make it romantic, but I was as unskilled in that department as the worst klutz.

Once, early in our relationship, Beth had admired diamond rings in a store window. I had been surprised, thinking they were too obvious. Now I had one of those rings in a little box in the secret pocket of my pants. It was my grandmother's ring that my dad had given to me just last week.

I was in a sweat every time I thought of how to word my proposal. Or thought of how to avoid pickpockets. At least I'd gotten my secret through airport security. I'd casually chosen a different line-up and showed it to the inspector who shrugged and told me to put it in the basket along with mundane items like my passport.

"Make love, not war." That was my main value, however out of date.

Beth asked too many questions to last long with Richard. I, simply a friend of hers at that point, may have fed numerous questions to her. I think she chose me because I was the opposite of Richard. And here we were in Cuba with me carrying a diamond ring and her packing a baby. I was totally in love, and afraid she might say no.

A song ended, and Beth asked, "One more, then upstairs, okay?" I was always ready to go to bed with her! Before I could speak, the next song had started.

To me, my dad had always been heroic. From my early teens, researching anything to do with Hemingway had been our hobby. When he talked about Hemingway, it was from an international political perspective, and when he looked at 1950's Cuba, it was from his own experience as a translator for diplomats and political leaders.

I used his expertise to start my doctoral dissertation. When the time came for me to visit the Finca Vigía for my thesis research, he was too sick to travel, and so I was here with Beth, determined to bring the manuscripts written by Mary home to read to him. I had prepared myself by studying the now unclassified FBI records about the unconfirmed manuscript and other, more disturbing, files that suggested FBI harassment of Hemingway. My plan was to use this online information, Mary's daily articles and Paporov's book as the primary sources for my thesis.

Finally, the band was done, not just this song but also the evening's entertainment. We joined in the applause and headed upstairs.

"So, according to your dad's research, no one but us knows about Hemingway's bunker, let alone Mary's description of their last week at the Finca, right?" asked Beth.

"I think it's so cool that my dad is apparently the only one who found out that the bunker existed and figured out how to get into it."

"And he knew that Mary's Manuscript B was most likely there?"

I unlocked our door and checked under the bed. Good, no sleeping refugee.

"When Mary first told Castro that she had put it in the secret room, she sounded secure in her memory of that incident. By her second visit alone to Cuba, she had become unsure of and almost nonchalant about Hemingway documents, to the point of commenting, coyly, that she had burned a lot of papers in her New York fireplace, especially drafts. When Castro reminded her that *Life* had not published her article because she had not submitted it, she froze, staring at him, and said clearly, definitely, 'I left the second part wrapped in a plastic bag, inside a tin box in the bunker. Only you and I know about it.'"

Beth wrapped herself in the blanket at the foot of the bed, then gestured to me to join her. "Tell me the rest again."

I was so happy she was interested. "Dad asked Castro why no one else knew about the bunker, and he said Mary had explained that the entrance to the stairs of the bunker is hidden by an optical illusion Ernest learned about from the Spanish Jesuits in their ancient monastery. During the Civil War he had rescued a Jesuit insurgent from a death Franco had ordered. The abbot was so grateful when Ernest arrived at their gates in the Basque back country with the wounded priest, he blessed Ernest then and there and pronounced that he would be under the protection of the Jesuits for the rest of his life in this world, that wherever he found a Jesuit house, he would have sanctuary."

"That's amazing!" Beth exclaimed. "And sanctuary is what we have agreed to offer Paulo. Hemingway would have done the same."

"I thought 'sanctuary' was the front of the church, the high altar area."

"It is, and for at least a thousand years it's also meant the place a person on the run can hide. The word 'sanctus' means 'holy,' and no one can attack another person in it. It's great as long as the people of the church offer it to the person on the run because someone, after all, has to provide food and drink."

"So even modern law in Canada respects this medieval tradition?" I had never quite believed that part of my dad's story.

"Yes, don't you read the newspapers? Occasionally there's a story of a church protecting a refugee so he isn't deported before his case can be tried."

"And your church will be cool with this?"

"They've done it before," she answered. "My parents are really into helping refugees. The only little hitch is that Paulo thinks we will meet him at St. Columba's in Ottawa."

"Your parents will take care of him, right?"

Beth reached into her jeans pocket, flipped open her Blackberry, and showed me the screen: "Sure, no problem. Take care of yourself."

"Hm," she murmured, kissing me. "I wonder if my parents suspect that I'm pregnant?"

I thought my heart would explode. Then and there, I should have asked her to marry me, but instead I made a lame joke. "Paulo will tell them."

I longed to read Mary's manuscript. How critical had Mary been of the FBI? I was worried that when word got out that she had dumped on Hoover from a great height, they might come after me. But really, Mary's opinion must have been small potatoes to them. Everyone back in mid-20th century America knew much more colorful and incriminating stories about the FBI and the CIA. Who else was to blame?

I had other questions burning in my brain. What was the story of the Russians who had lived, like Hemingway, in 1950's

Cuba? What about Castro, his friend Canadian Prime Minister Pierre Eliot Trudeau, and my dad, Trudeau's assistant
and translator? I was just a grad student, and thinking about
all these forceful personalities pushing their separate agendas
made me sweat all over. And I had no intention of letting José
or Alicia or Beth know that I was afraid.

I had hoped to have found Mary's article today and to have
read it before going to bed this night. Beth, in compensation,
had a different plan.

Thursday, July 21, 1960

"So, Mary, now I love you straight and true . . . and all I have
to tell you that I can write is that I love you."

Ernest Hemingway to Mary Welsh, 1944

Today is Ernest's birthday. He doesn't want to celebrate it
after last year's infamous 60th in Spain. What a disaster!
The three-day debauch left many of us wounded, including
me. Valerie will join us for a quiet party at lunchtime and
then get on with her job helping Ernest with his correspondence while hoping for a few minutes off with Julio, our
equally cute and charming groundskeeper whose English is
as limited as her Spanish. Come to think of it, he is far from
skilled as a groundskeeper for that matter. I guess I'll bake
the cake. The celebration of adult birthdays is a nuisance.

The bigger event is leaving Cuba in just a few days. I expect
we will both miss terribly our beloved *Pilar*, the sea, and the
perpetual summer. We haven't discussed what we're going
through. Ernest talks only to eulogize the past or to rant
about some imagined slight. If he stops to think about having to leave this beautiful island, he might simply ignore the
order and refuse to cooperate. Here's irony for those who
like it: he is being shoved into reverse exile, sent back to his
homeland. I don't see how it will be possible to budge him
from the Finca and the *Pilar*. He might be more inclined to
leave if I talk like it's a temporary visit to our Idaho friends.
Or the ones in Spain.

The *Pilar*, like the woman of that name in *For Whom the Bell
Tolls*, is solid, dark brown, old and durable. Ernest's ideal
mate is, as I try to be, witty and independent, tough, with
an actress's slim curves. I just hope I never look like I'm

wearing a corset to match an ugly hat, like his mother, poor witch. I have never met her but have always worried that he thinks I'm like her, "Graceless."

Unlike his classically awful mother, I have learned when not to intrude or comment. Perhaps I should have another look at what I've written and make sure I don't criticize him too much, especially his virility. But why not? He's blamed me, often enough and in public, for his impotence. And his endless flirtations! Is the ubiquitous Valerie simply being sweet? I can't criticize her helpful demeanor with me. She's a pretty bright girl. Little girls always know what they want to do. The men can't stop staring at her.

If Ernest is awkward with women and the whole love routine, he's totally comfortable in the death-dealing world of men. The article he's researching in Spain on the bullfight is a eulogy for that dying ritual. I remember, as well, the mammoth marlins and tuna he took such great pleasure in killing, the struggle that the man almost always wins, calling it ritual, art, religion. Bullshit! A relevant expletive. That's what is left after the bullfight, along with blood and guts.

Maybe I just don't understand the corrida. Ernest enunciates this word with great emphasis and delicacy as if it is the Holy Grail. He implies that I don't understand the tradition of bullfighting because I am a woman. I never argue that idiocy, out loud, at least. I am happy to cook the meat. In the old days the hunt was necessary and rituals, like the Mass, were believed to bring luck and safety. It's all primitive thinking, like Picasso sought in Africa and Ernest found in killing, especially in the chaos of wars.

His greatest love, even before writing, is booze, the villain of inappropriate idealism. During the filming of *The Old Man and the Sea*, we spent every evening at La Floridita. That's where Ernest, who nicknamed drinks as well as women, invented the Papa Doble: a double frozen daiquiri without sugar. He worried that Spencer Tracy, another brilliant drunk, wasn't right for the lead since he was overweight, hardly a starving Cuban fisherman, but after some drinking bouts, they became friendly. Spencer, the great drinker, couldn't match Ernest, and rumors started to drift out of the set that he was too hung over to get anything right. He insisted on eating supper at the Floridita so as not to impose on me, his lovely hostess. I could see that he just wanted to stay at the bar. Before long Kate Hepburn arrived, called by the director to straighten Spencer out so they could get the film done.

For all his selfishness, Ernest is a man of many friends. I used to wonder how he ever got any writing done when he had so many people to talk with, drink with, fish with. He has friends in bars and friends who are bartenders. Wherever he travels, he stays in great tourist spots. Most of these were made great tourist attractions by his presence. Oddly enough, he has no friends in Key West to draw us back.

And then his bewildered wives and lovers! He is a persuasive flirt, yet none of his affairs and marriages but ours lasted. His pattern is to charm each woman until she falls for him, irritate her so that she divorces him, and then establish a friendship with her. Oddly enough, he gets along better with his women after they break up. He sends them warm letters full of good advice. He even encourages them to be friends with each other. I was surprised when I found that I had actually grown to like Pauline. Bottom line, I am sticking with our marriage, even though it is in imminent danger of collapse.

For a long time we had many houseguests. They all have cleared out now, taking their hysteria with them. The worst-off were those who have been summoned before the House Un-American Activities Committee and labeled Red. Our offshore home was their haven, their sanctuary, Ernest their gracious host. No one accused him of being Christian, just Communist.

As time passed and the American celebrities were able to return to the States, Ernest spent more time with Cuban artists, attending and praising their shows. Ever generous to those in need, he would offer money to rebuild one artist's house when it was burned down by the police, and he would invite another to use the fruits and vegetables of his garden. I wondered at one point if he were trying to recreate Gertrude Stein's salon, but gradually he lost the energy to read all their writings and attend all their public events. Now he chooses instead to sit through the evenings in a bar with anyone or no one.

Cubans are more concerned with politics than art. Ernest has, all these years, happily bought drinks for young Cubans who were idealistic enough to fight with Castro but too new to the political scene to have attracted Hoover's attention.

With all these friends, however, he is too reckless, too trusting at times, and then paranoid. I wonder if there's a spy in the house reporting to Hoover that Mr. Hemingway talks about preparing to escape, and that the quiet Mrs. Hemingway has two hidden, packed suitcases. Ernest is always extreme in what he says and does. There's no way he can censure what comes out of his mouth. Nor does he even try. Careful talk didn't help his Hollywood friends, or his Cuban friends, or the refugees from the Spanish Civil War who also at one time hung about here.

I look at him and see a hurricane that must run its furious course. I look at him and see a bull, weakened by picadors, set up for a matador's final thrust.

Thursday, July 22, 2010

But in the night he woke and held her tight as though she were all of life and it was being taken from him. He held her feeling she was all of life there was and it was true. But she was sleeping well and soundly and she did not wake.

Ernest Hemingway, *For Whom the Bell Tolls*, 1939

Morning

Yesterday was too much excitement for this goody-goody from the boring capital of a straight-laced, friendly country. Living with my future wife and unborn child was one adjustment, but having an escaped convict under our bed was borderline traumatic.

I'd been awake in the night with intestinal cramps, the dreaded turista. Thankfully, medication solved the problem, all while Beth snored softly, spreadeagled across the bed, and Paulo beneath us snored like a steam engine crossed with a horny mallard.

Paulo, snoring? No way! He was put on a boat to Florida during the night. I told myself that he had disappeared from our life, but then I rolled over and peered down the length of the bed. Extended from under the bed, twitching, was one large foot.

So here we were, at dawn, and Paulo would be with us again when we got home to Toronto. He would be our very own refugee unless Beth's parents kept him in Ottawa. I sighed loudly, but no one responded, so I rolled over and snuggled in until all I could see of the world was Beth's hair. Maybe just such a predicament sparked the beginning of Hemingway's hair fetish.

Under my pillow was the desecrated Volume IV of the price-less and otherwise perfect late 17th century Venetian *Mappamondo Istorico* by Antonio Foresti, in 13 volumes. The volume's mangled evisceration was pointless in the absence of a crazy lady's diary.

It was, let's face it, B&E, yet a robbery that was not, thank God for one ray of sunshine, armed. Legalities can change from one country to the next. That's a euphemism for "I could get screwed."

Had I lost my grip? What would we name the baby? How/when/where would I propose marriage? Why don't women do the proposing?

"Distrust adjectives," said Pound and then Hemingway. What about adverbs? I had to escape the adverbs careening around my mind, bouncing back and forth between my ears.

Deep breath, mantra, slow breath, mantra, relax every muscle, mantra, find a good place.

I gave up trying to get back to sleep, got out of bed and started to organize my belongings as quietly as possible. I took the empty Volume 4 into the bathroom and stuffed it into the chest pack. Next I removed it because it was so bulky it made me look pregnant. If it came to lifeboats, that old thing was the first overboard. My ID was velcroed into my pant's secret pocket.

Beth stirred, moaned and rushed into the bathroom. I stood out of her way, then followed her to the toilet and knelt beside her, holding her hair back and not looking into the bowl. She was almost crying, and I was almost retching.

A peaceful silence settled on us. She reached up and flushed, then went over to the sink and splashed water from the tap on her face. She swigged from a bottle of water and spit it out.

I turned to look at her. Beautiful, smiling, heading back to bed. I caught her hand before she reached the door. "Beth, I love you. Will …"

A knock, more like a pounding, on the bathroom door came first, then an accented voice. "Please, Beth, it's my turn in there!"

Beth froze in horror. I spluttered, "It's okay, that's Paulo's voice!"

"That's okay?"

"Better than a stranger."

She saw my point and opened the door. We stood aside as he barreled in. "Thanks, man. Excuse me, Beth."

Beth went back to sleep. I curled in behind her, wondering if I would ever succeed in proposing, wondering why Paulo was back with us. I pretended to be asleep when he emerged from the bathroom and sat down on the foot of the bed.

Distracting myself, I kept slipping back into my current fantasy interview, sometimes with Steve Paikin on *The Agenda* and sometimes with Peter Mansbridge on *The National*. It would have been logical to have my debut interview on an American show but the only ones I could handle had been cancelled, one by several decades: *Oprah* and *Dick Cavett*. Those contemporary funny guys are way too sarcastic.

Q. How did you become interested in an American writer who lived much of his life in Cuba?

A. By the quality of his writing. And Sean O'Malley, my father, stationed in Washington in the '70's, heard a rumor about an unpublished and apparently incomplete article that Mary Hemingway had written for *Life*. The context was that Mary and her husband were harassed by the American FBI when they were living in Cuba. My father was intrigued enough to read all the Hemingway-in-Cuba books as they came out.

Q. Obviously you are too young to have met Hemingway. Did your father ever meet him?

A. No, but he did have the honor of meeting Cuban President Fidel Castro and American President Jimmy Carter and of working for our Prime Minister Pierre Trudeau. Castro and Carter were honorary pallbearers for Trudeau's funeral. Remember? The year was 2000. Trudeau, by the way, once tried to canoe from Florida to Cuba. A fascinating man. In 1976, when he was Prime Minister of Canada, he brought his gorgeous young wife, Margaret, to visit Cuba; she pronounced Castro one of the sexiest men in the world. My father was translator on that trip as well.

Q. Really? Now, tell me, was your father a CSIS spy?

A. Of course not.

And that question would not have been asked because I would have insisted that the interviewer sign an agreement on 'don't go there' questions. In my fantasies, I always spoke in eloquent, rhetorical sentences, expressing my intelligent, informed points smoothly. Smooth? I wished.

Q. How much effort do you put into looking like the young Hemingway of WWI?

A. None.

Q. Really? Now, tell me, …

I snapped out of the TVO studio and woke up under a languid old hotel fan with a pregnant fiancée. Today, I was determined, but now she was suffering morning sickness. And I had a refugee, idealistic and no doubt hungry, curled up at the foot of our bed, sound asleep. What on earth was I doing? My dad is still alive, and here I was pretending he was dead. Oedipus déjà vu. I remembered keeping the secret that he was a spy with such difficulty; my cred through the brutal years of adolescence could have used a boost.

Just a minute, Paulo in our bed? I guess he figured there was room. Lying on the edge of the mattress, I listened to Beth's next trip to the bathroom. It was that kind of morning: starts and stops.

An hour and a half later, Alicia began our tour of the Finca Vigía. As we mounted the steps to the landing at the top of the stairs, Beth admired the orchids growing around the trunk of the ceiba tree. Then her face took on the look of someone ready to jump on a colleague presenting an oral analysis full of holes to a grad class. "This isn't the ceiba tree in all the pictures you have shown me. It's not big enough!"

I looked at it and wondered what she meant.

Alicia answered, "You are observant, Beth. This is not the tree that was here in Hemingway's time. It was ancient and huge."

I asked, "So this one was never attacked by Mary?"

"No. Mary instructed a gardener by the name of Eduardo to cut off a piece of the root of the old tree that was ruining her floors. He phoned the Floridita and the bartender who answered handed the phone to Hemingway. Eduardo reported that he was about to start cutting the intruding root, and Hemingway swore that he would kill Eduardo if he did what Mary wanted. Eduardo was tempted to just quit and take off to his brother's place in the country, but there was no easy escape, with Mary as angry as her husband. He started cutting. When Hemingway arrived, shotgun in hand, Eduardo took off, running, and it was a miracle that he escaped alive. The powers of the ceiba tree had saved him."

"Really?" I spluttered. "It sounds to me like incompetence saved Eduardo's bacon."

Alicia glared at me. "Who are you to judge?"

"Moving right along," said Beth, her voice icy.

Alicia led us immediately into the house. She had obviously bribed the guard on the front steps; he turned his back as we approached the front door.

The inside of the house was off limits to tourists, and we found it empty. There was no evidence of renovations in progress on the building's structure or of restoration of the books. The smell of fresh paint still lingered, but it barely disguised the musty scent of pervasive mould.

"How long do we have inside this building?" I asked.

Alicia said, "We have the morning to explore as we please."

"Can we take pictures?"

She nodded and Beth pulled her Blackberry from her backpack.

Alicia said, "We must be discreet, though. The guides sometimes charge for pictures. If we are lucky, no one else will be around until lunch time."

We stepped through the front door and were immediately in the long, bright living room that stretched most of the length of the house. "It's just like all the pictures!" I exclaimed.

Alicia, looking amused, said to Beth, "Our Alf has a talent for stating the obvious." Beth didn't respond. She was busy lining up a photo of me looking at a wall full of the stuffed heads of African wildlife. Maybe she didn't like Alicia's use of the word "Our."

Beth said, "There's no one I know in Canada who does this anymore, except for the German neighbors of our friends up in Manitoulin."

"Does what?" Alicia asked. "Hunt or import stuffed heads?"

"Either. It's just too ..." she paused, searching for the right word, "politically incorrect."

"What's that mean?"

I burst out, "Oh, never mind. Let's do Hemingway here. Look, there are the chairs they sat on, and between them is the bar table he designed. Alicia, can you get a picture of the two of us? Come on, Beth. Sit down. My dad will love this!" I was close to hyperventilating. "Chill, chill," I told myself.

Alicia took several pictures, exclaiming at the speed of the Blackberry. "This is such a small machine to do everything!"

I was still obsessed with results. "First, let's look at the books. This wall. Beth, can you check a few books at random? Look for really old texts. Give them a sniff and feel for moisture. Also, since my thesis is on Hemingway's life here in the 50's, look for anything to do with the FBI, Castro's Revolution, Cuban History, Twentieth-Century Communism. Scholars know what was here in 1979. What would be very interesting is if what's now on the shelves doesn't match. Note only the grossly obvious discrepancies." I handed her a clipboard all ready to go, including sharpened pencil.

Alicia sighed as I turned to her. "Can you take pictures of the shelves on this wall, for starters? Close-ups, please, so we can read the titles!"

Beth was immediately busily absorbed by her job. Alicia started to mutter, "This is tedious!" I got the feeling that she had found a new word and liked using it.

"I'm going to check the shelves in Hemingway's bedroom and office," I announced. Beth looked at me, her eyebrows saying that she knew what I was up to. She called to Alicia to help her find something, anything, I trusted, except where I'd gone.

I slipped into the bedroom. This time I didn't have a headache from falling through the open window. The interior wall between the bedroom and the living room had a single deer head above the small portable Royal he must have used in his later years.

The first book I pulled out was *The Common Reader* by Virginia Woolf. I wondered if he found the Bloomsbury writers too precious. Beth's favorite literary character was Mrs. Dalloway. I can't stand her. *Who's Afraid of Virginia Woolf?* I am. Like anyone in his right mind.

No Canadian fiction in sight. Hemingway died just before Margaret Laurence kick-started the popularity of women novelists. A familiar book spine caught my eye: the first of Robertson Davies' Salterton Trilogy. I bet Hemingway didn't like Davies' humor; I grabbed the book and flipped through it. There was marginalia all right, sarcastic and unimpressed. "Just retribution!" I thought. Davies was equally sardonic when referring to those writers he considered inferior. In other words, all other Canadian authors.

"Get moving!" I muttered to myself. The bunker. This had been my second goal, finding the secret room where, according to Dad quoting Castro quoting Mary, she had left her description of the last two days, Sunday and Monday. What I wanted to do was examine the bunker thoroughly.

Beth and Alicia were at their task. I was going to be the only person to enter the bunker in 50 years.

I found myself looking, and seeing, as if through my dad's eyes. He had certainly thought it through. A man as paranoid as Hemingway, a man living in nuclear ground zero, 1960, would have had a bunker. A man with his fears of illness and of embassy officials might well have spent some part of his last week in Cuba in his secret room.

My dad had worked out the conjecture that the door to the secret room was an optical illusion, that there was a door that didn't make sense when seen from the back window that looked into the office. It did, however, open from the inside wall of the office.

I couldn't see it. Under the pressure of the moment, I felt a frustration that all of my dad's thinking seemed far-fetched. I felt like a child saddened that his parents' omniscience had been replaced by their all too human fallibility. There I was, about to prove that all those talks through Canadian winter evenings would pay off, and instead, suddenly, I was overwhelmed by doubt.

I tore into the office, around the desk, and there it was, the door. It led to the library but first into a mudroom, one wall still, after all these years, lined with boots and jackets, hip-waders and military uniforms. Behind the dust-covered boots was another, small door that apparently led to the basement, but didn't.

This was it, the door to the bunker. I pushed aside the clothes and yanked the door, but it didn't budge. Okay, what had my dad said? I had to believe that his plan would work, that I would soon be seeing what we had only imagined.

My dad had sent me into the back of the hall closet where he kept his favorite children's toys in the hope, I assumed, of someday becoming a grandfather. I still couldn't imagine how a magic kit for 10-to-14-year-olds was going to help us. I could remember, however, that it had enabled me to convince some of my friends that I was a trained magician. Some distracting chatter, a sliding panel that looked just like the real door, a wave of the magic wand and I could astound my friends every time.

Dad used it to explain how the door might work for someone who understood the magic of illusion. Here the distraction was a row of coats, the door behind them, too low for an ordinary door, and so not seen by anyone except its creators.

And me. I felt for the pressure point and found it in the door's upper left corner. A touch and it swung open to a narrow staircase that I followed down into a tiny room lit only by the flame of my lighter. I entered its doorway, resolving to sweep away the shoeprints that could otherwise point to the entrance even a decade into the future. Relief flooded through me. "Hey, Dad," I whispered, "you were right after all!"

I took a deep breath and stepped into the earthy stale air. Mice nests, mice droppings, mice smell. That was about it except for the two wooden chairs, the metal frames of the two small beds, an oil lamp and a pair of what looked like Hemingway's wire-frame glasses. I picked them up and slid them, spider webs and all, into my shirt pocket.

Feeling around in the near dark, I found a mouse bed. Gross! I jumped back to the bottom of the stairs, then returned to the bunks. Lifting the lighter toward the ceiling that was quite low, I saw, relatively intact, the floor of the bathroom above.

I brought the light back to the furniture. There, in the middle of the nearest bunk, was a metal cigar box. I stood there, astounded. The dust I had stirred up made me sneeze.

I opened the lid. Inside were papers, rolled in plastic, for all the world like a newspaper wrapped for a rainy day. I shook loose the plastic and pulled out the papers. The dim light confirmed that the top page was titled, "Sunday July 24, 1960," with a quotation from Pound.

The text began, "Wife pinch-hits for Ernest Hemingway!" I shoved the papers under my left arm, closed the metal box and pulled back from the room, trying to cover my tracks. I told myself that I had missed nothing of import, and that I had best skedaddle.

Once up the secret stairs and heading back into Hemingway's office, I found myself euphoric, still driven to make the most of my time alone. Seated at his desk, however, I realized that the rest of the manuscript could not have been kept in a drawer all these years. That was too obvious. It would have been found ages before. Whoever had taken it from the Foresti in the tower would not have turned around and put it in another hiding place in the next building. Surely in the half century since the manuscript had gone missing, every book, every drawer had been opened and every pocket checked.

I had taken the manuscript from the bunker. The manuscript I was stealing smelled musty but looked clean. I tore open my shirt and folded the old papers into my chest pack.

"Alf, come here! Have a look!" Beth's voice, coming from the living room, sounded enthusiastic. Alicia was laughing. I wondered if they could possibly have found something funny, or even important.

"Look," said Beth. "We're not going to find any valuable manuscript here. This place has been combed, everyone looking for what Hadley once lost or didn't lose."

I felt dizzy from the irony of my situation, but I couldn't tell her what I had just done. "So what were you laughing at?" I asked.

Alicia waved me over to the corner bookcase they had begun searching for previously unearthed treasures. The organization of the books into rooms, biographies in his bedroom, for example, seemed to be gone.

They had found, in the shelf below several Henry James novels, some Freudian critical books on Hemingway's early fiction. The analyses were devastating, and Hemingway's marginalia were furiously dismissive, grossly suggestive of the critics' sexual inadequacies.

The critics' comments were somewhat dull, but Hemingway's written responses reduced the three of us to helpless laughter. "Bullcrap" and "Insert assbackwards" were some of the milder and less original comments. He disliked the personal intrusion of biographical analysis and had often claimed, when in a more serious mood, "My typewriter is my analyst."

I wondered where they'd found these critical books since the shelf we were looking at had no gaps in it. Beth explained that these particular ones had been behind the books that were not in any discernable order. Sideways on the shelf, they fell forward when the front ones were carefully removed. It seemed as if all the books had been pulled, wiped and reshelved recently.

Alicia turned her back as I glanced at Beth who shrugged. My heart was racing. Anger on Hemingway's behalf, curiosity, excitement that in his marginalia I might have discovered something of significance, all these emotions were mixed together, and questions bounced around in my head. For now, I would pretend to be any interested tourist in case someone wandered in on us.

Alicia picked up a heavy dinner fork from the table set for 12 and pointed at the nearest linen napkin. "Look at these, and we'll talk about them later."

"Good quality, for starters," said Beth. "How is it these haven't been stolen?"

"Entire sets have been. What you see here are replicas."

As Beth and I headed down the pathway behind the house, Alicia deftly returned the Foresti to the tower and caught up with us as we passed the pool and stopped to admire, from a distance, the *Pilar*, in dry dock for several decades at that point.

I had not heard of anyone searching her for evidence of espionage; it had always been taken for granted that she was used for spy work—her speed and the skill of her crew had enabled her to disappear over the horizon whenever challenged.

Rumors about the *Pilar* had abounded, said Alicia, that Hemingway had assembled his friends to go deep sea fishing and drinking. Claiming to be searching for and protecting the Havana harbor against German U-boats was a front, the necessary justification for Hemingway's request to the Americans for free gas.

Later, the *Pilar* and Hemingway were connected, in the popular imagination, with the enormously successful book about an old fisherman out in the same waters, struggling to land the same great marlin into his much smaller boat.

Santiago was a fictional character, so he more easily maintained his heroic stature.

Who, I wondered, had chosen the deep rose paint for the bottom of *Pilar*'s hull and the cheerful turquoise for the top level of the deck? Most of the surfaces were polished mahogany trimmed by brass. Simple and practical, unlike Hemingway. Handsome and strong, like him.

My eyes were drawn to a long arrow painted on the port side of the prow. It was the familiar three-mountain arrow that Mary and Hemingway had designed for their stationery and silverware. I walked around the prow, looking up. The reverse image of the arrow pointed to the prow from the starboard. At the very front was what looked like a belt buckle. Beth and Alicia had noticed my absorption and joined me.

Alicia demanded, "What is the meaning of these symbols? They look like Santeria, but I haven't seen them before."

"These arrows are on the silverware we were just looking at," said Beth.

"The three points from the shaft of the arrows are the three hills of this island," I suggested.

"Oh, really?" Alicia looked embarrassed that she had not known all this. "We have half an hour left. Should we head back and look again at the cutlery?"

"And the linens," said Beth. "Do you think there was any superstitious meaning or not?"

"Santeria is the religion for many people who think Christians are superstitious." Alicia sounded a little irritated.

"Sorry," said Beth. "We are looking forward to the religion tour on Sunday."

"I save the best to the last," Alicia said, somewhat frostily.

Meanwhile I was still staring at the belt buckle design. "Have you got a close up picture of this?" Alicia and Beth were already down the path towards the pool.

A uniformed woman who immediately reminded me of a prison guard in a B-movie approached us. No, she approached me. Where did Beth and Alicia get to?

I was alone subjected to the woman's harassment accompanied by vigorous gesturing and shouting. She conveyed, in many words, that I had offended the gods and would suffer. My crime? Presuming to use my iPhone to auto everything, that was my sin. I turned and beat it back along the path.

What I couldn't determine was whether this woman had been offended that I had not paid her to take my picture with the *Pilar* or that I had presumed to take a picture of the holy boat. Was she concerned about the whole boat or just the symbols on the prow? Would an offering of cash have appeased the god of the *Pilar*? What was the woman's cut?

I caught up with Beth and Alicia, deep in conversation. They swung around at the sound of my steps, and Alicia demanded, "What's the matter?"

"Oh, nothing. I was just catching up with you."

"Who's that? I thought I saw a woman's dress back there."

"This crazy woman was mad at me for taking pictures of the *Pilar*."

"Oh, I hope you did not give her money!"

"No," I muttered.

Beth, who gives a handout to anyone who asks, made a harrumphing noise. Alicia marched back along the path, and we heard a loud duet of disagreement. Then Alicia reappeared, in high dudgeon. "Perhaps our tour of the Finca is finished for this morning," she said brusquely. "I will meet you later in town as arranged, for our tour of the historical sites."

I couldn't agree fast enough. Even better, Beth said our good-bye's, thank you's and see-you-later's.

Afternoon

I wondered where our refugee was at this point in the day. I, for one, needed some R & R.

Beth, amazingly, seemed positively bouncy as I dragged my feet around the Capitolio Nacional in search of Chinatown. Alicia had assured us that all the restaurants served delicious American-style Chinese food for the tourists.

What was my problem? I should, I know, have been ecstatic, having found part of the treasured manuscript. Instead, sweating and headachy, I found myself wishing I had never come to Cuba.

Beth took the lead, commenting that I looked sick or something and attempting to cheer me along. Oblivious to my real distress, she explained loudly that she was delighted to be taking care of me for a change.

I tried to focus on Beth's cheerful stories and exclamations of delight at the classically orange red trim of the architecture. This was Chinatown, for sure, and she was going to find a wonderful restaurant in the space of minutes.

Then I saw it. A big, dead, rat in the gutter, covered with flies and maggots. Gross!

I just missed stepping on it. And almost threw up, but instead grabbed Beth's elbow and swung her a quarter turn to the right so that we were facing a very ornate and colorful restaurant with tourists laughing and chattering, crowding the outdoor seating area. I longed for a cold beer.

Beth was happy with my sudden choice of restaurant although she did comment on my mood swing. I pretended to be fine, really, just wanting a cold beer in a long, v-shaped chilled glass.

We entered and the maitre d' explained that we had a choice: to be seated right away inside, at the back of the dining room, or wait a few minutes for a table out in the porch with the breeze and the view of people walking by. I chose the former.

The image of the dead rat was imprinted in my vision. Everywhere I turned, I saw it. I reached for and gulped down the ice water at my place. Beth tried to stop me because I hadn't double-checked that it was tourist water. The waiter gave her a thumbs up, but she was looking fixedly at me, and I felt both of them were assessing my behavior. I furtively attempted to adjust my chest pack to stop it from poking into my armpit.

Beth was ready to order right away. I struggled to regain a sense of normality and to speak as if nothing had happened. And nothing had happened, really.

"Your face is white," she said, and, leaning forward, touched my cheek. "You don't have a fever. Maybe you're just hungry. Why don't you order a full meal?" I ordered only white rice and iced tea. My taste for beer had evaporated.

The waiter deftly slid small plates of spring rolls with plum sauce in front of us, along with refills for our water glasses. He seemed to have forgotten my iced tea. I felt catatonic, unable to argue.

I managed to swallow one spring roll and slid the other onto Beth's plate. She nodded her gratitude and polished it off. Then came the main course. My plate had much more than simple rice. There was chicken, small bits, some with bumpy skin, some with protruding veins, some with fat. I swallowed hard and covered the chicken with rice. I'd seen the red-yellow insides of the rat, and the chicken was undercooked and looked the same.

"I can't eat this chicken," I mumbled.

"You didn't order chicken," Beth replied, then looked at my plate. "You don't have chicken."

"I covered it with rice."

"What?"

"I can't eat this."

"Do you want to leave?"

"No. You enjoy your meal. I'll just wait here."

The waiter by this point had picked up our distress and was hovering, concerned no doubt that patrons at neighboring tables would lose their appetites as well. He tried to get me to eat a piece of chicken by waving it in front of my nose.

I resorted to closing my eyes so I couldn't see the disgusting morsel that must have been entirely from the neck. I held my breath so I couldn't smell it. Beth told him I wasn't feeling well and asked him to take away my plate.

"Would you like anything else instead?"

"No!" I was about to strangle him.

What was he doing? I watched, mesmerized, as our waiter, having picked up my plate, walked through the swinging doors into the kitchen, pulled a fork from his back pocket and shoveled several mouthfuls into his mouth.

The doors swung closed behind him, and when another waiter swept through them, for an instant I could see our waiter standing at a stovetop, bent over my plate, cleaning it off.

Beth was speaking and, with great effort, I turned to listen and tried to talk, all the while vowing to myself that I would never again eat chicken in any form or Chinese food in any restaurant and that I would never tell Beth what had really happened.

I broke that last promise shortly thereafter when we had walked, in silence, towards Parque Central. Beth, finding a shaded bench, announced that we needed to sit and talk. I told her the whole story.

"You mean you found it? You didn't tell me?" Her voice was high. She paced back and forth in front of me. "Wow, this is exciting! You have Manuscript B here?"

I stared at her, speechless. What was she saying? I thought she'd freak out on me for being a thief and for putting myself and therefore her and the baby at risk by infuriating the heavily-armed police as well as the black market bandits in this strange country. Why was she so unpredictable?

The next U-turn came quickly. "I can't believe that you'd steal something from Hemingway's home! It's so out of character for you."

I felt my jaw drop at this point, and I rubbed my fists in my eyes, checking to see if I was in a nightmare. I asked, "Can you sit down?" She planted herself, arms crossed, in front of me. I decided to go for broke. "I also took a pair of Hemingway's spectacles."

Beth slumped on the bench beside me. "Can I see them?"

"Which?"

"The glasses first." I reached into my shirt pocket and was pulling out the specs when she stopped me by grasping my wrist. "No, we might be watched."

"I'm sorry."

I must have looked pretty pathetic because her next reaction seemed pitying. "Okay, you're okay. We can fix this. You haven't relaxed for an instant on this trip. We've got to spend some time doing nothing on the beach. That'll be good. Right now, let me see." She opened her tourist map and found the boulevard where we were sitting. "Look," she said, pointing to a large old building half a block away, "we need a little English break. How about some ethnically real tea?"

I grasped at that option. "Is that the English Hotel?" I pointed down the street, recognizing the tall columns and the outdoor coffee shop along the front of the hotel from the pictures we'd seen in travel books weeks before.

"Let's go!" We took only a few minutes to walk quickly down the street and reach the sidewalk that stretched along the shady café.

"Check out this huge café!" Beth exclaimed. We stood still, facing the entrance to the hotel on ground level and the imposing façade of three stories of ornate white stucco. The outdoor café consisted of rows upon rows of small tables for two across from the Parque Central. Looking to our left along the street we saw the Capitol buildings and to the right the gorgeously treed boulevard of the Paseo del Prado stretching towards the sea.

My dad had stayed at this hotel on the trip he had taken as translator for the Trudeaus. My mind was alliterating. "You're talking fast again," said Beth. "That must mean you're feeling better!"

I needed to know she was still onside. "Thanks for taking care of me. Have you ever had a Cuba Libre?"

"That's a rum and coke, right?"

"Cuba Libre sounds much better. How about you order tea and I'll order the drink and we can switch for the next round except no rum for you?"

Beth sank gratefully onto a chair and I sat opposite her, relieved to feel the cool breeze created by overhead fans and to order our drinks in English.

When I was about to explain how I'd been freaked out by the rat, I stopped. She was opening the mystery thriller I had lent her, *Cuba Libre* by Elmore Leonard. How, I wondered, could she concentrate on reading? I didn't ask. Our rule was never to speak when the other was reading.

So I sat there, keeping myself silent and still. This was the very place Leonard described in that book, the place where the English-speaking reporters could meet fairly safely as the Spanish and American militias fought for control of the island in 1898.

My dad had given me the book for Christmas and I'd finished it before Boxing Day. Now I could see that Leonard had described the place perfectly. I imagined telling my dad about my misadventure, and I missed his being with us. I listened to nearby conversations in English.

Beth closed the book. "I can't read anything just now."

"I've been waiting for you to say that! I couldn't imagine how you can read while so much is happening outside the book." I pointed at the cup and saucer waiting by her hand. "Would you like to pour me some tea, my lady, some liberated Lady Grey tea?"

She smiled and reached her cup and saucer towards me. "Those little cucumber sandwiches look delicious! Where would Lane have found cucumbers in Havana?"

"Surely cucumbers are available in Havana all year round!"

"Especially for ready money?"

"I'd really like marmite on toast!"

Beth and I had just a short distance to walk to meet Alicia for our History of Havana tour. What I wanted to do, right then and there, was read Mary's manuscript of her last two days in Cuba with Hemingway, but I didn't dare pull it out from under my shirt in case someone was tailing us.

I was still in a kind of shock that I had acted out my dad's dream, and my own, in opening the bunker and finding the document.

Stealing it. That was what was stressing me the most. I felt detached from myself, looking at the world as if from a distance, pulled toward Beth who was trying to re-establish our normal interaction. As I was.

I thought, as we started to walk down the boulevard, that perhaps we should be leaving the country before we were arrested. Tense, expecting the ancient car horns all around us to be those of the police bearing down on me, I kept telling myself everything was really okay, and everything would work out.

Half an hour later, we had found the meeting place, the glass-walled display case containing the *Gramma*. This was the boat used by Castro in the Cuban Revolution. Sure enough, we found ourselves waiting for Alicia.

I wondered what Beth remembered from her reading about the 1898 revolution. She remembered snippets. "'Remember the Maine!' was the rallying cry of the Americans, as if they were the victims, right?"

"They claimed to be victims, to work PR."

"Wasn't this the war where the first Roosevelt yelled 'Charge!' and ran up a staircase brandishing a broom, and everyone thought he was nuts?" Beth could occasionally be frivolous.

"That was Teddy, the crazy brother of the two old ladies who were serial killers, in *Arsenic and Old Lace*."

"I'm also thinking about your Cuba Libre. Coca Cola is a classic American product. How did it get to be part of Cuba's liberation?"

"PR again. I guess the Americans were helping to free their neighbor island from the Spanish colonial masters. Would any Cubans have believed that story?"

Beth liked to talk fast during conversations. "Didn't Trudeau yell 'Viva Cuba Libre' at a huge public rally when he visited in 1976?"

"Yeah, and 'Viva Castro!' Charles de Gaulle came to Expo '67 in Montreal and at one of the big celebrations of Canada's 100th birthday shouted, 'Vive le Québec Libre!' De Gaulle was insulting his host. Trudeau was supporting his."

"Who else was Castro friends with?"

"He'd choose friends who were heroic and charismatic, like Che, or idealistic and brilliant, like Trudeau. President Kennedy? I doubt it. Castro found him too reckless, and Castro was probably not impressed by JFK's glamor."

Beth said, "Batista, he must have hated Castro, and vice versa."

"And Castro was not impressed by Peron who was the glamor boy of Latin America."

"Peron's wife was the topic of a Broadway hit, *Evita*. Señora Castro .... Wait! Is there one?"

We watched Alicia meandering along. She never rushed and was always interested in her surroundings or her companions. I, however, was impatient to read Mary's manuscript, not trudge around the city, being told what I already knew.

"Keep with the tour," I told myself over and over as Alicia answered Beth's question about Castro's wife.

The tour was decidedly boring, as Alicia walked us around Castro's Havana. We started with Revolution Square. Che's huge, handsome portrait must have irritated Castro during all those rallies, all those speeches. You'd think he would have cut them shorter!

After Alicia had recited the essential information concerning the great historical events that had occurred in the Square, she flipped open her cell. It was of a vintage that no one in Canada would stoop to keep in use. I asked where she was planning to take us, and when she listed the National Hotel and Tropicana where so many American and European celebrities had partied during Prohibition, I turned to Beth. "I've had enough touring.

What about you?"

Alicia stopped figuring out how to work speed dial and looked at me, surprised. "Well," answered Beth, "if you don't mind missing Beach, Bums, Boobs, Bands and Booze, I'm cool with not keeping with the tour for once. Okay with you, Alicia?"

As I expected, Alicia seemed a little hurt, but I didn't want to explain, then and there, that Beth and I wanted to retreat to our room primarily in order to read a newly-discovered manuscript.

"What are you doing for dinner?" Alicia asked, somewhat plaintively.

Beth said, "Come on, why don't you walk with us back to our hotel? I think José said he'd touch base with us there, about 4 o'clock. Then the two of you can do your own thing and we'll chill a bit."

I wondered if José would also seem to prefer our company. Alicia had to stop working on her clients' guilt to pressure them into spending time with her. I was a Canadian, but I was not polite all the time.

Evening

When we reached the hotel after our obviously truncated tour, José was chatting with Fede and seemed happy to report that he had managed to communicate with Tomás and to ascertain that he knew something about the whereabouts of Mary's manuscript.

I felt hesitant and did not tell him what was in my chest pack. On the other hand, if he had some new information, I certainly wanted it. I had to assess if we could actually trust José. Beth seemed to glow as she smiled at him. That was it. Enough chatting. I thanked both José and Alicia and agreed to meet them the next day to hunt for Mary's manuscript.

As soon as they were out on the street, I gently took both of Beth's hands and spoke in a soft voice so that Fede couldn't hear. "Sorry, sweet, but I want to read 'Sunday-Monday.' And I definitely don't want anyone, especially people connected with the black market, to be involved. Okay?"

Beth nodded. "Let's go upstairs and start reading!" She sounded intrigued but didn't ask any more questions until we were both ready. I suppose I was playing up the precautions against being bugged that my dad had drilled into me as a child.

"Before you read, there's some context you should know." We sat, cross-legged, on the bed. "My dad informed me of everything Castro told him in their conversations of 1976 and 2000. When Mary came back to Cuba in August 1961 to collect her treasures, she asked René to help her retrieve Hemingway's unpublished drafts and such from the bank vault downtown. That was fine, but when they climbed up the tower and looked in Foresti, Volume IV, her manuscript was not there. She exploded in fury, but she believed René when he said that he had put it there.

"In her hand she still held the original 'Sunday-Monday,' that she had planned to leave with 'Tuesday-Saturday' in the tower.

"Now she simply wanted to leave it to its fate in the bunker. That's where it belonged, she told René. He guessed that to her it represented mostly painful memories that she did not want anymore.

"René asked, 'What bunker?' and she just kept still and quiet, then changed the subject. While René made a simple dinner for the two of them, she briefly entered the bunker."

"And you could very well be the first person to enter that bunker since then," said Beth.

"So," I said, "here we are, fifty years later, in Havana, figuring out what happened. Only you and I know I've been inside Hemingway's bunker. Only you and I will know, in a matter of minutes, the contents of Mary's 'Sunday-Monday.'"

"Awesome!" Beth exclaimed.

"I want to keep our escapades quiet and Mary's article secret until we are home. Then I will have time to work out a strategy for knocking them dead with my thesis."

"How about I read the Sunday part and you read the Monday?"

"Okay. Here it is." I handed her the papers, surprised to feel a little afraid to actually find out what Mary had to say.

As Beth read "Sunday" aloud, I began to pace the length of the room. She paused only once, to ask for a drink of water. We glanced at each other but made no comments. Beth looked, however, as horrified and sad as I felt. She read the last line: "The high tower had crumbled."

"Echoes of Eliot?" I was trying to sound academic and casual.

Beth blew her nose. "That just about destroys my image of fun-in-the-sun Cuba!" Silence. She picked it up and flipped back a few pages, reading to herself.

"You up for the last day? Maybe there's a happy ending?"

"Yeah, right!" She handed me the document and said, "Just a minute. I need something to eat." She grabbed her backpack, pulled out a granola bar and settled back on the bed.

I resumed pacing and flipped to the last page. "Look, Beth! Mary signed and dated the manuscript."

"That proves she wrote this part anyway," said Beth. "Go on! Read it out loud."

When I reached Mary's description of the manuscript as looking "like a newspaper still folded in a waterproof pouch," I stopped and looked at Beth. "Just what I thought!"

She nodded and I read on, sad that it would soon end, then that it had ended too soon. Who was the nastier, Ernest Hemingway or Mary? Who deserved pity or praise?

I stood up and paced the length of the room, then back, then again. Beth shook herself out of her funk. "Come on. Let's find some real food and talk later."

Not long afterwards, manuscript safe in my chest pack, Beth and I had eaten our favorite dish and were a bit more relaxed, listening to the flamenco band and trying to think about nothing. Fede had provided me with a beer and I was surprised to find the bottle empty. Beth's orange juice and bubbly water was likewise gone.

As I turned to ask her if she wanted anything else, Fede came by our table, discreetly making the "Watch out, you're bugged" gesture he'd taught me the night Uncle Ed first came by. Cuba was starting to annoy me.

A familiar voice whispered in my ear, "You should be very wary of crime at the Finca." We turned about and found Uncle Edmond and Aunt Sylvia standing right behind us.

I was so wired up by reading Mary's manuscript that I chattered on like an idiot. "We are so worried about the ethics of

```

people taking books from the Finca. But what about all those books he brought here during the war?"

Aunt Sylvia asked, "Do you think he paid for them all?"

"Have it your own way. Road to hell paved with unbought stuffed dogs. Not my fault."

Uncle Ed's innate pomposity shone through. "How did you become so drunk?"

Exaggerating each syllable, I said, "I was pretending to be Bill, in *The Sun Also Rises*, appropriating his voice. Do you have a problem with that?"

I guess Beth wanted to prove she could argue with anyone or everyone in the O'Malley family. "The Haida sculpture in front of the Canadian Embassy in DC, you know, the building that looks like an iron in white marble…"

"On Washington Avenue?" I was trying to help her.

"Yes, and out front there's a carved Haida canoe made by a great sculptor, Bill Reid. But he was half white, so why is his carving representing the Haida people?"

"But that canoe represents Canada, not one tribe," scoffed Uncle Ed. "I don't see what the issue is here."

Fury pulsed through my veins. "Aren't Haida people Canadians?"

He persisted. "So before the whites arrived, do you think the Haida never intermarried with or attacked or stole from other tribes?"

Beth assumed an impressively snotty tone. "Talk to the Greeks
```

about the Elgin Marbles, so nicely displayed in the British Museum!"

Uncle Edmond was enjoying irritating us. Even as I recognized his strategy I had no choice but to invite them to our table and pull out a chair for Aunt Sylvia. My dear uncle proceeded to quote back, word for word, everything Beth and I had said during our meal. I was embarrassed, furious, and impressed by his memory and lip-reading skills.

Proudly, he patted the front pocket on his shirt. I felt obliged to look in it but couldn't see anything in particular until he leaned on the back of my chair while patting my shoulder. In another minute or two he gestured that it was quite easy to bug me. I got the point.

Edmond sat back and I wondered how long the chair would manage to hold him. No supersized furniture here.

I was angry, as well, that we had got stuck with Paulo. Well, we had boasted about how Beth's church does refugee sanctuary. It was time to get serious. The responsibilities of adulthood yawned before me.

Edmond said, "Your heroic quest for the manuscripts might have been easier if you'd followed normal channels like getting a letter from your Department Head approved by the Cuban Embassy in Ottawa. Then you could have taken it, bright and early some weekday morning, to the Canadian Embassy here. Some official could have escorted you through the Finca and the José Marti Library and answered all your questions."

I was drooling with the temptation to wave Manuscript B in his face, then to tell him that we were hoping to find Manuscript A in a day or two.

"Is there any way you could put some valuable papers in a

diplomatic pouch to avoid customs stealing them from me?"

"Of course, if they're being exported legitimately. If you want diplomatic immunity and it turns out that you're smuggling, both your dad and I will be hung out to dry by our bosses. Did you think of that?"

I was so stupid! Then again, he was so sure of himself that I always wanted to do the opposite of whatever he instructed.

Uncle Ed continued. "Nowadays, with Cuba opening up to entrepreneurs, there's more likelihood of making a buck. The treasures of the Finca are just waiting to be sold to rich American academics on research jaunts." I wasn't sure whether he meant people like me, but I sure wasn't about to ask.

Beth and I played footsies as Uncle Ed gave another lecture on being careful not to fall prey to every danger from bugging devices to armed robbers. We thanked him for his concern, thereby implicitly hinting that we were planning to ignore the specifics of his advice, and that we could take care of ourselves. As if.

Long afterwards, my relatives stood up to leave. Beth chose that moment to keep the argument going. "We need to learn as much as possible about Hemingway this week," she said, "so we can't spend every minute worrying about what someone who is probably not particularly interested in us might overhear."

"Canadian students wreak havoc on political and economic ties with Cuba," I chimed. Beth and I laughed. The other two did not.

"Very well, Beth." They both sat down again, and Uncle Edmond sternly motioned us to lean forward. "Let us recall and discuss my brother's discoveries about Hemingway's relation-

ship with the FBI." We nodded and he proceeded. "Mary contacted Castro in 1977 to request a visitor's visa for a few days
in Cuba. He promptly responded and assigned Julio Menendez
as her escort. When she arrived, she was surprised that Julio
had been Castro's man all along. Julio reassured her that the
manuscript was in good hands."

I had to set the record straight. That was an egregious cliché
but I was not at my best. "What Julio knew or didn't know
was not of particular importance to Mary at that time," I said.
"She was here with Hollywood director Sidney Pollack, talking about making a movie about her life with Hemingway in
Cuba, and she didn't want Pollack to see the manuscripts."

Aunt Sylvia opened her mouth to speak. This was a first!
"Maybe she just wanted to move on with her own life and
forget about her husband's aches and pains."

What was that about? There was a pause that could, in another
context, have been called pregnant.

Into the silence that ensued I continued telling them that Julio
rather pompously had assured Mary that she could just forget about the missing papers since they were not where she
had left them and were probably unlikely to reappear. Mary
laughed and said that what she couldn't remember she could
simply make up, and when she had trouble making something
up, Pollack could easily throw in some details that would
make her look good.

"Basically," I said, "Mary and Julio agreed not to look for her
1960 manuscript because it didn't really reflect well on her
Mrs. Hem business."

Beth looked at me. "That's just what she said! How could such
a self-centered person as Mary not keep track of a manuscript
that was so rah rah Mary?"

I answered quickly, before Uncle Ed could notice Beth's slip. "By 1977 she was seriously soused most of the time, and she had trouble keeping track of so many documents, mostly his, some hers, sitting around in all the places they had lived."

"She had no children to talk to?" asked Aunt Sylvia.

"No, and apparently no trustworthy friends or siblings, either." I noticed that Uncle Ed was nodding his head. I imagined that he was telling himself to sit back and listen since Beth and I obviously knew what we were doing.

Or not.

There was a pause between songs and we all relaxed from the strain of communicating without being overheard. I felt the need to redirect the conversation. "I tried to get into the bunker this morning. The doors are so misleading in that corner of the house." I was surprised by my need to maintain some level of secrecy, and to boast. Beth was kicking me under the table.

Edmond made more pompous throat-clearing noises. He reminded me of a wheezing porpoise. "Well, Hemingway had learned a trick or two abroad. It's not surprising that his secret room with its secret entrance has never been discovered, indeed, rarely even mentioned."

I was on a roll. "Mary probably wasn't sure about having put her papers there in the first place. And she probably liked not telling know-it-all Hemingway scholars and publishers about the bunker. Meanwhile, her carbon copy had been stolen, or maybe she'd accidentally burned it. She was burning a lot of letters, notes and papers at that point."

I tried to sort out what I was doing. Why had I been so delib-erately obscure, let alone rude, to Uncle Edmond? He was just honoring the request of his dying brother-in-law, to watch out for me, his careless nephew.

Still, when my relatives had said good night and headed out to the taxi that would take them back to their hotel with its crowded beach, Beth and I shared a sense of triumph. The big spy hadn't figured out our secret. Or had he? And had we been at least civil to my aunt? What other grief was my irritating uncle going to inflict on us over the next few days?

Beth sat for a minute or two in silence. Then she smiled and I felt relief wash over me. "We should be nicer," she said. As if that were easy!

I was confused, as well, by what we had read. "So did the FBI force Hemingway out of Cuba? Or had he heard that Castro was confiscating all foreigners' properties? Or did he need to return to the States for medical care?"

It was Beth's turn to look horrified. "I can't imagine him voluntarily going for shock treatments!"

"I'm afraid to say it might have been much worse than that. Maybe the shock therapy was not all that voluntary. We know that the FBI communicated with Hemingway's doctors at the Mayo Clinic."

"You make it sound like *Cuckoo's Nest!*" said Beth.

"They're out there."

Friday, July 22, 1960

"I felt that gigantic bloody emptiness and nothingness, couldn't ever fuck, fight, write and was all for death."
　　　　　　Ernest Hemingway to John Dos Passos, 1936

Cuba has been a wonderful place to live, but here, too, we are being crowded out, bugged, in both senses of the word, mainly by J. Edgar Hoover. Hoover must have spent all his adult life worrying about Ernest or someone like him exposing his nasty tricks, his self-promotion, his sexual secrets. Irreverent, spontaneous types like Ernest drive guys like Hoover nuts. Ernest's idea of a "joke" is to "accidentally" call the Federal Bureau of Investigation "the Gestapo."

J. Edgar Hoover is obsessed with control. He set up the FBI in 1924 and has been spying on American citizens at home and abroad ever since. Hoover really hit his stride once Fascism was beaten and Communism the next big threat. Tweedledee or Tweedledum? Rumor has it that school children studying Orwell's *Animal Farm* can't tell whether the allegorical pig is fascist or communist. So what, I ask, is the difference? The animal good guys are democrats. At least that is clear.

Today, I am writing, up in the tower, after supper. Every other day, it's been early morning but today I was too busy packing. It was my first chance because Ernest hadn't come home when I woke up at dawn. He would absolutely freak out if he'd seen me packing. Now it's done. I don't see how I'm going to get him on the ferry.

And where was he this morning? The last time he pulled an all-nighter he rolled in about noon after losing all our cash on hand at a cockfight. It would be more accurate to say he was rolled in, dragged by a few of his fishing buddies and his loyal friend, José Luis. The cockfight, Ernest claims in his more sober moments, is a Santeria ritual. I think it's a poor country's bullfight. José Luis doesn't express an opinion; he just wants to take care of his friend as best he can.

When I'd hidden our two suitcases containing our essentials under my bed, I wandered around the house, looking for him. Valerie was reading down the lane in the old gazebo, and I made sure she was packed and asked if she had her papers in order for our departure on Monday.

She said Ernest and José Luis and the other men had escorted her back to the Finca well before midnight. They were heading to the Embassy party that she and José Luis tried to tell him was scheduled for Sunday at 8 pm. Ernest insisted that the party was Friday night and that he wanted to introduce his Cuban fishing friends to the American Ambassador and tell him how evil Hoover is.

I sighed, and Valerie said that José Luis had told her to tell me not to worry. He was watching out for Papa.

Valerie and I sat silently for a minute or two, and then she laughed as she described the conversation, earlier in the evening at the Floridita, when Papa was asking some Cubans why Cuba has no bullfighting and telling them how they should set it up as a tourist attraction and as a means of teaching moral values to the young men. On and on he had waxed eloquent, and she didn't know whether he was just joking or what.

Then, when he was on what he announced was his last drink ever at the Floridita, he began to rail against Julio. Valerie obviously finds the young Cuban more interesting than Ernest. Can't say I blame her. I thanked her for helping out with Ernest and headed back to the house, wondering when he would be back and what I had to do before Monday morning.

I also wondered what, if anything, Valerie was up to with Julio. Why were her relationships my business? Ernest, the paranoid, sees spies everywhere. I don't go looking for spies, but I had suspected Julio since I first saw him listening to Ernest. What I noticed was that Julio understands English; he had said, when we first met him, that he knew only Spanish. I didn't tell Ernest. What was the point? If we fired Julio, another informant would take his place. If Valerie is involved with Julio, however, that might become complicated, but not for me.

Hoover is at the root of our troubles. What right had the Federal Bureau of Investigation to operate in Cuba? What right had Hoover to order Ernest to return to the US?

Then there are the taxes. For years Ernest has been convinced that the Internal Revenue Service is hounding him, that he has paid taxes at a ridiculously high rate, that we are facing an old age of poverty. I ignored this ranting until he asked me to bring in an auditor and have him go through our papers. I called Scribner's who sent down someone they said would impress us as reliable and thorough. After a day of looking through our papers and asking us questions, the man agreed with Ernest's fears. Hoover is using the IRS to harass him by stealing his legitimate income. Ernest is still a rich man, thanks to the enormous royalties from *For Whom the Bell Tolls* and *The Old Man and the Sea*. He is one rich man who does not evade taxes. His motivation is fear.

And when my rich man finally makes it home in a taxi from his bender, he is almost catatonic. José Luis is in bad shape as well, but the good doctor, with René's help, carries Ernest up onto the deck and into the house. I thought they'd all collapse in the living room and celebrate with a drink. Instead, they drag him into his bedroom. René Villarreal is a quiet one, and he is reliable, our Majordomo. We are lucky to have such good men around us in Cuba.

I follow as far as the living room and make myself a gin and tonic. No one is talking with me. Waiting there, looking out the front window at the ancient ceiba tree, I wonder if it had ever seen such a messy human situation as this great writer being driven mad by his own government. Or are we making the whole story up? Conspiracy theories are an American indulgence. It started with the Constitution ensuring the citizens' right to bear arms against our government. The citizens of working democracies start with the assumption that their elected officials represent them. It doesn't occur to them to buy weapons to defend themselves against their own government.

"Do you know a big Yankee? They're going to kill a Yankee." Valerie, quickly absorbing Ernest's assumptions, heard this at the café where she sometimes hangs out, taking a break, I suppose, from us old folks. I wonder if Julio meets her there. Their plot is romance, but they can't escape our spy story.

Does she know, or care, that Ernest was once an American spy? In 1942 he and Martha worked for the Central Intelligence Agency in China.

When he settled at the Finca Vigía, he organized the Crook Factory, a group of his friends claiming that they were amateur spies warding off German U-boats by patrolling the entrance to the Havana harbor. Who knows what they were doing beyond drinking? Perhaps Ernest was simply tricking the American government into buying gas for their fishing expeditions. I never heard of any German subs sunk in Cuban waters, but I did hear Ernest claim to have liberated the Paris Ritz from German occupation. Was he self-deluded, regressing into childish fantasies, or spinning yarns?

It's easy to see why Hoover thinks Ernest is a threat. Here he is, the tremendously popular American writer, choosing to live on this island, Cuba, where Russians have gained a foothold. Ernest is also a writer of popular books supporting "enemy" (socialist) values. I find this astounding but such have been the accusations against *For Whom the Bell Tolls* and *The Old Man and the Sea*.

Also, as a former spy, Ernest might know a fraud or an incapable agent when he sees one, and Hoover must be quite simply afraid of Ernest writing an exposé of his poor record as Director of the Federal Bureau of Investigation.

Now you see why Hoover must not read what I'm writing until it is published in *Life*. Then I'll be his enemy, too, and I'll be honored to stand up beside my husband and be counted as loyal Americans in our rejection of Hoover's authority. Until then I just don't want him trying to sabotage my publication schedule.

Ernest is inherently belligerent and seems to enjoy fighting Hoover. I, on the other hand, am scared, mainly because I've seen how ingeniously he can make a person's life miserable. What will he do to us once we're back in the States?

Even here in Cuba Hoover's men continue to torment Ernest. Someone at the American Embassy calls him every day and says something like, "Hey, Yankee, leave Cuba or else!" They know he's paranoid, the heartless boors. Apparent strangers in the streets of Havana yell, "Shocking!" when he walks by. Ernest is convinced they are threatening to torture him.

I have started to keep the pages I've typed in the locked drawer of my desk. The carbon copies are folded tightly and slid into a belt I wear around my ribs, under my blouse. It's very hot and unattractive in terms of my figure, not that I have to worry about Ernest or anyone else noticing.

I have one more theory, perhaps snobbish, about Hoover. If Ernest's instinct is to go to bat for the underdog, he comes from an upper middle-class background and has enjoyed world travel and the good life. Hoover, on the other hand, had to struggle to achieve advancement and hates those he sees as well-connected snobs. Hoover must know that Ernest despises him.

The day passed as I wrote about Hoover. He's been an unarticulated threat hanging over my head for too long. It's dark and there's no party that I can hear at the pool or in the guesthouse. Half an hour ago I saw Ernest's bedroom light go out. Perhaps they're all asleep. Perhaps Julio and some others are downtown, meeting their handlers, reporting all the unAmerican comments made by the man who bought their drinks, reporting that he seems unaware of any plans to return to the US of A.

I once asked Ernest if he was trying to write *Guernica*. He answered, "My life is *Guernica*."

Friday, July 23, 2010

"Is Helen going to have a baby?" George said.
"Yes."
"When?"
"Late next summer."
"Are you glad?"
"Yes. Now."

Ernest Hemingway, "*Cross-Country Snow*," 1924

Morning

I awoke to the sound of Beth throwing up in the bathroom.
Soon she was back in bed, cuddling up to me for warmth
which seemed a little odd in Cuba, so I wrapped the blanket
and my arms tight around her, and she fell back to sleep.

I knew I wouldn't get to sleep again, but that was fine. I wondered when she would stop losing weight and start putting it
on. Beth rolled over in her sleep and murmured, "A while. A
few more whiles." What was she dreaming?

In the meantime, with the room quiet, empty of intruders, I
was able to assess our situation. I needed to read Manuscript
B through at one sitting and determine if it was indeed worth
taking all these crazy risks for, then think through and discuss
with Beth what we needed to do. Priorities: get ourselves
home safe and sound; get what I needed for my thesis; make
my dad proud; help the Santiago families, especially José,
Alicia and Paulo.

This last item on my list was tricky. They had to work it out
for themselves. Alicia needed to whine less and José had to get
out of the underground economy. And Paulo, too bad he had to
leave. I wondered where Paulo was.

But my big plan for today was proposing. I had to do it. Wearing the ring on my pinkie finger and keeping my left hand in my pocket when Beth was awake, that was way too distracting. I was determined that today without fail I would ask the question.

Surely the right moment would present itself on our bus tour to the cigar factory and whatever else we had signed up for through Alicia's tourist agency. Not that I thought a cigar factory was romantic. What it comes down to, what I really want to know is why, in this day and age, it has to be the guy asking.

I did want to persuade Tomás to let me have Mary's Manuscript A. If he indeed had it. There were, in every scenario I could imagine, too many "if's" for my liking.

What if, for example, José was lying when he vaguely hinted that his family had all kinds of Hemingway treasures? Alicia had more reliable business ethics, I thought. Still, how much had she been kept in the dark? By her husband.

I crept to the bathroom, picking up Manuscript B from the desk on the way. I closed the door, flicked on the light and spread a clean towel on the floor, as far from the plumbing as possible. Voila, a surrogate desk.

Reading Manuscript B yesterday with Beth had given me nightmares all night long. I needed to see if I remembered it accurately.

The white 8 ½ x 11 inch paper was of plain, high quality stock, and thick, a pleasure to touch. But not to smell.

My dad and I had waited for just such a moment, except we'd assumed that we'd both be reading the complete manuscript together. Using my iPhone, I snapped pictures of the first few pages of the manuscript and emailed them to my dad. I wondered if he would be able to read them. Would he be awake right then, also too excited to sleep?

I hoped he was feeling well enough to enjoy my discovery. He didn't know enough about what I was doing to worry about us. He didn't know that I was afraid to start reading it again. I didn't know why I was afraid to start reading.

I sat on the towel and blew my nose. It was like standing on the high tower diving board, ready to do a cannon ball, imagining doing it and imagining not.

Once I'd started, I was totally absorbed. It read like the last two of a series of newsmagazine articles, all right. The author's fear, anger and pride seemed mixed equal parts with dislike of her husband, and at times, love. Her voice was proud, sometimes panicked, and often ambivalent about exposing her husband's vulnerabilities and her own.

By the time I was done reading Mary's description of their last, painful days on this island, I was on a major downer. That a heroic man should come to such a state was totally tragic.

I wondered what I could do to make sure my dad didn't suffer like that. Of course, he wouldn't. He was loved and respected, and well cared for by his society. He had not asked his mother for the gun that his father had used to commit suicide. He would go gentle into that good night. Hemingway had raged.

And poor old Mary, so easily forgotten, yet determined to be heard. Childless, and so easily dismissed, she had raged as well.

Well, old Hem was sure daunted in private. I couldn't believe the violence that he barely contained. How did Mary manage to stay with him?

And those FBI agents, were they his paranoia, or Hoover's?

I thought, "George and Martha, sad, sad, sad."

As I dwelled on their misery, I realized that I hadn't known Mary's life, or his life, or anyone's life could be so awful.

Did my dad know how wretched these two were? And did Hemingway know that he was heading back to the society of electroshock therapy in its rough early stages, the land where his enemy, J. Edgar Hoover, had willing workers everywhere?

Hemingway, that strong bull of a man, only lasted a year in the States. And Mary stayed with him to the end. Was she his Judas?

I sat there, manuscript still glued to my hands, on the floor of that bathroom of that Cuban hotel, wondering what had led me there and what I should do next.

A light knock on the door snapped me out of my self-absorbed trance. "Alf, are you alright? Can I come in?"

I sprang to the door. "Sorry, yes, come in."

Beth wasn't in a huge rush so that was good. Still, I left her and flopped down on the bed. A few minutes later, she joined me. "What were you doing, reading Mary again? You looked pretty freaked out."

"Yeah, her last few days with Hemingway in Cuba were brutal. Loveless, unloved."

"So?"

"So what should we do now?"

"What do you mean? Get dressed, for starters."

"What are the odds that the FBI are trailing us right now? Like today, on this tour?"

Beth turned from the closet where she was pulling out a white sleeveless dress I had never seen before. She looked right at me. "They're not about to follow our bus all over the island!"

My worries started to fade as Beth continued, "We should make more of an effort to enjoy life. Let's shower and put on some clean clothes and meet Alicia. How long do we have? I hope there's time for breakfast!"

The day got a little better when Alicia met us. "Are you two sure you're up for a full-day bus trip to Vinales?" asked Alicia.

"Yeah, I think we'll relax if we can get out of all the craziness here. You okay, Beth?" She nodded, almost imperceptibly. Because I was grasping my chair with my left hand, neither noticed the ring, diamond inside my palm, on my little finger.

Spending ten hours in a bus, touring around, that sounded like a good break from all the noise and heat of the city. I've been told that I have a Candide-like naivety about country life. So did Hemingway. Across the river and into the trees, he was the Impressionist of perfect words.

Alicia was explaining how Paulo's crossing to Florida had been delayed a few hours because of high winds, but he had left not long after midnight and was presumably now at an uncle's house in Miami.

José was driving, since the usual man was sick. Off we went, somewhat apprehensively, Beth clutching the barf bag Alicia provided.

José, Alicia confided, had never driven such a large vehicle. The tour bus for our group of 12 Canadians turned out to be a rather old mini-bus, and not at all comfortable.

The streets were so narrow in the old city it was a miracle that we got out of town without taking down one of the several construction scaffolds on each street. The odd thing was that most of these renovation sites were dust-covered. Alicia said that workers refused to proceed until paid, so many projects took years, and in the meantime the scaffolds served the purpose of propping up the buildings that would otherwise have collapsed.

We passed one active worksite and looked right in, like at the theatre, to a scene of busy nailing and painting. Nowhere in sight was there a hard hat or a warning sign, let alone a covered walkway for pedestrians. "Up to code," now there's a first world concept.

Once out of the city we passed farms that seemed not only third world but also centuries old. There were few tractors or other implements, only two-wheeled carts pushed by human muscle or pulled by oxen. Houses were tiny, rundown shacks made of weathered boards with thatched roofs. We watched José maneuver through a village, again very dusty and rundown. Then we were moving through what looked like wasteland, too rocky to support any kind of farming or business.

I could see, behind us, an approaching car. It zoomed past us, its engine roaring, its speed creating a dust cloud. There was enough traffic that José had to pay attention to his driving. In the tiny village of Machureutu he wove his way through a crowd of young men lounging along the sidewalk. "You see these guys?" he asked rhetorically.

I asked, "What are they doing here in the middle of nowhere, looking for a bus load of gringos to hijack?"

José caught my eye in his rear-view mirror and grimaced.

Eventually Alicia stood up and announced to the group that we would be stopping soon at a cigar factory in Pinar del Rio. If we were approached by begging children in the street, we would be advised not to pull out our wallets since if we gave anything to one, we would immediately be swarmed. And we should beware of pickpockets. However, inside the factory we would be safe and we could purchase cigars.

She was certainly a skilled travel guide, and yet she, like all the Cubans we met, was unable to register for a travel visa. She had told us that, moreover, she had no money for travel to the city of her dreams, Paris. What I didn't understand was how she didn't seem particularly upset by her people's poverty.

"L'amour est un oiseau rebelle," the cigarette factory song from *Carmen*, was playing on a tinny tape deck. The sweet pungent odour of fresh tobacco leaves filled the air. We filed along the centre aisle of the factory that was set up like a school room with a woman at each desk. A man sat at the front of the room, reading aloud to them.

Most of the women made no eye contact as they rolled the popular varieties of cigars and stacked them in piles on plates for packaging. Everywhere little charms marked the job space of the workers.

A few women hiked up their skirts so they could roll the tobacco leaves on their bare thighs while they pointed to their tin cans for tips. How awkward! One managed to roll a Romeo and Juliette on her attractive thigh, sing along with Carmen, smile and nod toward her coin collection, make lewd comments to the man reading, and call out to the male tourists walking past her desk. I avoided her eyes. Alicia explained to the group how the more expensive cigars were made using higher quality tobacco leaves.

Beth shook her head and, gesturing to all the workers in the crowded room, asked, "Who'd have thought it?" She was feeling better. We were both feeling better.

Beth and I stopped in the next room where men worked, dressed in the sleeveless white undershirts that a fellow grad student once told me were called wife beaters. I guess the nickname was connected to Marlon Brando shouting, "Stella!" Every male of my dad's generation longed to make that mating call. I didn't think it would work with Beth.

In the last room in the cigar factory, wooden boxes were made for each brand, and in a corner there was a small shop. We bought two cartons of the "Romeo and Juliette" brand.

Alicia was encouraging the tourists to return to the bus. I couldn't help asking the obvious. "How is it you've told us that, unlike other Caribbean islands, Cuba has no children begging from tourists? What about these kids and the kids in Cojimar?"

"Okay, in a few tourist places." That was a bit vague. I realized that since neither she nor I had ever been to another Caribbean island, neither of us knew what we were talking about.

Alicia explained to the group that, aside from Havana and a few other places visited by tourists, the people were not bothered by poverty. For them, life was better than in the past. There was milk and education for all the children and health care for everyone, and this was why the people still supported Castro.

As well, I thought, he kept order with his army and jails. But how could she say the people weren't bothered by poverty? How about the people who served meals and cleaned washrooms in gated resorts along the north shore, like where my aunt and uncle were staying?

"Did Hemingway and Mary ever notice the poverty of the people?" I asked.

"Until yesterday I thought they did not," said Alicia, "but last night I was reading the book you gave me, *Hemingway en Cuba*. Yuri Paporov writes that Hemingway was a supporter of Castro's Revolution."

Beth turned to me. "I still think it's amazing that you've brought this heavy book with you, hoping to find someone who would read it and tell you what it's about."

"It's not so heavy, it's paperback." I turned so I could include her in my conversation with Alicia. "I have this goal to get it published in English because then it will be easier to use Paporov's ideas in my thesis. Imagine, a book written by a Russian about Hemingway in 1950's Cuba! It's my silver mine."

"And the gold mine is Mary's story, right?" asked Beth.

"Right. You can imagine, though, that since it first came out, this book, researched and written by a Russian diplomat, has been disparaged and then ignored by the literary establishment in the States. Especially since Paporov disappeared back to Russia."

"Can you guess which words I did not understand in the last thing you said?" asked Alicia. It took just a few minutes for the necessary English lesson.

"Oh, right," said Beth. I could practically hear her thinking she'd have to refresh her memory of the details on this background information.

Alicia said, "Whoever did the translation into Spanish was not an expert. Have you approached the publisher?"

"I sent an email, but no answer."

The road through farmland and tiny villages was straight and paved, so José joined the conversation. "My father told me that it was René who was the loyal friend to Hemingway. He used to visit and talk with Tomás, before I was born. I wonder if he knows where Mary's manuscripts are?"

I answered. "From what I've heard, Julio, who took the article from Hemingway at the ferry customs, could have taken it to Castro, his boss. More likely, Julio didn't really think it was of any particular interest so he gave it to René who took it to the Finca and put it in the Foresti Volume IV, up in the tower as Mary had instructed."

Beth joined in. "It is strange to think about this famous American writer and his wife being so intimidated that they hid her description of their last week on the island."

"What happened to René once they left Cuba?" Alicia asked me.

"According to my dad, René, as Majordomo, was the only Cuban friend still on the Hemingway payroll. He was basically the guard and Tomás was the only long-time friend of Hemingway to whom René confided what he knew about Mary's manuscript. Julio was the only other person who knew about it, and his knowledge was limited. He had, however, been close to Hemingway during that last week."

Beth asked me, "Is Julio still around? Maybe you could interview him. He sounds Machiavellian. Maybe he noticed something that Mary might have missed."

"If he's still in this vale of tears, he'll be very old, but maybe I should. Good idea, thanks."

"You're welcome. You know, I'm hungry. When's lunch?"

Alicia answered, "Over an hour." She turned from Beth to
me. "I'll try to contact Julio. When do you have some time in
your schedule?" Beth suggested that we could make ourselves
available any time before our departure on Monday.

As Beth shared a sandwich with Alicia, I chatted casually with
José and looked out the window at the changed landscape of
the Vinales Valley. We were now driving through an obviously
fertile land with magnificent flowering plants such as jasmin,
hibiscus, and orchids along the fences dividing the fields. The
scent of the blooms sweetened the air.

Alicia turned and spoke to the tourist group, "We will soon
arrive at our second last stop on today's tour. We will hike
along a path in a cave until we come to a river where there
are boats to take us farther into the underground world. It is a
holy place for the native people of Cuba because of the spirits
they believe live there and make it so mysteriously beautiful.
Please note the lush vegetation outside the caves. You can see
the three ages of Cuba: native palm trees, colonial sugar cane
fields, and modern hydro lines.

"After exploring the cave, we will have a leisurely meal at the
picnic area outside it. You can see the pavilion up ahead of us,
on the right. That will be about an hour from now, so if you
are as hungry as my friend Beth, you might want to reach into
your lunch bag right now."

I felt in my backpack. On top were the cigars I had bought
for Tomás, a bribery José had told me would most likely be
effective. There were also a few very expensive cigars for the
celebration of the birth of the baby. I told myself, "Get engaged! Today!"

Beth whispered, "Where is Manuscript B right now?" I silently patted my ribs.

I couldn't hold back my question. "So, Alicia, where is Mary's manuscript?"

Alicia was about to answer, but José interrupted. "We must go and visit Tomás. First, pray that this is not our last Friday."

Afternoon

"Here we are, ladies and gentlemen, at the Indian Caves," announced Alicia in her best tour guide voice. I resolved to ask my question until I had a satisfactory answer.

I squeezed Beth's hand with my ringless hand. "Let's keep with the tour." I kept rehearsing various versions of my first priority question.

As we stood to get off the bus, I looked out the side window to the entrance to the cave. Half a dozen young men, lounging in their wife-beater shirts and grimy jeans, were watching us. One of them growled at José when he approached them at the mouth of the cave.

Alicia muttered to me, "This isn't safe." She called, "José!"

The men laughed at José, mocking him. He looked back at Alicia, his face a contortion of fear mixed with frustration. I told myself that I had no idea what their dynamics were and no business in finding out.

We were at the mouth of a cave that was supposed to be interesting. Beth had been to Capri and was not feeling too enthusiastic about getting in a boat and floating around in the dark. I was claustrophobic at the very thought of the cave but was not about to admit it.

I had, however, found out in advance that it was lit by strings of electric lights, so it wouldn't be too bad. Still, I had been counting on having to stay behind, on the bus, with Beth. Unfortunately, all the other tourists were grumbling slightly, and Alicia was relying on us to be role models. Beth, daughter of two teachers, obediently switched into goody two-shoes mode.

I had resolved not to allow myself to call her my fiancée again, even in my mind, until she was.

I dutifully, bravely, followed her out into the hot sun and along the rock face that led to the cave. José came to walk close beside me and, with his tour guide smile rigid on his face, whispered sideways. "Quick, give me your chest pack!" I was too stunned to object and seconds later he was buttoning up his shirt and fading into the crowd as we were joined by a couple of other young men who hopped off an ancient diesel tractor that had just pulled up.

One of them looked familiar and for an instant I thought it was Luis, but then realized that was impossible. They skirted around us and took off quickly along the pathway we were to take to our goal, an underground river and a small lake reached only by taking a boat through a tunnel. I'd read about this lake. It was supposed to be where an Indian maiden had met and loved a young man from an enemy tribe. More Romeo and Juliet.

As we hiked along the path beside the river, we quickly left the daylight behind. Our way was lit by an overhead string of electric lights. Alicia pointed out stalagmites and stalactites and explained their formation. Creepy, dark shadows lurked around bends in the path. I walked ahead of Beth, closely watching.

Eventually, the path ended at a large wooden wharf to which were tied three old, flat-bottomed wooden boats, each powered by a small outboard motor operated by a bored boatman.

And on the wharf, apparently waiting for us, were the young men wearing wife beaters. How did all these people come together? The boats knocked faintly against the dock and what must have been a generator for the lights purred somewhere in the darkness.

Alicia and José looked at each other as if deciding something. "Come on, José!" called one of the newcomers who laughed as he blew out an invisible candle.

José backed slowly away from our group and moved towards but not into the gang as they got into one boat and Alicia urged us into the two other boats. She began her tourist guide spiel about the Indian lovers.

When the two tour boats were almost loaded, out of nowhere appeared a woman who looked like the caricature of a prostitute in a 1940's Hollywood movie as she wiggled in her high heels and tight, short skirt to the edge of the dock. A middle-aged guy in the boat ahead of us called for the boatman to wait until they could squeeze in "the charming lady."

I told myself to stop imagining things and helped Beth into the third boat. She sat down, staring at the woman in the boat ahead of us as her admirer gallantly helped her to a seat beside him on the back bench. He pulled her onto his lap, and they were soon all over each other.

José, at the front of that boat, helped some older tourists climb out, and I helped them clamber into our boat. They were grumbling their disapproval of the whole scene but most of them couldn't help watching the couple who had progressed to the floor of their boat that was now empty except for the boatman who ignored their rolling ride as the boat came close to tipping over. The men in wife beaters cheered. The boat did not leave the dock.

The river water was dark as our over-crowded boat slowly approached the pool famed for its beautiful stillness. The boatmen turned off their engines, and as Alicia finished her story of the Indians, I felt an ancient presence. I was about to speak to Beth when I was stopped by total silence.

I held Beth's hand in the darkness. With my other hand I protected her face from being scraped by the rocks leaning out over the water. The engines turned and caught, and the boats moved on through our nightmare.

"Are you alright, Beth?" She answered by nodding her head against my shoulder.

Why had we got ourselves into this situation? I could hear nothing except for the small engines putting away and the tourists' nervous whispering as we eased along the wall of the cavernous gorge.

I had to declare myself to her, then and there. I slid the ring off my little finger and found her left hand, luckily next to me. Wordlessly I slid the ring onto her ring finger, and closed her hand with the diamond pointing into her grip. She sat totally motionless. I had no idea what she was thinking or about to do, but I was no longer afraid of the darkened cave.

Apparently ignoring my quasi-romantic move, Beth pulled her Blackberry from her pocket and passed it to Alicia. For an instant I felt hope, remembering Beth asking how to call the Cuban equivalent to 911, before I realized that the solid stone walls would block any phone calls. Anyway, the nearest police station would be too far away to do us any good.

I dreaded whatever was about to happen to us and prayed that it wouldn't last long. I hoped even more that I would be able to protect Beth and the baby.

My eyes had somewhat adjusted to the darkness when flash-lights started to light the cave, and I realized we had stopped against another shelf-like rock. José was grabbed and yanked out of our boat onto the shelf where half a dozen men waited for us, waving guns and flashlights in our eyes and shouting, "Men, out of the boat!" Beth tried to push me down out of sight, but I was grabbed by the elbow and pulled across her lap. I hoped I hadn't hurt the baby.

With the other men I was dropped on the shelf rock and searched. The thieves were clearly in a hurry as they felt us all down for our valuables, except for José who stood motionless against the wall of the cave. They found nothing on me except my wallet. One of them went through it, pulled out its bills and tossed it back in the boat.

Next the robbers demanded that the women's purses and all the backpacks be put on the rock to be emptied of anything of value. Inside a few minutes, the robbers' bags were full. They took off in the first boat, deeper into the cave, leaving us in the darkness, our boat with the women still in it, along with our empty wallets and even emptier bags. My iPhone was gone, but they left the cigars I had bought.

Someone was crying. "Beth," I called softly, "you okay?" She answered yes, somewhat hesitantly, and I was happier in that moment than I had ever been in my life.

Then I remembered the traditional proposal line in 19th century English novels and, as sweat dripped down my face, I spoke, just loudly enough for her to hear, and anyone else nearby who was listening, "Beth, will you do me the honor of becoming my bride and make me the happiest man in the world?"

She answered, "Yes, I will."

Alicia clapped her hands. "Yes! Wonderful!"

Instead of more laughter and applause, the other tourists produced grumbling and fearful yelling. I heard one voice exclaim, "We've just been robbed, you idiot," and I didn't know what to do next.

"Way to go, Gringo!" It was José, sarcastic, sounding tired. "Great timing." He was on the end of the rock shelf, now in the light from the boatman's flashlight. "Don't worry, I still have your pouch."

"So," one of the tourists grumbled at us, "are you in league with the robbers?"

Alicia, however, was still cheering. "I thought he'd never propose! I thought I saw him put the ring in his mouth to swallow it."

"I didn't do that."

Beth held up her hand. "Can someone shine a light on this ring! I want to see it." She loved it, just as I had hoped for so long, and hugged and kissed me, laughing and showing it around.

Alicia still looked worried, but also relieved by our happiness. She said to me, "You should not have kept her waiting so long!"

"What? You were waiting so long?" I was devastated as I pretended to be surprised. Beth protested that Alicia was exaggerating.

The return through the complicated series of caves was less tense. In the distance we could see the light of day, and that was more welcoming than the dark threats of our entrance.

Back at the dock, the "charming lady" was nowhere in sight, her admirer sitting disheveled on the back bench of the boat, one hand holding his black eye, the other his empty wallet. The boatman was fishing off the edge of the dock.

The hike back to the entrance was made in hostile silence. Beth and I walked at the back of the group to enjoy talking about our future as a married couple and the story of our love. Alicia joined us briefly to tell us that the police were on their way.

We had an extended picnic at the new wooden pavilion for tourists near the start of the path into the cave. Some of the tourists blamed José and Alicia for the robbery and the high-risk day. Some looked at Beth and me suspiciously, but we, in our own bubble of joy, ignored them.

One guy reminded me of my dad's next-door neighbor who was a crass radio talk-show host. This one assumed the leader-ship role, organizing the other tourists into checking what had been stolen and reassuring them that he would for sure, right away, get them back, pronto, to the gated community.

He waved his arms to get the attention of the group and shouted, "Will you promise that you will never ever leave our beloved community until it's time to catch the plane back to civilization?"

"We will!" several shouted.

"What's that?" he bellowed. "I want everyone to try that again. Tell me, will YOU stay in our gated community until it's time for our plane?"

"We will!" everyone shouted. José and Alicia looked almost fearful. Where did the instant demagoguery come from?

Fede had packed lunch bags for us and we shared them with Alicia and José whose much smaller lunches looked like left-overs from the previous night's bar at the National Hotel.

The ranter soon had most of his crowd tight around him, glancing occasionally over their shoulders at us, as if we were in cahoots with their oppressors. He complained loudly that we were obviously out of contact with the police and that he would organize a class action suit against the tour agency. His flock was making grumbling noises, especially when sirens were heard in the distance, coming towards us.

The police arrived with a good supply of bottled water, and that improved the group's collective mood. For the first time since arriving in Cuba, I felt oddly relaxed. That didn't last long. It seemed to take forever for the police to take down our information. Sitting there waiting, I found myself aghast that we had been put in such danger. I could understand why the group was so angry.

"José, was that guy with the bandages Luis?" I asked.

"No way. Luis is still in jail, so we are clear." José laughed, and I wasn't sure I saw the humor, or believed him, for that matter. He continued, "We're lucky no one resisted." Great, I thought, the perfect crime.

The picnic lunch having been consumed, the other tourists could not relax and enjoy the lush vistas of the valley. Their main concern was to reach the resort safely and quickly. Can't say I disagreed. Soon we were boarding the bus.

The Lothario had wilted after his starring role in the cave. He got on the bus and then got out again and went around to José's door. Beth and I giggled, telling jokes as we imagined the information he was seeking. The other three men travel-ing with him were looking very irritated. I guessed that one of them was his brother-in-law. Or had been.

Once we were ready to leave, José passed my chest pack to me. Instead of putting it on, I just shoved it in my bag. Alicia picked up Paporov's book from the bench where she had put it hours before and where it had rested undisturbed while Beth and I had been robbed and had become engaged to be married.

"What should I read to you?" asked Alicia. She really knew how to change the subject. She still seemed blasé about the violence we had experienced.

"Is there anything in the book about a loving marriage?" I asked. Thinking through Hemingway's novels and stories, not many such pairings sprang to mind, except for the one with Catherine dying in the rain. Beth would not die in childbirth.

"Do you want every word or the general ideas?" Alicia wanted to know. "I think you'll get more out of it if I sum it up for you."

As she flipped through the book, diligently searching for the best chapter, Beth and I looked at each other, quizzically at first, but then nodding in agreement. Beth, for once ignoring an opportunity to learn something from a book, politely asked Alicia not to bother with Paporov since we had too much on our minds. Alicia looked relieved and moved up to the front seat where she chatted with José.

Beth played with her new ring, and we talked about wedding rings. Feeling secure for the first time in hours, we soon found ourselves dozing into sleep, and I remembered that she had not been tired all the time before she became pregnant. She'd get over the tiredness and nausea before long.

I wondered, for the first time, if she'd wanted to get pregnant in order to pressure me into marriage. No, she could have snagged any guy she wanted into marriage, with or without pregnancy. Why did she choose me? Why did she choose pregnancy? I had no answers, but I was so happy I really didn't need them. I wondered, for an instant, if she knew I'd chosen her? I had. Definitely!

The people around us started cheering when the bus reached the downtown marketplace, and Beth and I woke up, disoriented and stiff. We looked at each other, and I felt shy that I could be so much in love. We didn't speak.

Three policemen and one lady cop were there to meet us. They said we had two options, discuss our losses in the robbery and then go to the public washroom in the hotel nearby or do those things in the reverse order. The tourists were loudly congratulating each other that they had less than half an hour's drive to their resort. They seemed totally unaware that the police and Alicia and José might understand and be insulted by their chatter.

Alicia spoke quietly to Beth and me. "We'll come by your hotel as soon as we're free. My mother is preparing a feast for you tonight because she wants to meet you."

I was a little put out by Alicia's assumption that we would join her in obeying her mother's whim, but I told myself this was a great opportunity to experience a genuine Cuban household.

The Cuban police, in halting English, informed our group that they had reported all our stolen credit cards. They gave us a phone number to call to discuss replacing them and asked us to meet individually with the police to have our stolen goods returned. They had found less cash than we had reported. On the other hand, no passports had been taken.

There was a rumble of complaints from the tourists. I could see the police were irritated, so I whispered my plan to Beth. She nodded and I spoke out, first asking Alicia to translate.

Beth and I volunteered as a couple to be first to meet the officers under the tree, and we wondered if it would be acceptable for the rest of the tourists in our group if they could have a choice between meeting officers after us under the tree or coming the next morning to the police station. The police nodded agreement, and within a minute everyone was signed up to meet after Beth and me.

José and Alicia gallantly undertook to wait to drive all the tourists back to the resort after their talks with the police, and as Beth and I walked back to our hotel, we wondered if our friends would be thanked or tipped for their extra time and effort. Probably not, since most of the group suspected José of being in cahoots with the robbers. They seemed to think the same of me.

"You know," I said to Beth as we turned up our street, "the police gave me 40 US dollars more than I reported stolen."

"Me, too," said Beth. "I reported 90 dollars stolen, which is what I lost, and they gave me 150."

"Hey, they must have liked you better."

"But the thing is, I didn't object. And neither did you. And everyone else got less back than they claimed."

"Guilty. And who knows if everyone else was lying or not?" I hated this kind of talk.

"Well, we deserved some reward for smoothing things out," Beth said, "for helping the situation instead of just sitting there, whining."

"The jerk with the hooker got zero dollars back. That was pretty funny. She'd cleaned him out in the boat."

"The fool says in his heart, 'there is no God,'" concluded Beth.

Sometimes I don't get what Beth's talking about. I was relieved to walk into our hotel and find, as expected, Fede smiling a welcome. Our friends, Fede, José and Alicia, seemed to be somehow involved, perhaps even complicit, in the robbery. After all, José knew when to take my chest pack. Still, I trusted and liked them on a personal level. What about the hooker? She wouldn't hang around an underground cave all day. Surely our relative prosperity made honesty easier for us.

It suddenly struck me. One of the robbers who had held us up in the cave looked like one of the guards at the Finca. Our friends seemed implicated in and responsible for more than one crime. But so was I. I had been lucky no one had searched me when I left the Finca.

We headed up the stairs, holding hands. It would be some time before Alicia and José would be done driving the tourists back to their resort. Beth and I fell into bed.

Evening

It was almost dark when Alicia and José knocked at our door and asked, almost formally, if we would care for dinner with her family. I was about to open a bottle of bubbly that I'd bought to toast our engagement, but Alicia suggested that, since she and Beth wanted no more than a sip, we should bring it to dinner. Her parents ran a casa particular, basically a Cuban version of bed and breakfast. Both generations wanted to celebrate our engagement.

"We also can celebrate Paulo's safe journey," said Beth.

"He'll be out of our hair until Tuesday," I said, sighing. They all looked at me and I realized I'd said the wrong thing. "That was an American joke."

"We are all American. Remember?" José sounded offended, as usual.

Well, no more guilt. I turned to Beth and used my stage whisper. "I wonder if we should invite them to our wedding?"

"I wonder if we can get a visa to go to their wedding?" Alicia asked José in the same voice.

"And have they any idea how expensive it would be for us to go all that way?" José responded.

"Could we get married here?" I asked.

Once we were walking along the early evening streets, Mary's Manuscript B almost comfortable in my chest pack, a semi-relaxed mood settled on us. I wondered if our newfound friendship would last after we boarded the plane home on Monday afternoon.

At the top of the street we passed the pub where Beth had danced with the pro. That sleaze bucket was hovering at the door, watching us. I didn't meet his eyes.

Alicia's parents welcomed us warmly. It was a traditional household and immediately Alicia joined her mother in the kitchen and helped serve dinner while the men drank beer and laughed together.

Her father, apparently the grandson of Carlos Gutierrez, peppered me with questions about my connection to Hemingway. I managed to steer the conversation around to the black market in possessions from the Finca. He talked quite openly about José's struggle with Luis for control of what he called "the Hemingway business."

José stood at a tiny bar and gave us a lesson in making mojitos and, for Beth, a virgin mojito. He explained how to crush the mint and lime in the bottom of the glass, then pour in white sugar and crush the three ingredients together. He tossed small ice cubes into the glass and poured light rum over them, then soda water to fill the glass. He carefully stirred the drink and garnished it with a long mint leaf and stuck in a straw. He didn't specify quantities but we could see that the drink was customized to the drinker: lots of lime and rum, or not much sugar or rum.

I thought of the tall glasses my dad had. The first thing I'd do when I saw him next would be to put three of these glasses in his freezer and unpack a cooler with all the ingredients. That would be fun, especially when we told him that we were expecting and were wondering when and where we would be married. Even if Uncle Edmund had already told him everything, he would act surprised.

My parents had broken up when my mom left us in Washington. I hoped that the same fate would not be Beth's and mine, but it nagged at the back of my mind. I couldn't tell her because that would freak her out. In my nightmares I kept mixing together my Beth, my mother and Catherine Barkley. And, in the past two nights, Alicia.

Hemingway, like Frederic Henry, had been superstitious. It seemed to be an easy, thoughtless substitute for religion, a compulsion in psychiatric lingo. Back in Canada, it was the old folks and the poorly educated who were superstitious. And maybe also the immigrants. Thoughts like this would get me in trouble in Canada as well as Cuba, so I kept them to myself.

Hemingway's religious characters were simply superstitious. How was being superstitious different from being religious? I had to talk with Beth about this because she, unlike me, had been brought up in the church and she talked the talk, to use half a cliché. I knew, however, lots of scientific types who were superstitious as well, and I'd heard of brilliant religious scholars who routinely knocked on wood for luck.

"Hey, Alf," called Alicia, "come back from your dreaming."
I had been staring at the dining table, having polished off the
best meal of our trip: shellfish with rice, black beans and potatoes.

José was putting on his jacket before escorting Beth and me to
our hotel. Alicia was going to help her mother clean up.

She asked to borrow the Paporov book a little longer, and we
arranged to meet in the hotel foyer in the morning to go to
Cojimar and visit Tomás.

We walked quickly through the near-empty evening streets of
the downtown. We could have walked on our own back to the
hotel, but José's presence was certainly reassuring. Our plan,
however, was to spend the evening out celebrating our engagement, and so I suggested that he drop us off at El Floridita.

Off he went and we dove into the noise and cigar smoke of the
bar. Visiting El Floridita was an experience! It occurred to me
it was typical of places I've read about that turn out to be just
like what I've read and then imagined, except the real place is
usually smaller and noisier.

We found a seat across the bar from the crowded Hemingway
corner and set ourselves to soaking up the scene. "Cuba's
Brain Drain," "The Middle-Class Pirates," "Graduate Student
Flees from Cuban Jail to Sanctuary in Canada." Beth stopped,
clearly on a magazine title roll, except since I couldn't hear a
word she said, she resorted to printing on a paper napkin.

The waiter arrived with a flourish and, in English, asked us
what we would like. At least that's what I thought he asked, so
I shouted, "Hola. A Papa Doble, that's a double daiquiri without sugar, and a Shirley Temple."

The waiter looked at me with disdain. That was okay. He

informed me, I imagined, that he knew what a Papa Doble was. Nobly resisting the temptation to tell him what was in a Shirley Temple, I nodded and smiled. "Gracias." I realized then that Beth has the reassuring capability of overlooking my embarrassing moments.

She simply proceeded. "Let's think about the Finca."

"The fun-filled Finca?" I interrupted.

She looked at me sternly. "The Finca Vigía without gunshots. Maybe we shouldn't go near the place again."

My first reaction was anger. Then I realized she had a good point. We had no idea about how safe we would be at the Finca. I needed, however, to find Manuscript A and I might have to go back there if Tomás didn't have it. Maybe Beth and Alicia could do something else, something safe, while José made sure I didn't steal anything else from the Finca.

Beth lifted a strand of her heavy blonde hair off her flushed neck and restored it to the double French braid that prevented her from sweating too much in the island heat. I couldn't imagine why most Cuban women wore their hair long. Women puzzle me.

We looked around at the clientele, mostly tourists it seemed, but certainly none from the wild tour that afternoon.

Beth was studying the food menu. "I could use a Big Mac right now."

"Well, anything like that here?"

"Not really. What did Hemingway eat here?"

"Expensive seafood. Does that sound good?"

She nodded. "I didn't want to ask for seconds at Alicia's place."

I smiled. "I wonder if it's a boy or a girl."

The waiter brought our drinks. Mine was incredibly sour, probably the first double I'd had in a year or so.

I ordered two of the day's special that, according to the menu, had been the favorite of Papa and Mary. I wondered if it was a huge meal as I'd read had been served in Hemingway's time. Probably not. The picture in the menu suggested that it was beautifully plated, as Toronto waiters liked to say.

Our meals arrived, and the waiter smiled as we looked at the very attractive surf and turf. He filled up our water glasses. Beth sat, gazing at the fragrant meal. "Wow! Fantastic!" It tasted great as well, even the inevitable potatoes. My belt was unusually tight.

Beth watched me ease it looser. "Maybe you shouldn't be eating for two."

"This is going to be a five-pound holiday, for me anyway. Okay, no dessert. Besides, as Hemingway said, 'any man who eats dessert is not drinking enough.'" We polished off our meal while we looked around. "How come," I asked, "no one's getting his picture taken with a hand on the Hemingway statue there?"

Beth looked around. "Wow, that's an imposing statue! Life-size."

"You probably didn't see it when we walked in because of the crowd. It's new. The corner stool where he sat used to be chained off so it was always empty. Kind of a cool gesture, eh?"

"Or snotty. And I think the painting over the bar is overly heroic."

"Talk about snotty! That's a gorgeous bar, don't you think? This must have been one of the classiest drinking places in the Caribbean at one time." The bar was painted a shining black and a deep red. Its lights reflected in the brass trim, and its largest feature was a painting, on the wall behind it, of the old Havana harbor. And this had been Hemingway's favorite place for entertaining his Hollywood friends.

Beth resumed worrying about our safety. "Maybe we should rethink our tours with Alicia and José. Today was definitely hairy."

"Well, they can't keep the tourism business going if tourists get shot!"

"Visiting Tomás should be fine tomorrow."

"You're right." I was so lucky to have found her!

Beth, unaware of my rush of grateful love, looked around us. "So, this is the bar where Hemingway held court. I guess he needed to have lots of admirers. He didn't seem able to focus on one woman and love her enough to be happily married, just the two of them."

"Maybe he couldn't love anyone because he loved the booze more than any person."

"Why didn't someone tell him to stop?"

"There were people who talked to him about why and how he should stop, like his good friend Doctor Herrara, but no one loved him enough to stand up to him, I guess."

"Mary didn't?"

"Well, the cynical view of the scholars is that Mary had him figured out. He grew tired of women quickly and, once he'd fallen for the next wife or lover, he'd irritate his current woman until she left him. There are rumors that at times he was abusive. Mary got him to write her into his will as his sole heir and as literary executor, and then she hung in there and never left him. Brilliant, eh?"

"That's so brutal!"

"You mean his behavior or hers?"

"Both!"

"It's scary, though," I blurted, "what can happen in a marriage!"

"It won't happen with us. We're both too sensitive."

We stared at our empty plates. When I straightened up, Beth did, too. She asked, as the waiter cleared our table, "Is there a gentler, kinder story?"

"Well, partly, but it's also really not credible. It features Mary as innocent and loving and Hemingway as abusive and manipulative. The opposite extreme, with Hemingway as victim and Mary as villain, doesn't ring true either. The feminists have always argued that Mary's been basically maligned by all the male scholars who blame her for Hemingway losing his potency as a writer as well as a lover."

"What do you think?"

"I think it's too bad that he got so drunk, but that doesn't excuse his being abusive, if in fact he was. I think a lot of people

can't imagine their favorite writer being abusive so they tend
to dislike his alleged victims, or at least Mary, the woman who
stuck around the longest."

Beth said softly, "I hope Alicia's not abused."

"Surely not!" I said. "You know, it's only a short walk down
Calle Obispo to the hotel. How about we walk instead of taking a cab?"

"Sure."

We were a bit nervous walking down to Calle Mercaderes, but
there were people all around us and police at every intersection, guns at the ready.

In a few minutes we were being greeted by Fede behind the
bar. "Decaf?"

We looked at each other and nodded.

"Has Paulo left yet?" Beth asked.

"Sí, I think so," Fede answered.

"Fede, why was Paulo in prison?" Beth asked.

Fede frowned at us. "Paulo has never been in prison."

Beth glanced at me and I looked at her. There was a moment
of fear between us.

Trying to effect calm in my voice, I smiled at Fede. "Perhaps
we misunderstood the bilingual conversation the other day."

"Are you hungry?" Fede asked.

"Actually," Beth laughed, "we had two dinners tonight." As she told him about our day's adventures, she flashed her ring. I couldn't believe she would do that girly ring flash, and I couldn't believe how delighted I felt!

"Congratulations!" Fede reached across the bar to kiss Beth on both cheeks and shook hands with me. "May I offer you some champagne on the house?"

"No thanks, man. We've had enough alcohol today. The coffee will be great."

Fede looked a little surprised but also happy to make us his best decaf espresso. "I heard that there was a robbery in the Indian Caves. I hope that you were not involved!"

"Yes, we were. Listen, Fede, can you tell us if it is safe for us to go to more tourist spots?"

"Sí, sí. There are very few crimes against tourists in Cuba."

"But we've seen crimes every day so far!"

Fede laughed. "Then you should not have any more trouble." He turned his back to finish the swirl of milk topping our coffees. He set them down on the bar before us. Beautiful! The milk pattern for both of us was a heart.

I put my arm around Beth's shoulder. We drank the coffee watching Fede clean up the bar. As we headed up the stairs to our room, the flamenco dancers were heading out the front door. Fede said, "Buenas noches."

I asked Beth, "What time is it?"

"Half past kissing time, time to kiss again."

When Beth was ready for sleep, she found me pretending to read with Hemingway's wire-rimmed spectacles. "Oh my God!" she gasped. "Not the stolen glasses again."

I smiled and nodded slowly. My humor was not having its desired effect.

Beth sputtered, "How could you even think of taking those from the Finca?"

Saturday, July 23, 1960

She was the single artificer of the world
In which she sang.
And when she sang, the sea,
Whatever self it had, became the self
That was her song, for she was the maker.

Wallace Stevens, "The Idea of Order at Key West," 1934

Saturday morning, I'm up here alone, writing again. Open-ing a window of my tower, I hear the trees full of birdsong. What about our household? Only Valerie will leave Cuba with us. René will stay in charge of the Finca, and a number of others will maintain the place, still paid by Ernest who talks in terms of our being back in August. My throat con-stricts. I am convinced that neither Ernest nor I will ever live here again. This is my last Saturday morning here.

And where is our famous writer? Even a few years ago, Ernest would have bounced back from the previous day's hangover and been up and showered, hair crisply brushed, wearing a clean shirt and shorts, favorite hat and moccasins. He'd be writing, whistling to himself, totally concentrated. Now, he suffers too much pain, physical and emotional, to produce the kind of writing that once made him proud and happy. When he tries to rid himself of his troubles by writing of better times and better friends, he is even more saddened. When he primes his muse with alcohol, he draws murky poison.

I'm almost concerned enough to go down to see if he is still breathing, if he needs help, but José Luis comes out the front door and waves cheerily up at me. He has often expressed a polite interest in my writing but he has never come up the tower. Today he strides off down the driveway, and I hear a car, probably a taxi, coming to meet him. What will Ernest do without his long-time friend to care for him? Obviously Ernest is still alive. I return to my typewriter.

You've heard of Batista? My dear American reader, did you know that in the 1940's and 1950's, Fulgencio Batista worked with the American mafia to profit from the Cuban black markets in prostitution, gambling and drugs? One night in 1957 when Ernest was in Miami, Batista's drunken soldiers invaded the Finca, looking for socialists. The thugs threatened me with guns, then shot Ernest's dog instead of me. They were lawless mercenaries, and Fidel Castro, in his early days, made himself popular by promising he would rid the government of the corrupt Batista and his followers.

Ernest was so determined to help Castro's revolution against Batista's puppet government that he donated $10,000 to the Communist rebels in Cuba. When some of them invaded the Finca, both Ernest and I were away. René phoned us and said the rebels were demanding all his guns and his car. Ernest said, "Let them have whatever they need." A few months later, they returned what they had taken, unused, because of their respect for Ernest. The car was even gassed up. This story seems made up to me, probably by Ernest since it reflects so well on him.

Ernest is a wild card by nature, definitely larger than life. In earlier wars he blurred the lines between soldier and reporter and once faced an inquiry by the military. He was lucky he wasn't court-martialed for exceeding the rules of engagement laid down for journalists. I don't see the point of military heroes, however, or any kind of fighting. It is not evident that Ernest is actually helping the people of Cuba. Perhaps he is merely indulging his need to stir the pot to get people's attention.

Ernest has rather unusual social skills. Whenever he is in the company of someone important, he manages to insult that person. When he is with working-class people, he is charming, so polite he's almost patronizing. Nevertheless, he has been consistent in his instinct to support the underdog, and socialism has seemed to him to be the best means for doing that in Spain and Cuba. Is that treasonous? In 1942 he invited representatives from both sides of the Spanish Civil War to meet here at the Finca. Is that treasonous? Hoover has never done anything constructive or creative; still, because he knows which way the wind blows, he is paid by the American government to persecute Ernest. Who is the better man?

René surprises me by calling up from the base of the tower. His voice sounds urgent. I look down from my window, and he's mimicking holding the telephone to his ear, gesturing that I come down. I hurry downstairs, and at the door to the second level, we meet. He says a call had just come in from New York, and a stranger had told him to warn Ernest that FBI special agent Gerald Thacker of the American Consulate in Cuba wants to meet Ernest today or else he will denounce him as a Communist at this Monday's House Un-American Activities Committee.

That's not news. Thacker has already told Ernest this a month or two ago. He'd also said that Ernest's reputation as a Communist sympathizer is a problem for the United States of America and that it would be helpful for him to go home. The FBI guys seem to like using unusual verb forms such as the passive voice when they threaten their compatriots. When I tell René all this he looks at his feet and then around the room, everywhere but at me. Finally, he says that Thacker had told him to warn us that we won't be safe if we stay here any longer, that the Federal Bureau of Investigation can bring pressure to bear.

So, this is the main reason for us to leave on Monday. I smile and say to René, "Remember the Maine." I tell him how much we will miss him and all the other workers around the Finca, and how we'll be back when the political climate improves. René just nods and nods, looking at the ground. He assures me sadly that he will help us get off the island safely.

I wonder why Thacker made that call today. Had his agents reported that we were preparing to leave in two days? Maybe I've hidden our suitcases too well from Ernest. Maybe he said something careless or defiant to someone, and that's got back to the FBI. Even though I try to sound confident with René, I feel more and more discouraged and fearful.

Another irony is that Americans have been told that Fidel Castro is a monster and their own leaders and representatives abroad are honorable men. My experience is the opposite. Certainly Castro is a man acting with his people's best interests at heart.

He is, however, like Ernest, a wild card. Oddly enough, they have only met once in all these years they have both lived on this little island. Ernest organized a fishing tournament just this past May, and Castro turned up and won it, fair and square. Once the pictures of the two great men and the prize-winning marlin had been taken, they talked for half an hour and seemed to enjoy each other's company. When I asked Ernest what they talked about, he said he had briefly told Castro that the American government wanted us to come home and that he needed American medical help. Ernest's Spanish was good enough for that conversation and on that day his mind seemed clear.

Castro told Ernest that he had, for years, assigned some men from his inner circle to shadow us, and that he would maintain that protection until we were off the island. Ernest thanked Castro and agreed that we would continue to act as if we did not know this. Castro also promised that he would preserve the Finca for our return. In other words, he would not let the FBI or the black market tear it apart.

After the fishing competition Castro made another gratifying comment when he told Ernest how much he admired his novels. Of course he loved *The Old Man and the Sea*, but he said he found *For Whom the Bell Tolls* the most useful. Why? Because in the early 1950's he read and reread the pages describing guerrilla warfare techniques, and when he launched his invasion of the island, his plans were based on what he had read. We were both amazed by how quixotic this complex and idealistic man really is, especially in light of the very distorted portrait of his character in the American press.

I once asked Ernest, if Castro is such a good man, what about all the executions of his own people? Ernest said it was necessary to clean up from Batista's corrupt regime and then to establish health care and education for all the people. It is a strict rule, with many young men executed or thrown in jail, but the people appreciate that they're better off than the people of most Caribbean islands and also better off than before Castro took power. I also wonder whether Castro's success owes something (if not almost everything) to his Russian occupiers.

Ernest said that he had told Castro about my manuscript and explained that I wanted to take it through customs for publication by *Life* Magazine. He also expressed our concern that either Cuban officials or FBI agents would confiscate and destroy it. Castro said he'd speak to our protectors who were trained to handle much more difficult situations. I thanked Ernest for arranging this and said that I would tell René of my hiding place for the manuscript if we somehow were unable to get it through customs. I also told Ernest that I wanted him to wear it in his chest pack and only give it to René if he felt the FBI was going to do a body search on him. I didn't tell Ernest where the hiding spot was. He would flip if he knew I'd desecrated his collection. I shouldn't have done that.

After the fishing contest Ernest contacted one of Castro's deputies and offered to help Castro write his speech for the United Nations in September. Castro instead sent a speech-writer to talk with him. Ernest emphasized that Castro needed to understand American values in order to succeed in communicating with both United Nations leaders and, through the media, with average American citizens. I just hope Castro can get into and out of New York without being assassinated. Even on his own island he has to sleep in a different place every night.

I am now going to find Ernest. It's been hours since I've talked with him and I am struck by my recurring fear that he's dead. No, René and Valerie are moving about normally. What he said in a dreary time last winter echoes in my mind: "I'm through with all that running around. I got in wrong." He's been made to feel like a failure by American authorities. How sad it is to witness a great man lose his talent and his confidence, to see him cut off from the people and places he loves, to watch him lose himself!

It is almost time for us to leave this violent, beautiful island, its third world poverty only slightly ameliorated by a revolution in the name of noble goals. It strikes me that Cuba, like Ernest, has been buffeted by foreign as well as internal powers for too long, but I do not have the energy to think anymore today. Perhaps there is no need to hide what I am writing, but for now I will put my typed pages and the copies out of sight. I am tired, my head aching as usual when there's a storm brewing.

Better dead than red? Better read than dead.

Saturday, July 24, 2010

"A man," Harry Morgan said, looking at them both. "One man alone ain't got. No man alone now." He stopped. "No matter how a man alone ain't got no bloody fucking chance."

He shut his eyes. It had taken him a long time to get it out and it had taken him all of his life to learn it.

Ernest Hemingway, *To Have and Have Not*, 1937

Morning

I woke in a panic, dreaming of Castro charging at me like a raging bull, followed by Uncle Edmond awkwardly patting Aunt Sylvia's shoulder as she grieved, then Paulo, like a fool, singing the children's song, "The cat came back, the very next day." Finally, I wandered endlessly around an unfamiliar Cojimar, unable to find Tomás's house. I woke up. What was this? I forced myself back to sleep to dream these scenarios better.

Then Beth was beside me, sitting at her parents' dining table, along with siblings, in-laws and old folk. Her father, a quiet man in a gregarious family, was quizzing me about my prospects. I wasn't able to hear one important sentence he said, something about his knee and France. His brother-in-law, across the table from me, picked up my distress and said, "Oh, he's just telling you about his war."

I leaned closer to Beth's dad and listened hard. "I was in the military, like your dad, but I was wounded by a land mine off the coast of France." I froze. What was I going to do with that? Beth was cheerily talking to her crazy aunt about our wedding plans.

I was on my own. I swallowed compulsively. This was the test. I saw it. What I didn't know was whether it was a test of discernment, of sobriety, or of social skills. Well, my analytical skills generally outrank what is now called emotional intelligence, and although I'd had two beers, I decided to play my trump.

"Excuse me, sir, but a landmine explodes on land and 'off the coast of France' refers to being on a boat out on the Atlantic, so I don't see how you were wounded."

I heard Beth gasp and wished I were in a dream instead of awake. But I was in a dream and not, alas, awake.

The chatter around the table subsided into meaningful glances and under-the-breath snickering. Beth sat staring at her plate, smiling to herself. That gave me the courage to look her dad straight in the eye. He stood up and announced, loudly for once, "Do you know that you are the first person to ever listen to me tell that story? And the first person to call me on its obvious lie. My son!"

Beth was shaking me. I woke up, sweating, gasping. "What? What are you doing?" I had no idea where I was.

"Alf, wake up! You're okay! It's just a nightmare!" I recognized her voice and started to calm down. I held on tight to her until I could forget it.

Beth sat on the side of the bed, slowly braiding her hair into an elegant double French braid. I was rummaging in my suitcase. My clean wardrobe options were limited.

"I seem to be over morning sickness," she said.

I'd noticed that but had hesitated to comment on it. "Do you suppose Alicia is pregnant? She was looking pretty queasy for the past two mornings."

"Top secret, but you're right. It's just that she doesn't want to tell anyone, including José, until she's three months."

"Why not tell him?"

"She's not sure he'll be pleased."

"Is she afraid of him or what?"

"I don't know. It's just that they had agreed not to have children until they were on a better financial footing. They're living with her parents still."

"I wondered yesterday why she disappeared so quickly at lunch and why she's been whining. So has he."

"He's so macho he can't stand being poor and underemployed. Also, he's jealous."

"Jealous?"

"Of you, silly."

"Good grief. Well, I suppose he's jealous that he doesn't have you." That was my effort at gallantry. It was also true.

"He's not my type."

I felt relief to hear that, jealous as I was of José. And every other male who had ever looked at her. Stupid. I felt more relief as she went on to tell me how she'd lain awake planning our wedding for mid-summer's night. By having it soon, she would still be able to get into a regular wedding dress and make a grand entrance to Mendelssohn's "Wedding March."

I suggested that we could make a grand exit, too, being piped out. She looked surprised. I realized I had never told her about my cousin Jake who wore the McLeod tartan after his mother's side. Beth had only heard about the O'Malleys, Irish who had fled, hungry, to Canada during the potato famine with a gift of the blarney, some handmade glassware and linens, some deep animosities and not much else.

In any case, Beth and I would make our own way together, however much our parents groaned and called us immature. We both liked pipers.

"I know what my dad would like me to be doing right now," I said, finally squinting at the clock. "We've slept in! We said we'd be at Tomás's place by now!"

"I'll call Fede to order us a quick breakfast and a taxi. How long will it take us to get downstairs?"

Fifteen minutes later we were in a taxi, driven, to my relief, by no one we knew. It was another beautiful day and I was with my ladylove. In my chest pack was Manuscript B. It was good not to have Alicia and José around all the time.

The driver was chatty, but despite Beth, the sunshine and Manuscript B, I began to feel dragged down again. It seemed, on this trip, that whenever I thought something was fantastic, something miserable screwed it up. As we drove along I tried to explain this to Beth, and she said she felt the same. "On TV ads everyone in the Caribbean looks so sexy and glamorous in their skimpy clothing, happily running hand in hand along the sunny beach, and we haven't even got to a beach."

"Yeah, we've just seen greed and violence. I've kept expecting, day after day, to see the TV version." I checked the driver's expression. He didn't seem to be listening to, or understanding, our back seat talk.

She nodded. "And here we saved up to have a good time. Self-ish or what?"

"Or simply rich."

"So are we going to be lucky this morning?" Beth asked.

"Do you mean, get lucky?" I gave her my lascivious leer.

"Find the rest of Mary's manuscript, silly. José said he's going to be at Tomás's place this morning."

"To translate or to make sure we don't steal something?"

"Both, I guess," she said.

"And Uncle Ed keeps warning us about poverty and gangs and violence. Maybe he is right, and this is why Aunt Sylvia is always looking so worried."

"Maybe we're hopelessly naïve staying in a downtown hotel, getting involved with the locals."

"But we don't like all-inclusive resorts. It's boring doing noth-ing but eat, drink, swim, sleep, gamble, tan, read and pay for entertainment. And how else would I have done any research on Hemingway?"

"Right. But have you ever had an all-inclusive kind of holi-day?" she asked.

"My dad opposed it on ethical grounds. I went once with my cousins and their parents to Disney World. Bored me out of my frigging tree."

"Inclusive in church doublespeak means that gays are wel-come." Beth was undoing the French braid she had so rhythmically and beautifully braided. Her hair was now thick and curly, covering her neck and resting on her shoulders. "The all-inclusive gated places aren't safe either. Your Aunt Sylvia says it's easy for staff to let their dealers and prostitutes in through the back door. Lots of tourists are down here for the adrenalin of danger, the paid sex, and that endangers everyone. Indignant types like her husband are quickly labeled as interfering, and that's why she's so nervous. He's been threatened."

"That could mean we're in danger by association. I just want to get you and our baby home."

"But we have friends. We can trust Alicia and Paulo." Beth looked certain about this.

"Paulo's not here," I said.

"Details, details," she said, her voice light-hearted. Her expression was more serious.

"José?" I asked.

"He's the wild card. We've no idea how he's going to act one day to the next."

"For us or for them?"

She sounded confident. "For sure, what you and I have got to do is stay together, not get separated."

"Right." She seemed to feel that we'd solved all our problems. I was still worried.

She flashed her happy-with-life smile. "You know, I've been thinking of a pop quiz you could use in your Hemingway class."

"How? What quiz?" I was still in fear mode. Sometimes I thought that my mind didn't hop around as much as hers did. Perhaps I wasn't ADHD anymore. Or perhaps we both were. Pity our kid. Yikes! Maybe teachers label kids who are smart and bored ADHD in self-defense.

"These are the questions I thought up this morning when I was waiting for you to wake up: 'Castro read *For Whom the Bell Tolls* to learn about guerilla warfare techniques.' True or false?"

"True," I said.

"Right. 'Mary and Ernest Hemingway owned more than 50 cats in Cuba.' True or false?"

"True."

"One more: 'Castro did not cheat to win the fishing contest organized by Hemingway.' True or false?"

"They're all true!"

"That's so it's easy to mark."

The taxi had stopped in front of the Hemingway monument erected by the fishermen of the town. Still laughing as we got out, we looked around. To our left were the ruins of a castle. To the right, around the still water of the harbor, was La Terraza bar.

Tomás was sitting by the entrance to the bar with some other old guys. They looked as if they'd been there, motionless, since Hemingway's time. Positively dusty.

I was about to kiss Beth when it occurred to me it was right here that I'd made an awkward scene on our first day in

Cuba. Maybe, in fact, all those old guys were parked on their stools in anticipation of another such show. I imagined Tomás spreading the word, the others snorting.

"Want me to pick you up and twirl you around?"

"I was hoping that you were going to propose then and there."

"I was trying to. How about we just go talk with Tomás?"

Beth smiled, and I could see she understood. I smiled, and I could see she was happy.

"There's José." I waved to him as he came up the path and greeted us as old friends. He said Alicia had asked Julio to meet us at Tomás's house that morning.

Tomás silently led us inside La Terraza, past the long, polished wooden bar and into the lounge. There we looked out over the large natural harbor that was home to hundreds of small fishing boats. He pointed out the dry dock where the *Pilar* had been so painstakingly repaired, all expenses paid by the Hemingway Estate. I noticed that Tomás ignored the role of Mary who was the Hemingway Estate.

Now the *Pilar* was back at the Finca where it belonged. It hadn't been out to sea since May 1960 for the great fishing contest Hemingway had hosted and Castro had won. May 1960, a few weeks before the great man left, in July. All this, that Tomás had told us before, was probably not precisely true but we politely nodded as he told it, tears in his eyes, having learned the sentimentality that tourists love.

José was politely translating. I asked Tomás if Mary Hemingway had ever talked to him on the trips she had made to Cuba after her husband died. Tomás replied that she had given the *Pilar* to his father. I'd heard this. He confirmed that Mary had paid for the boat's overhaul but really it was only good for tourists to look at.

Tomás talked at some length in Spanish, looking right at me as if I could understand. Finally he stood up and started his slow shuffle out of the building. José explained that Tomás wanted us to come to his house.

"What was he saying, just now?" asked Beth.

"He was talking about his son, Manuel, the one Manu in *The Old Man and the Sea* was based on. My father, as you know. He spent many summers playing with Hemingway's sons. Hemingway, who sometimes wanted to play with them all as well, would pitch for their baseball games because he wanted to teach them baseball."

Beth, José and I followed Tomás past his friends on their stools and along to his street. We kept listening to José. It was amazing to be so close to people so close to Hemingway, but still I felt we were circling the information that Tomás knew I wanted, the location of Mary's manuscript of days Tuesday to Saturday. Was he teasing me or what?

It was José who brought up the topic. "Alicia and I were talking last night about whether or not Grandpa knows where the manuscript is. I was telling him this morning, before you arrived, that if the FBI actually harassed Hemingway during his last year here, her story might bring that wrongdoing to light."

I nodded and spoke loudly so Tomás could hear. "The FBI made Hemingway's last years miserable. Not just him. Mary had to endure so much as well. Scholars often treat her as a bitchy complainer, but when I think about the FBI files on Hemingway, her claims of their mistreatment in the last sections of her article seem justified. Imagine going through all that!"

"Why did Hemingway use your father as the model for the boy Manu instead of one of his sons?" Beth asked.

I groaned to myself. Way to get off topic! But maybe it was good to keep circling.

José answered Beth, "I would say that Hemingway was a difficult father. He and his sons did not get along. My father was the genuine Cuban boy that Hemingway needed in the story."

"Did he die young?"

"When I was 10 years old."

José paused, then continued. "Once he almost got killed when Hemingway had set up a baseball game, but the boys wanted to play 'Manuel the Matador.' Hemingway was angry and very drunk but decided that he would teach these boys about bullfighting. When Tomás saw his son take a hit to the stomach, he grabbed him and started to pull him out of the game, and Hemingway got mad and challenged Tomás to a boxing match then and there."

"Did they come to blows?" I asked. "Hemingway must have weighed twice what your grandfather did back then."

"And neither of them had boxing gloves or whatever Hemingway was dreaming about, so they just wrestled. Tomás was bruised all over, but he managed to rescue his son. It was a long time before the two men talked again, and the next summer Hemingway's boys did not come to Cuba."

"Did your grandfather ever meet Hadley? Did she ever escort Bumby to Cuba for his visits with Hemingway?"

"Everyone asks that and the answer is no. And our family called the son 'Jack,' not 'Bumby.'"

"Everyone really wants to know if Hadley maybe left a suitcase here."

"And you also want to know if Mary left a manuscript here." We laughed, not without a level of tension. As we were about to enter Tomás's house, I could feel my fingertips tingling in anticipation.

In the living room, we greeted Isabel, José's grandmother, and we all sat down. She gestured to José, and he excused himself and returned almost immediately with a tray full of sweating bottles of pop. He served his grandmother, then Beth, his grandfather and then he stopped in front of me. "The last morning drink I served you was a mojito."

"Gracias, amigo."

When José was settled, ready to translate, with his own Coke in hand, Tomás picked up his story. "Mary was a lonely woman when she came back after Ernesto died. She had worked so hard to get rich. She had become rich, but then she had nothing to do." Tomás sighed.

José looked right at us. "He does not like to talk about the painful times. I will tell you what he cannot."

I nodded at them both.

"Mary had married and stayed with Hemingway for money, and so she suspected that anyone who was friendly to her was after her money. She was also suspicious because she was convinced that the FBI was following her, after his death, harassing her as they had once tormented both of them in Cuba. She trusted my grandfather because Ernesto had trusted him, even though they had the big fight once." José looked proud, in a good way.

A knock at the door distracted everyone. The visitor was another old guy, and I knew right away that he was Julio Menendez, Hemingway's groundskeeper. Here was another real person from the pages of Mary's story. He had been at the airport for the relay handoff, the lateral pass, of Manuscript A, which had kept it out of the hands of the FBI. Julio had received it from Hemingway and passed it to René who walked out the door and, presumably, straight back to the Finca.

Julio was a bright, handsome man, probably in his early or mid 80's, fluent—or at least courtly—in English. I was full of questions for him.

Julio said he wanted to speak privately with Tomás, and José invited us to let them talk in the living room while we looked at Tomás's collection of Hemingway memorabilia in the hallway.

Beth asked José, "It must have set you apart from your school friends to have grown up with the ghost of this great man everywhere. Were you proud that your father was 'the boy' and your great grandfather was 'the old man'?"

José neglected his usual male posturing and looked out a window for a minute. I imagined that no one had ever asked him about his reactions before. As he hesitated to speak, Beth and I absorbed ourselves in looking at the artifacts in the hallway and commenting on their condition. I wished I could take pictures, but it was just as well I couldn't since I didn't want to disturb the level of trust we had established over the week. I kept telling myself that my goal for the day was to locate Manuscript A.

"You know how kids are," José began abruptly. "They called the book *The Old Man and the Secret* and called my great grandfather Santiago and my grandfather Santiago as well.

My father they called 'the boy' and me 'the boy's boy.' Alicia and I both have a great grandfather who had been first mate of the *Pilar* and had told Hemingway stories of the legendary old man who almost conquered the monster marlin. Before their time, before Hemingway came along, that story was just a local fishermen's story."

"The-One-That-Got-Away kind of story?" I laughed, but he looked at me suspiciously. Jokes definitely do not work in another language or culture. I should have known that! I resumed pulling books off the shelf, one at a time, noting that most of them were paperback copies of Hemingway's novels in English, apparently unread.

"Did you hang around the Finca Vigía often?" Beth asked. She was probably thinking that she could repair the damage my social gaffe had caused. Meanwhile, having given the library a cursory glance, I was looking for Mary's manuscript, aware that José was watching me and that Beth was watching both of us.

"The good times were over by then. The place was empty. Children were no longer allowed."

A hard-cover edition of *The Old Man and the Sea* caught my eye, and I lifted it out, flipped it open, and froze. Beth's voice and José's came to me as if drowned out by the breakers of a summer storm.

Beth took the book from me. "Look, it's inscribed: 'To Gregorio Fuentes, my first and best Santiago, E. Hemingway, 1952.' Wow, this is signed by Hemingway!"

I took it back. "It's a first edition, with the Scribner "A" on the publication page, inscribed, with the dust cover intact, the whole thing in pristine condition!"

"This book, it is valuable?" José was sounding very interested.

"With Hemingway's signature, over $20,000 USD," I answered him.

"What's that in Cuban currency?" Beth asked. "Are you sure this book is worth so much?"

"Yes! In American dollars. I've no idea what it's worth to this family."

"What are you going to do about it?" she asked.

"Nothing!" I answered. "It obviously belongs to them."

"Isn't that great?" she demanded.

"Ask José," I answered.

"Here's your chance to start over," Beth said to him. "You can sell this and have enough to buy your own house with Alicia. And you can have children. And I should stop telling you what to do."

Beth handed the book to José who stood silently, examining it. He flipped on the hallway light. "You know, I have only read Hemingway's Cuban and Spanish books."

Immediately I outlined a reading program starting with the Nick Adams stories and ending with the European war novels. Beth put her hand on my arm. "Slow down."

José would need time to absorb the implications of this find. I was glad that I had recognized the value of the book for him and for Alicia. "Now's as good a time as any to look in this bookcase for Mary's manuscript," said José. My heart started racing again. Great idea.

"It will be a pile of loose typing paper, probably twenty pages, one-sided. I expect the back of each page will have blue smudges from the carbon paper. That's how Manuscript B looks." I could tell neither of them was listening to me. They were busy peering behind other books, testing the solidity of the wall behind the bookcase.

"We should do this more methodically," announced Beth, and I could hear her giving orders to our future children sitting at breakfast not to forget their money for book fair day. "Let's check each book, starting at the top shelf on the left. José, you lift them down and put them up in their present order. Alf, you flip through each one, looking for whatever."

"I know what I'm looking for, dear," I said, resisting the urge to call her "Boss." Or "Mother." I pointed out that she was doing nothing.

"I'm doing the thinking," she claimed.

Beth was definitely not doing the watching, though, because I turned around to find Tomás and Julio standing behind us, looking somewhat bemused.

"Shall we finish our conversation in the sitting room?" Tomás asked. I noticed that Tomás echoed Julio's elegant way of speaking and moving.

José stood back for the older generation to proceed, then waved Beth and me to follow while he, I saw in a backwards glance, carried *The Old Man* to his seat where he slid it into his ubiquitous backpack. He knew I'd seen this move and was okay with it.

Tomás spoke in Spanish, and José translated. "Julio is *Profesor Emérito de la Literatura Cubana en la UniverSidad de la Habana*, and a friend of mine going back to the time of Hemingway's troubles. I have asked him what I should do with the papers René gave me. I will let him tell you himself."

I leaned forward in my chair.

Smiling at Tomás, Julio began. "If Mary's manuscript describing Hemingway's last few days in Cuba demonstrates FBI harassment of our great friend, it will be significant evidence that the United States' interference in our Revolution was unwarranted, illegal and destructive. Why? Because both Ernest and Mary Hemingway are still remembered in literary circles. This we have maintained for all these years." Julio turned to me. "Tomás told me that you have some of the pages. May I see them?"

I looked at Beth who nodded. I hesitated, my hand on the front of my shirt. "What I want to do is find the rest of the manuscript. Do you know where it is?"

Julio shook his head. "I am sorry to say that I do not know. What are you planning to do with Mary's story once you find the whole thing?"

"If he finds the whole thing," put in José.

"When it is published, it will clarify the role of the United States in Cuban politics in the past, just as you said."

Julio added, "And it will encourage the Cuban people to be more careful of preserving their heritage."

"It seems to me," I said, "that the FBI's Hemingway file is still sensitive to the Americans as well as to the Cubans."

"But why is it important to a Canadian?" Julio asked.

"I plan to use it, along with reference to Paporov, as the basis of my doctoral dissertation about the FBI's harassment of Hemingway in Cuba."

I began to explain about Paporov's book, but a wave of Julio's hand interrupted me. "I know who Paporov is and what his *Hemingway en Cuba* says." I was surprised by the impatience in Julio's voice.

"Did you ever read Mary's article?" I asked.

Julio answered, "No, I never had access to it. I passed the papers Ernesto gave me to René at the ferry terminal. I never saw them again."

The room fell silent, and Tomás turned his puzzled face to José for clarification. José whispered briefly in his ear.

I decided that it might help to lay all my cards on the table. "My father and I have worked together on where to find Mary's manuscript for as long as I can remember, and now he has had a stroke and I want him to read it." Beth reached over and squeezed my hand.

José interrupted. "This is our rich boy. I want, I deserve, I get."

I ignored him and pressed on. "I found the pages relating to their last two days at the Finca, and now I want to find the rest. Maybe I will donate it to a Cuban museum. I know several Canadian and American universities that would take good care of it in their libraries." I was making the last bit up.

"You cannot take this document out of Cuba!" Julio exclaimed. "Do you know that there are active negotiations in progress between Cuba and the United States to remove the embargo that was begun half a century ago? It is time for Cuba to stand strong but also diplomatic!"

Inwardly I agreed. "All I need is a copy of the whole thing." Beth quietly hummed a warning that I interpreted to mean, "Don't back down any further!"

"That is good." Julio looked satisfied, ready to move on. "I remember meeting your father at the United Nations when Castro gave his great speech. Your father was there with the Canadian delegation as translator. He was one of the first people I knew to call for nuclear disarmament." He paused. "Would you consider leaving the manuscript with my university's library?" he asked.

I looked at Julio. "Will you make a copy for me? Will you use your connections to publish an English edition of Paporov?"

Tomás was shaking his head slightly. I was sure he could not follow the conversation.

"Certainly. I can see how you can use that as well, for your thesis." Julio paused, then asked, "Have you photocopies of those pages you are holding?"

"These are Mary's writings about their last Sunday and Monday in Cuba." I wanted him to know I meant business. "I took pictures of a few pages on my iPhone, before it was stolen, and sent them to my father. What I'm saying is that part of the manuscript has been found and copied; the original is this, the photos are in my father's care, and the eversion, if such a word exists, is in the clouds. Your island can't be kept isolated any longer."

Julio held out his hand to receive the originals but I held them tight against my chest and said, "Before you or anyone else touches this manuscript, I want to have read, verified the legitimacy of, and copied, the entire Manuscript A, the description written by Mary Hemingway, for *Life* Magazine, of Tuesday to Saturday."

His hand retreated and was restrained by his other hand. He said, "You have, I presume, seen the files on the Internet written by the FBI about their surveillance of Hemingway, even their correspondence with his doctor at the Mayo Clinic, the one who gave him electro-shock treatments, the one who called him a 'problem' patient, the one who approved Hemingway's decision to register at the Mayo under an assumed name in order to maintain his privacy." His voice rose half an octave during that speech.

"My God!" José said. "Did all this really happen? And it's now on the Internet?"

I nodded. We sat in silence, and I stared at Julio, willing José to stay put and not run off with the first edition of *Old Man*. I could hear Beth's breathing close beside me.

When the tension in the room had somewhat dissipated, I turned to Tomás and asked, "Where is the manuscript of the first five days of Mary's story? That is what I need."

There was a brief exchange between Tomás and José who then turned to me. "Let Julio have a look at what you have under your shirt."

"Then Tomás will tell me?"

"Yes."

I pulled out Manuscript B and handed it to this man I had never met before.

Julio carefully unfolded it and read or at least skimmed through it all quickly. He looked tense. Perhaps as he found references to himself, perhaps as he discovered the FBI's mistreatment of Hemingway.

I said, "There are several FBI letters on their website that are totally blacked out."

"Whatever for?" José demanded.

"For reasons of national security, I suppose."

"It's 50 years since all this happened and the Freedom of Information Act is now bringing it to public attention, and the FBI still treats it as sensitive?" Julio wondered.

I nodded. "Hemingway scholars have been watching and commenting on such postings as they've surfaced over the past few years."

Beth asked, "Did the Hemingways know, before they moved back to the States, that they were being watched so closely?"

"They didn't know it, but he certainly feared it," I explained. "Hemingway was paranoid and terribly afraid of being imprisoned in a mental institution, like Ezra Pound. It was a classic Catch-22 situation."

Beth turned to Julio. "You were there, with the Hemingways. Did you think they were harassed by the FBI?"

Julio looked, first at Beth, then around the room until he was staring at me. "Yes. At the time I did not take it all seriously. I was young and thought that I was tough and that the big American hero made a big fuss over everything."

I asked, "Can you remember a specific incident beyond what you have just read in this manuscript?"

"No, but I am eager to read the rest of it."

"Could you contact other people who were involved?" I asked, conscious of the close attention being paid by everyone in the room.

"Are you referring to René and Valerie?" Julio asked.

"Yes," I said.

"I have not been in touch with them in decades, but if you'll give me your questions, I'll phone them both, and ask them for you."

"That's amazing! Thank you."

"Your father was a good man. Give him my regards."

I could sense our conversation was ending, but I had one more question. "Is there anyone else still available for questioning?" Julio smiled and shook his head, then turned away.

Everyone in the room seemed to be talking at once. Beth caught Julio's attention with her next question to me. "Living in fear like that must have damaged Hemingway's writing."

I tried to explain, hoping that Julio would agree with me. "He submitted to his publishers a lot of incomplete texts in the 1950's, so badly done that various editors and family members tried to improve the manuscripts. He was devastated and furious. Other manuscripts were stuck somewhere in the process of being published, presumably under pressure from the FBI."

"How can we ever know what really happened?" Beth asked.

I said, "In the 1950's he wrote several manuscripts that he did not submit; he put them in a bank vault and called them his life insurance. After his death, Mary submitted them, and then after her death, his sons published still others as well."

"If that is the case," said Julio, "and the manuscripts have been improved, or if the opposite is true and the manuscripts have been deliberately or inadvertently worsened by agents or family members, how can we call these writings his?"

"I hope to address these questions in my dissertation, Professor. I will ask my advisor to invite you to be an External Examiner. I will be greatly honored if you can do this."

He flashed a charming smile, and I glanced over at Beth who raised one eyebrow. This was shaping up to be a great day!

Julio had resumed reading Manuscript B. José pulled the first edition *The Old Man and the Sea* from his backpack and showed it to his grandfather. I guessed that he explained its great value, for Tomás started to react noisily, and José placed his finger on his grandfather's lips.

A delicious smell entered the living room, and I heard Alicia's voice telling someone in the kitchen that she had bought lobster, caught fresh that morning. Manuscript A, like *Old Man*, would obviously have to wait.

Julio stood up abruptly and thanked me as he handed back Manuscript B and shook hands all around. He excused himself, assuring me he would be most honored to be kept informed about the progress of my quest.

Why was he taking off? We watched him leave and heaved a collective sigh of relief. Beth hugged me and then turned to Tomás. "Do you now believe that the book that José is holding and the manuscript Alf has are genuinely valuable?" José translated and Tomás nodded.

José asked him, "Are you going to tell Alf where to find Mary's Manuscript?"

Tomás smiled and José continued, "How about right after we eat lunch?"

Tomás shook his head.

"What?" I nearly exploded.

"I think I will tell you now," said Tomás, directly to me.

Alicia and Isabel chose that moment to bring the tureen of lobster stew into the main room. Beth looked at me in exasperation. José laughed, set his treasure on the top shelf of the bookcase, and patted my shoulder. "Patience, patience," he said.

Right, fine, I didn't give a damn. I grabbed the chair Tomás pointed to as he asked me to have a seat. In the past I would have accidentally kicked it and diffused my frustration by jumping up and down with a stubbed toe.

"You've got to trust, man." Paulo's words. Paulo's voice. Paulo?

I gasped. "You should be in Canada by now, with Beth's parents! What are you doing here?"

"Alf, my friend, you might try to sound a little friendly!"

Beth said, "My parents must be frantic, worried about you. They were all set to meet you yesterday, at St. Colomba's Church in Ottawa."

"Oh, Beth, I am sorry," said Paulo. "How is the baby?"

I blurted, "Forget about the baby! Forget about your parents! I want to hear what Tomás has to say about the manuscript right now!"

No one said a word. No one moved.

Then Beth turned on me. "Why don't you just get lost? You only care about this manuscript, not about me or your own child!" She sat down with her head in her hands.

Frustrated, hurt and confused, I turned and ran out the door.

Afternoon

"Alf, come back!" I didn't because it was not Beth's voice. I had never seen her angry like this. How could she have let me down and challenged me in front of all those strangers? As if I only cared about Mary's Manuscript!

What a mess! I walked and ran until I collapsed, still panicked, beside the monument. She was right. I was a total loser. I'd known this all my life, and only since I'd known her had I hoped I could be happy, normal. Now I knew I was wrong.

I was wheezing, and when I opened my eyes I could only see a tunnel, like the blurry circle in a dark field with shooting bars of light. I thought of my father dying. I sank further into silent panic.

"Alf! What is going on with you, man?" I could hear José and feel his hand tight on my shoulder, but not see him. "Your face is so white! What's your problem? You are all upset by a woman yelling at you for ten seconds! Hey, man, toughen up!"

I was trying to figure out how to react to his insults. It was normal for women to scream rejection at a man? Not in Canada. Maybe Beth would have changed her mind. Maybe she hadn't meant what she'd said. But the Beth I knew didn't change her mind or say what she didn't mean. Damn! And what about my dad?

It occurred to me that I couldn't just march off then and there and leave Beth, pregnant, in Cuba.

The first thing I saw when my sight returned was the row of old men on their stools outside La Terraza. They weren't laughing this time. I tried to imagine what they were thinking.

"Are you going to come back? Lunch is getting cold. Here, have some water." José took a bottle of water and dumped some on me. I grabbed it and poured the rest on him. The next thing I knew we were wrestling. And I was losing, pinned to the ground by a guy much lighter but also, obviously, more muscular.

I suddenly felt flooded with gratitude that José was my friend. Of sorts. And happy that my father had enjoyed a good life. The row of old men all had his face, his smile. These ones, though, looked like they'd enjoyed their noon meal.

José stood up and offered to help pull me up. "Too bad you're going back to Canada so soon. I could teach you how to build up some muscles, how to stand up for yourself."

Once back on my feet, more or less stable, I remained defiant. "I don't want to learn to fight, and my fiancée ...." I was hit again by grief at the thought of losing not only my father but also Beth and the baby.

"I have to do this myself," I told José. We walked back to Tomás's house and, within sight of the front door, José disappeared. I stood there.

Beth appeared and we looked at each other. She shrugged and asked, "You hungry?" I shook my head.

Beth demanded, "Why did you leave me?" A rush of anger made me start to turn away from her, but I didn't. I had heard fear and sadness in her voice. She was afraid, not angry. I was both.

I would not run away. I had to stand still and wait for her to come to me. I knew this had to happen.

"Alf?"

"Yes?"

"Are you still mad at me?"

I stood silent. She was used to my quick capitulation, used to being right. The shape of her shoes and the pastel colors of children's crayon drawings on the wall of the house absorbed all my attention. At least that's what I pretended.

She took a shaky breath. "I'm sorry, okay? Is that what you want?"

"No, Beth, I want you."

"Hey there, Beth! Why the sad face?"

I groaned, "Just what we need, the holy fool!"

Paulo reached out to grab my shoulder. "Beth, he's a joker in life, like me." He made the insulting words sound friendly. Still, I wished he would take his interfering foolishness elsewhere.

Beth also sounded exasperated. "What kind of husband does a fool make?"

I objected. "I'm not a fool any more than you are! And you make mistakes sometimes, like even imagining that Richard was anything but a crook!"

"Hey, Beth," interrupted Paulo. "This is your man! Goofy, a little goofy. But I like him! And you, too! "

"What?" She glared at him.

"Chill out, Beth, chill out! Why did you freak out on us?"

"It's none of your business." Beth was now angry at Paulo.

"Of course it is my business!" Paulo winked at me. "I'm glad I came back."

"Why did you come back?" I asked.

"Do you not think I am needed here?"

"Okay, then, can you tell me what I need to do to reassure Beth that everything is alright between the two of us?"

"You are doing the work here, Alfredo! You have understood. Now, Beth, a good man is hard to find. What that means is not what you think. Do you know what I am saying?"

Beth heaved a great sigh. I feared another explosion and began to wonder if she was mad at herself. She sure wasn't cooling down. There was a long silence.

"Beth, I am sorry. Do you forgive me?" I took the initiative.

"For what?"

"Whatever. Everything."

"Yes." She paused. We smiled at each other, then started feeling around in our pockets for tissues.

"I bet you anything," Paulo said, cheerfully, "that this was your first big argument."

"The next thing you'll say is, 'It's all one,'" said Beth.

"Of course," he replied, and turned to me. "It is all one. You agree?"

We all went inside. Beth thanked Isabel and Alicia for the meal, and I apologized for disturbing it with our argument. Alicia served us leftovers, and dragged Paulo away as he sat himself down and began to help himself to seconds.

Alone at the dining table, we lapsed again into an awkward silence. "Next time we have a fight," I whispered, "we will not need Paulo as self-appointed counselor."

Beth nodded. We ate, barely tasting the food.

Tomás tried to explain where he thought the papers might be. What he said didn't make sense to any of us, something about voodoo and the ceiba tree. I suspected that I was not the only one feeling that we had wasted an entire morning when we could have been doing something more productive or at least more fun.

Alicia volunteered to stay with the old folks and try to coax some specific information out of Tomás when he woke up from his afternoon nap, but we talked her into coming with us. Beth, José, Paulo, and I were all excited to find Mary's Manuscript A without any more of Tomás's ambiguous help. At least I still had Manuscript B in my chest pack. I wished again and again that those thieves hadn't taken our iPhones. Manuscript A could have been so easily copied and sent to Canada.

José fussed over Luis's taxi's engine until I produced enough cash to half fill the gas tank. Beth sat close to me so I could reassure her, over and over, that I loved her.

As we drove, all squished together in the old taxi, I replayed in my mind the conversation with Tomás about the old ceiba tree's roots growing under the house and causing the tiles of the floor to push up and out of place.

"It happened more than once, I believe," Tomás had said. "I think that it damaged both the floor of the dining room and the floor of Mary's bedroom. René told me."

"Is her bedroom open to the public?" I asked Alicia. "The outside windows are small and high up, so no one could look in and see her."

Earlier in the week Alicia had shown us the boarded up windows on the front of the house at the right-hand end, as seen from the Guest House tree. That, she had told us, was Mary's room, at the corner of the house closest to the ceiba.

I told the others in the car about my idea that we should start our search for the manuscript in Mary's room. José pointed out that there was another interior room, called the Venetian room. Just between the office and the dining room, it was where the brother of a very young Venetian countess had spent six months before she and their mother arrived. The family was fleeing post-war shortages in the old country, and intrigued by the attentions of the great man whose wife pretended not to notice.

"What has Adrianna Ivancich got to do with finding Mary's Manuscript?" I asked.

"Maybe nothing," José answered.

"That's easy," said Beth decisively. "From what Tomás said, the two rooms that the ceiba tree grew its roots under were Mary's and the dining room. The Venetian room is next to the dining room so it might well have places in the floor damaged by the roots."

"Did Julio ever meet these Venetians?" I asked.

"No," José answered, "I don't imagine so. Actually," he stopped to think, "the Venetians were at the Finca long before the Hemingways had to leave the country."

"That makes more sense," I nodded. "Right after the war." The conversation lagged. It was good to relax.

"By the way," I said a few minutes later to Beth, "I owe you a couple of magazine titles. How about 'Little Finca of Horrors' and '*Veni, vidi, vigía*'?"

"Good." She nodded. "I've been thinking of essay topics for you to use."

"You mean when I have a fulltime job at a gorgeous university?" Somehow the ideal place always looked, in my mind, like McMaster or Victoria College, UofT.

As our taxi pulled up to Hemingway's house once again, I looked around and my imagination flipped to how easy it could be for any sniper to take us out. "Beth," I whispered, "listen, how about you wait for me here in the taxi, just in case Luis or some maniac decides to take a shot at us? This is a wild west show!"

"Hemingway as prototypical Survivor," Beth said. Then, seeing my puzzled expression, she asked, "How about 'Isn't it pretty to think so? The Deconstruction of it'? Alf, you're worrying too much."

"Right," I agreed. "One more: 'Like a white elephant: Hemingway's weight issue.'" She laughed, and I remembered that it was only a few days before that I had wanted to check out Hemingway's daily record of his weight on the bathroom wall. It was time to finish up my business at the Finca Vigía and get my fiancée and our unborn child home safe and sound.

All around the Finca Vigía that day were tourists and curators. We would have to blend in and conduct our search when we had the chance. I wished Julio and Tomás were with us. They could have done an excellent job of deflecting attention.

In the taxi we had decided that Alicia and Beth would examine the floor tiles of the Venetian room and Paulo and I would check out Mary's room. José would spread a few bribes around to get us inside the house. I pulled out my wallet once again. It was much thinner than a few days before.

In Mary's room, Paulo waited quietly for me to tell him my plan for finding the manuscript. Well, that was nice of him. Too bad I had no plan.

He asked, "How about we look in any big old books that Mary might have cut out the pages from?"

"There are no big old books in her room." I was suddenly too tired to think and flopped down on the bed. If one of the guides could see me, I'd be in deep dooda. I hoped to find the tiles that had replaced the ones damaged by the intrusive ceiba tree, lift out those tiles and, voila, the hiding spot of the manuscript would be revealed.

I explained all this to Paulo. He said, "Someone hid this manuscript under the tiles about 50 years ago. Did the ceiba roots incident that Tomás told us about not happen years before that?"

"That could present a problem."

"You mean that the Hemingways would spend years tripping over uneven tiles?"

"Well, he was pretty convinced that harming a ceiba tree was bad karma or whatever the voodoo term is for luck."

"You have to speak with a more respectful voice." Paulo sounded genuinely offended. I didn't know that was possible. I had, however, spoken like an arrogant know-it-all.

"Sorry, Paulo," I tried lamely.

"Good. Hemingway at least learned about our religion."

He wandered about the room, somewhat aimlessly, since the floor tiles looked totally flat. I noticed a baseball bat leaning against the head of the bed. I went over and picked it up, pretending that I was a major league player, warming up for my time at bat. "What else did Tomás say about where to find the manuscript? Anything remotely useful?"

"Maybe Tomás doesn't want you to find it," Paulo said quietly.

"Why not?"

"Stop looking so irritated!"

"I'm trying not to hit you over the head with this bat! Where do you get off pretending to sound so wise all the time?"

"What is that doing in Mary's bedroom?"

"Protection against Hemingway?" I wondered. "Or Batista's thugs?"

I remembered Tomás mentioning voodoo symbols when we were talking about finding the manuscript. I didn't see any piece of cutlery or napkin lying about.

"Maybe the symbols are small and hard to see," said Paulo, dropping to his knees in one corner of the room. Well, at least he wasn't being pompous for a change. I started on my hands and knees, on the other side of the room, to examine the tiles for any scratches and images. Nothing.

Beth joined us. "We did the same thing in the Venetian room but it's smaller so we got done first." Alicia and José appeared as well, and the room felt suddenly crowded. We were all on our hands and knees, looking.

Paulo crawled under the bed. We heard a quiet call for help and looked at each other. He was stuck. I was delighted and mimed looking about for him, even calling his name. The others copied me. We had trouble not laughing.

"Help! I can't breathe!"

"Okay, just a sec! José, grab the foot of the bed!" I positioned myself at the head of the bed and quietly ordered him, "Now! Lift!" I hoisted my end but Paulo was still stuck.

What was José doing, just standing there?

Beth whispered, "José, here! Lift here! Alicia, lift with Alf!" With the four of us lifting together, the bed was free of the floor and Paulo rolled out from beneath it.

"Why did you take so long?" Paulo demanded of José.

"I did not know what he was saying."

"I said, 'Lift the foot of the bed.' That's simple."

"Oh, you mean the bottom of the bed."

Beth laughed. "Translator needed! Your father should be here. So, Paulo, did you see any voodoo under the bed?"

I was rubbing my sore biceps, barely even listening when Paulo answered, "I think so. It was dark under there."

"You mean you want us to move this frigging bed? Again?" I felt the urge to throttle him. Again. I picked up the baseball bat with a menacing grin.

"Stop! Put it down!" Paulo ran at me, grabbed the baseball bat. Gently bouncing it on the floor, he traced my steps to the head of the bed where I had, of necessity, stopped. "The floor sounded hollow here," he said. "That's why I wanted to see what was under the bed." He threw himself onto the floor again.

José nodded. "Come on, Professor. Use those muscles."

I glared at him and hoisted. "My end is heavier, you know!"

"Listen!" Paulo yelled. I resisted the urge to drop the bed on him and instead followed José's lead and shifted it sideways before dropping it because I couldn't hold it any longer.

Beth was listening to the hollow sound Paulo made as he continued to explore the various sounds made by the bat as it bounced on different tiles. She pointed to one. "That's a good spot!" Beth and Paulo reminded me of my grandmother who claimed to be a water witch. Using a v-shaped branch of a willow tree, she could follow an underground river to help a farmer know where to dig a well.

A shape appeared on a tile. "Look!" I yelled, and Alicia hissed at me to be quiet. Squatting down, I ran my fingers over the corner of one of the tiles that had sounded hollow when Paulo dropped the bat on the other corner. The rest of the tile was hidden by the bed.

Beth whispered, "There are tiny marks here. They look like the symbols we saw on the bow of the *Pilar*. Remember? The arrow with the three stylized hills of Cuba and the belt buckle one? The same symbols are on the cutlery and the linens."

"What marks? What symbols?" asked Paulo.

I spluttered, "Beth, I think you may be right. Whoever hid Mary's Manuscript used the same symbols to mark the spot. I suspect it was Tomás. We need to look under this tile!"

José asked, "How do we pry up flagstone tiles? They've been mortared in place for half a century or more."

"'There's a crack, a crack in everything. That's how the light gets in.' Or a knife in this case. That was my dad's favorite Cohen song. Anyone got a knife?"

"When did he die?" asked Paulo, suddenly worried.

"He's not dead! Can you stop acting like a bloody Delphic Oracle or something?"

"You said your dad's favorite song was, not is. There's a crack in the mortar."

José handed me a jackknife and said, "You dig." For all his grumpiness, this guy was sure useful.

I dug with José's knife. Paulo used a nail file Beth found on the dresser. "Listen, don't be too rough on that," José told him.

"The file will break easily."

"Trust me, man!" Paulo continued working at the loose mortar.

I kept jiggling and tugging. I got my fingers into the widening crack and pulled. The tile came up with a jolt. There, nestled among the roots, was a box, a tin box just like the one I'd found to contain Manuscript B. I lifted it out gently.

Paulo sat back, watching me. José let out a low whistle. I opened the box, and found a pile of pages, about twice as many as the first group now in my chest pack. The top one was blank except for weird painted symbols, not like the ones Hemingway and Mary had put on their boat and serviettes, but ancient, troubling shapes. I drew back.

Alicia was whispering frantically, and I was reluctant to pay attention.

Paulo saved our bacon right then. As I carefully checked that the papers were what I expected and inserted them into my chest pack, he closed the box and buried it again under the tiles, so that the area did not look even slightly disturbed. Just before the door was flung open, we lifted the bed back in place. José smiled at the guide who nodded, then left.

I was exhilarated but then realized the danger we were still in. What we needed was to get the hell off the property. I was good at getting into trouble, but not so great at getting out of it.

Paulo said, "It is about time to leave."

I interrupted him with what I later acknowledged was a less than brilliant suggestion. "How about we make a run for the taxi?"

José looked ready to shake me. "Listen, we pretend to be tourists who have found ourselves lost from our tour. We wander about, not altogether, and meet at the taxi. You two go through the house and Alicia and Paulo and I will go out the front door and around the building. Go!"

I was starting to feel hopeful, but still had the urge to slug Paulo. I looked around at the others. "Brush the dust off your clothes." They all did this, and so did I.

I checked my chest pack and Paulo experimented with various hiding spots in his clothing for the small picture of Ernest and Mary he had taken from her bedside table. He chose the front of his underpants. I guess he wanted a souvenir.

"Good luck!" he said, and I knocked gently on the wooden dresser.

Leaving the bedroom first, Beth and I made our way toward the Venetian room, stopping to pretend to admire the head of a gazelle on the dining room wall and then the view out the door to the terrace. I turned and tried the door of the Venetian room. Locked. Why?

I glanced through the wide open living room window and saw Paulo talking casually to Alicia who was looking toward us. I had the urge to sprint for the front door. So far I hadn't met a single tourist or guide. A few minutes later Beth and I had caught up to the others. José urged us along the driveway after Paulo. I prayed there would be no gunshots as we fled.

Once in the car that had been parked just inside the front gates, we roared onto the road into town. Paulo slumped down in the passenger seat. José concentrated on the road. That was good given the speed we were moving. Beth checked out the back window and yelled, "No one behind us!" Alicia looked casually happy, as if what we were doing was not a big deal.

José swore under his breath and Paulo settled back to watch
Beth. When she turned her head to speak to me, Paulo pulled
the old photograph from his pants. Beth opened her mouth to
speak, and I put my finger on her lips, then pointed at my chest
pack and gave her the thumbs up. Triumph lit her face as she
mouthed the word, "Yes!"

Evening

We rode in silence long after the danger of being tailed had
passed, all the way back to the driveway of Tomás's neighbor.

I unfastened the strap to my chest pack and pulled it out from
under my shirt. By this time we were inside Tomás's house.
Julio had returned, perhaps in anticipation of our discovery. I
decided it was my turn to tease the others by slowing down.
It occurred to me that this was becoming a public event, and
therefore posed more dangerous problems.

Once in the living room, with Tomás, Isabel, and Julio in the
chairs and the rest of us crowded around them, cross-legged
on the floor, I gently pulled out the long-hidden and very
musty Manuscript A, unfolded the pages, and read the beginning out loud:

"'Wife pinch-hits for Ernest Hemingway!' Or imagine this
headline: 'Ghost writer for Nobel Laureate pens memoir!' I
realize, of course, that the editor and the readers are interested
in me only as Wife of Ernest Hemingway. I can, nevertheless,
bear witness to our last week in Cuba. I can, in fact, attest that
we are being booted out."

Julio interrupted. "Where did you find it?"

Paulo stood up, one hand behind his back, and said, "Let me
tell." And tell he did, with every detail. When he came to the
discovery of the symbols on the tile under the bed, he omitted

the part about getting himself stuck. He pulled the picture of
the Hemingways out of a pocket and held it up so they could
admire it.

Tomás slowly unfolded a fine cotton napkin he had been holding so we could see the engraved symbols. These were the
same as on all the Hemingway linens, the same as on the prow
of the *Pilar*. For once our friends were rendered speechless.
The old man reached over to the painted cover page of the
manuscript and said, "What Hemingway painted on this page
was very old. There was a spell on everything under that page
that protected them. Paulo was able to find the manuscript
because he has the gift of healing instead of harming."

Alicia added, "He has learned from his Santeria friends."

That was a conversation stopper! Did they really believe this?
I looked at Beth. Her eyes were popping.

We stood up, and I reached out and took Manuscript A from
Tomás. So much for being a polite Canadian. I carefully
zipped it into my chest pack and strapped it on again, then
pulled on my shirt.

"We need a taxi," said Beth.

"We'll walk down to La Terraza and pick up one there," I said.

"So," said Alicia, "you're on your own for tonight?"

I paused in the doorway with Beth. "Thanks so much for
your help, everyone. I hope we all found what we were looking for." I had been upset with Tomás all day because he had
seemed to be putting me off. As we said goodbye it occurred
to me that he might have forgotten where he had put the manuscript and didn't want to admit it.

The other factor was that Tomás did not trust museums. I understood but did not agree. I appreciated that no one was stopping me from taking the manuscript with me. That discussion about taking it out of the country could wait. I hoped.

We shook hands and hugged each person and finally were on our own. Not for long. We turned to see Julio coming toward us as we headed to the bar to catch a taxi.

"I must tell you something privately," Julio said.

"Please, go ahead, sir," I answered. "We can walk together."

"Your father and I spent a few hours together the evening of Castro's one New York press conference. Somehow, despite our different backgrounds and our strangeness to each other, we understood each other. We went to a restaurant near the United Nations complex and then to a bar outside Grand Central Station that was supposed to be Cuban but both seemed full of spies so we just walked and walked, down Broadway to the bottom of Manhattan where we could have caught the ferry to the Statue of Liberty. Instead we just looked at it, both of us marveling at the troubled idealism of that young, strong country we could never understand.

"What I want you to know is how your father spoke with such confidence and hope for the future of the world and with such fear of a war that could wipe out every human being including all Americans. He could not understand how ordinary people as well as political leaders around the world did not grasp the enormity, the tragic folly of the nuclear arms race."

I had the sense that I was once more talking with my father, the one person in my life, until Beth, who could look, unblinking, at the possibilities of the future. Julio walked along with us in silence.

Beth turned to Julio. "Did Mary love Hemingway? What do you think?"

"In her way, yes." He paused. "She put so much effort into keeping a smile on her face when really she was lonely and totally dependent on him financially. She knew that no one was interested in her. I felt sorry for her." Julio cleared his throat rather awkwardly.

"What about Hemingway?" I asked. "Did he know about the stockpile of Soviet bombs on the island?"

"He must have," said Julio.

"But did nothing?"

"His Nobel Prize was for Literature, not Peace. He was absorbed by his own great pains all the time I knew him."

I wondered, not for the first time, if I should change my major.

Julio was talking quietly. "Now that, oh, never mind. Did your dad ever speak to Valerie Danby-Smith or say anything about her?"

"No, sir."

Poor guy, after all these years, still looking for contact with the past. Maybe he was worried about what Mary had written about his relationship with Valerie.

We had reached La Terraza and I asked at the bar for a taxi. There was nothing to be done but to say goodbye again to Julio who decided to return to Tomás's home.

In any case, the complete manuscript was now in my hands. It was amazing that they all had allowed me to take it with me.

Back in our hotel room, the old-fashioned phone was blinking an orange knob and beeping an annoying noise. This could only be a message from someone with grey hair. My dad? No, it was dear Uncle and Aunt. She left the message, presumably because Edmond knew I was tired of listening to him. They'd tried to find us today but hoped to meet us before they went home tomorrow. It was important. She would call us again in the morning.

I looked around for a toast to Hemingway. There were no glasses except those scented by toothpaste, and no fluid except bottled water. We chose imaginary wine glasses and invisible wine. I smiled at Beth and said, "To Hemingway's ghost!"

She lifted hers and said, "Bung-o!"

"Did you see that we had no struggle with anyone about keeping the manuscript, no argument with Tomás who had buried it there, no objection from Julio, no trick by José to steal it?"

We organized ourselves, beginning to plan our return home as we discussed dinner. Beth felt the need of a quick nap so, as she went to bed, I carefully picked up Mary's manuscript of Tuesday to Saturday and began to read her long-hidden secrets.

When I was done, I was saddened and Beth was sound asleep. I took one of the cigars we had bought out into the foyer. There was an ashtray I had noticed a few days before, and I hoped to find solace with every puff. I watched the dancers and musicians setting up for the evening show, while thinking about past, present and future.

For one thing, I, Alf, because of my argument with Beth earlier that day, was wondering why I was so concerned with Mary's manuscript and so interested in Ernest Hemingway.

I had to make Beth and our baby my first priority in life. Throwing myself enthusiastically into making enough money to support our family's well-being would, from day to day, trump the demands of my career. And of my interests. And supporting our family included supporting Beth's career goals.

First, I needed to clarify for myself the importance of Hemingway to my father and to myself. No, first I needed to resist the urge to smoke a cigar on an empty stomach. I butted it out regretfully, but packaged the rest up for sharing with my dad.

For all his crude behavior and fascination with violence, Hemingway was a dreamer like Gatsby. He was a reporter who supported the victims of war and the first American after Henry James to hold his own in the complex society called Europe. Hemingway suffered and described the diseases that characterized his century in the United States of America: depression, violence, alcoholism. He was a prototype of the citizen who distrusted his government, the idealist who rejected his religion, the man who hated his mother. He traveled to and lived in beautiful places with beautiful people.

What had that got to do with me?

The music began, as loudly as usual, and my mouth tasted dry and sour. I was suddenly tired from all that had happened that day.

Hemingway was the artist in search of the right word, and this last point was what counted the most, what I shared with my father. We were two readers who admired a writer's sentences.

Isn't it pretty to think so?

Sunday, July 24, 1960

"This would be a good year to release poets."

Ernest Hemingway, *Time* Magazine,
after receiving the Nobel Prize, 1954

This was our last full day in Cuba, so full that I had no time or energy for writing. What happened on this day and the next was so painful and exhausting that I didn't even try. By Wednesday July 27 I started and it took me that day and next to record all that happened as my husband and I left our home and separated.

On Sunday morning I was so low I could barely swallow. At dawn I wandered around the whole property, saying good-bye to it. The one spy I found was so startled he almost shot me.

When it was 9 am and Ernest still hadn't appeared, I went to wake him up and tell him I had breakfast served for him. I found him lying on the bed in all his clothes. He looked at the wall and did not say anything. I asked if I could help in any way. No response, so I took one of his painkillers and my headache eased away as I said goodbye to the rooms in the house.

I climbed up to my tower room and sat down to write, trying to remember the story of Rapunzel. Marriage with Ernest had never been a fairy tale. My hair had never been long enough. Seriously, he was never a prince. When he isn't behaving like the grandiose world-famous author, he is acting like an immature boy, a latter-day Huck Finn defiant of civilization. And he carries a life's weight of bad memories that conspire to lump together the many women he's been drawn to and make me a stand-in for them all. He's haunted most by his mother, the evil enchantress, but maybe she's been unfairly blamed as well.

I can't walk out on him when he's in this state and, to be honest, I'm also hanging in there for my inheritance. I figure I deserve a rich old age after he kills himself as he keeps saying he will. Okay, I obviously just decided that I no longer want this to be published. What the hell? I'll keep writing. I can always edit out the true bits that might impede my inheritance. Practical Mary strikes again.

Sunday? We don't attend church. Ernest converted to Roman Catholicism so that he could marry Pauline. Neither being a Catholic nor being married to Pauline lasted. If anyone ever needed forgiveness, it's me. I meant to write it's him. Forgiveness from whom? Somewhere in an argument or a laugh we lost what few beliefs we had. The simple-minded religion of the mid-West States, the superstitious Catholicism of Southern Europe, neither works. Ernest finds solace in the grace and skill of the bullfighter. I pretend when I am with him, but the corrida doesn't save my soul.

The one ecclesiastical type in Cuba that Ernest respects is the Baptist pastor. This old guy whose church is in a former circus building across the street from the government buildings has kept it open since the Revolution. How does a Baptist church survive in a Communist country? Well, the pastor was at university with Castro, and they shared a mission, to help the poor. He told Ernest, once, that Castro wanted a democracy, like in the States, but swung over to the Russians since they were the only ones willing to help him get rid of Batista. Ironic name. Ernest, in any political or religious discussion, looks to see who is helping the underdog. That's good enough for me.

David, however, now there's a believer who is a hazard to those around him. He sometimes comes by on a Sunday morning, ever confident that he will save our souls. I wonder if he knows that today is his last chance. A handsome young man from the Dominican Republic, he loves to tell us how he was saved by Jesus and how he, in turn, has saved thousands for Jesus. I don't talk to David because of his crazy religious mishmash. And I try to save my husband from this young man's demons. Endlessly fascinated by his stories, Ernest has, in turn, tried to save David.

Last week, David told us, he was called to return home to head up a mission to Haiti, the mission he'd fled a year ago. He's told us many times how he'd built up such a following for healing in Port-au-Prince that he attracted the Devil who alone had the power to kill him. At revival meetings he was able to see the Devil enter into people in the crowd, and when he shouted at those people, "Devil, be gone!" they would be exorcized of their temporary possession, and he would be safe. However, the Devil kept coming every week and the chief missionary, whose name, believe it or not, was Saul, had told David to stay away, that all these appearances of the Devil were scaring off the people.

God told David to fool the Devil by dressing in working clothes instead of his customary preaching suit. And when he did that, the Devil couldn't find him, and David was able to preach and heal hundreds. Still, Saul was afraid and sent him away for one year. This past week David had heard that the chief had died, the year was up, and the people were calling for him to lead them.

During his year in Cuba, every time David came by the house, Ernest asked him about his progress in learning to read and write. He encouraged David to seek an education because it could provide him a step out of poverty and voodooism, and he promised to pay David's expenses for him to study for three years in a Roman Catholic or Episcopal seminary in the States as soon as he had completed the prerequisite secondary education. I could tell this was too complicated, too slow, for David. He preferred the glamour of fighting his devils. I still wonder what his real name was.

Centuries ago, when they were kidnapped and brought to Cuba, the Africans that the whites enslaved kept their religions by disguising their gods as Christian saints with Christian stories. Generations later, David and the other islanders who called themselves Christians were still using Santeria customs, and the black magic of the vibrant African tradition was dangerous to someone as emotionally unbalanced as Ernest.

Today there was no escaping chaos. I could feel it coming. The sound of Ernest practically bustling from the main house to the foot of the tower made me groan to myself, but I went to the window when he called up. He and José Luis were going for a drink at the long bar at La Terraza in Cojimar followed by checking on the *Pilar* and maybe having a swim. Did I want to come? Juan would drive and René would pack a picnic lunch. They wanted a woman's company, and Valerie was out with Julio. David needed a lift to the port there to meet a fisherman who would take him back to Port-au-Prince. Of course José Luis was along for the ride.

My mood lifted. René was setting out breakfast, and so we sat down in the dining room under the blank stares of the stuffed wild animal heads from Africa. José Luis joined us, watching in silence as David, who had just arrived, ate with the concentration of someone who has known great hunger. Over the year he'd been living in Cuba, he had put on weight and no longer fit his one suit. I saw he was wearing Ernest's most expensive three-piece blue pinstripe.

Ernest had become euphoric, manic. "I'm under the protection of the Jesuits," he said with a laugh in his voice. "You know who they are?" David shook his head. "They're the brightest and the best of the Catholics. Superb academics." David looked at him in amazement.

"I don't see them doing a particularly good job of protecting you," I said.

David started to launch into his spiel about Jesus overcoming devils, but José Luis interrupted, pointing out that he'd just seen René carry our lunch out to the car. We piled into it and rolled down the windows.

It was one of those days of high wind, humidity and heat, the barometric pressure howling migraine. The *Pilar*, in dry dock for repairs, looked trapped and bruised. She would regain her dignity by the time of our return from Idaho. I felt myself relaxing as I imagined taking her out into the Gulf Stream, just Ernest and me.

But Ernest was not at peace. When we reached Cojimar he headed straight for the dock and turned back to call us to join him. He was shouting, over the crash of the waves, "Let's go swimming! Skinny dip time!"

José Luis looked at him as if disgusted. "This is not the Finca!" Usually José Luis was more tolerant.

Ernest walked slowly up to us and asked, with a dangerous calm, "What's the problem, Dr. Herrera?"

José Luis looked to me for help. I said, sounding anxious even to myself, "How about we come to your place? That's a private beach, isn't it? And why don't we have lunch here first?"

Ernest was muttering something. No one could hear him so we just headed into la Terraza. René opened the lunch basket, the others set out the food on a long table, and I ordered bottles of chilled beer and wine from the bar. We had so much fun, eating, drinking and telling stories. For once I was the centre of the group and Ernest was by himself, at the end of the table.

We were rushed, however, because we all wanted to see David safely onto his boat. It was a good-size fisherman's boat that could handle the rough waves. It would be a long ride across the top of the island, then south to Haiti. Our boy caught it just in time. Off David went from the pier, too faithful or inexperienced to recognize a dangerous ocean.

When he was out of sight, our mood was plummeting until I suggested we retrieve Ernest's Nobel Prize medal from El Santuario de Nuestra Señora de la Caridad del Cobre in the southeast of the island, near Santiago de Cuba. José Luis, who attempted to correct my pronunciation of those many words, gave up after one try. He had turned into a bit of a damper, saying that the priest in charge of El Cobre would make us say confessions and besides, it was too far to drive there and back in one day. Ernest said we should have driven David there in the first place because then he'd have had just a short boat ride to Port-Au-Prince. The rest of us were giggling for some reason and insisting that we head to the beach. René suggested that José Luis invite us to his home. It was just a short drive.

I will never in my life again see a beach as beautiful as that cove of white sand. It was a small dent in the north shore of the island whose beach stretched for miles in either direction: pure white sand, large waves rolling in and undertow rushing out, large Royal palm trees, their tops dipping in the gusty breeze. The breakers were so large they drowned

out our conversation. Just as well, we had nothing much
to say. Ernest started to strip off his clothes, and José Luis
insisted that we borrow bathing suits from his box of extras,
even though his wife was off at work, as were his children.
We were all eager to accommodate the rules of his house,
except for Ernest who was too big anyway to borrow trunks
from anyone.

We laughed as we jumped around in the knee-high water. It
was harder to keep standing as the minutes passed and the
waves grew more powerful. I could hear worry creep into
José Luis's voice. A wave toppled me like a doll, and Ernest
caught my arm as the undertow swept me out. René rushed
towards us, shouting at us to get out of the water. Ernest
looked at him, not comprehending, but I pulled at him
and he picked me up like a bride and carried me out of the
water, laughing. That was the second time he saved my life.
Perhaps he is my prince, after all.

We took showers because of the sand that was weighing
down our bathing suits and matting my hair. My nose had
been cleaned out by the salty water when I somersaulted.
Ernest was happily sunburned.

José Luis said he would call it a day and stay home to have
a nap before his wife and children came home. We headed
back to the Finca in silence, everything having been said.
Limp from having absorbed sun, waves and blowing sand,
we shared a close comraderie, except Ernest who stared out
the window of his passenger seat, moving only to fiddle
with the no-draft. Our silence, at first congenial, grew awkward and impatient. As we approached Havana he announced that he wanted to go to the US Embassy to explain
why he had changed his plans, and that we were not leaving
tomorrow.

Juan didn't say anything. He just turned at the next inter-section and drove us there. Ernest got out and opened my back door, so I went in with him. It felt like the employees were expecting him. The Ambassador addressed him impa-tiently, and that was the match that lit the fuse.

The next hour couldn't have been worse if the Devil himself had planned it. Yelling, threatening, pounding on desks, Ernest went berserk. Finally, I grabbed his arm and yelled at him to stop, and he swung around. For a second I thought he would hit me. Instead he seemed to deflate, and he shuf-fled past me, out the door, and back into the car. I followed, head held high, refusing to acknowledge the Ambassador's nervous offers of help in managing Ernest. When I reached the car, I formally thanked Juan and René for waiting, then got in and slammed the door, dignity intact.

The Ambassador, however, wasn't finished. As we all sat, trapped in the car, he knocked on my window and I lowered it, doing my best to hide my irritation. I was told to have my husband at the ferry the next morning half an hour before it was to leave. Two men from the Embassy would escort him to Key West and put him into the custody of the Florida Federal Bureau of Investigation. I stared straight ahead at the back of Ernest's motionless neck. Why were we just giv-ing in? Why should he be in custody?

Finally we were back at the Finca. My head was swimming with the several martinis I had swallowed as soon as we were dropped off. I found myself alone in the living room, packing a few things, not bothering to tidy up as I always had done when we left on trips. I just filled up our suitcases with random treasures, memories. A huge bruise appeared on my forehead after I ran into a doorway while heading for the bathroom.

It seemed like just a minute or two later that Ernest's voice was calling me to wake up, for Christ's sake, and there he was, obviously panicked, and me still drunk, sprawled on the couch. "What the hell are you doing here?" I can't remember who asked that.

Ernest and Valerie found their way back to the living room where he kept his bar precisely as he wanted it. She sat down, then got up from my chair and cheerily asked what I would like to drink. René mixed it, and someone said this was our farewell party. Julio and René were talking *sotto voce* in the doorway to the dining room.

Ernest told me, earnestly, so I would know it was a joke, that the bartenders from all the downtown bars would soon arrive with their best drinks already mixed for a celebratory taste-testing of Cuban rums.

"Yeah, sure," I slurred. "What time is it anyway?" No one answered.

Ernest said he hoped the FBI goons stalking the Finca were jealous. They deserved it for shadowing us instead of guarding us from Batista's thugs. Ernest was breathing heavily. In fact, he looked as if he didn't quite recognize me.

The next thing I knew it was dark outside. I was vaguely aware of Julio and René running towards us and Ernest telling them, "Listen, stay out of this. You aren't with me." I insisted that Valerie, Julio and René run for their rooms and pretend to be sleeping since it sounded like we were being invaded. Julio followed Valerie.

"Sh! Get in here!" I pulled Ernest into the kitchen, towards the back entrance to the house, and through the door that seemed to link the boot room and the bathroom, the door that no one ever noticed. "You've got to hide. In the bunker! It's you they're after!"

Ernest allowed himself to be led down the stairs to the secret room. No one knew about it since we alone had constructed a bomb shelter one weekend years ago. "Come on. We'll both sleep it off tonight."

We talked instead, and we were quiet when we heard the FBI men tossing things about upstairs, looking everywhere but where we were, and then going away. I whispered, "What are they doing here? We've said we'll get on the ferry." I reached for a bottle of water and drained it. Ernest did the same.

He said, "They're just strutting their power over us."

"We'll be more compliant if we're scared?"

"Something like that."

"So what's our plan of escape for tomorrow? Today."

"We wake only Juan and René at 3 am and they drive us to Cojimar. I spoke to Gregorio. He said he'll take us wherever we want to go in the *Pilar*."

"It's 4:30 now, and the *Pilar* is in dry dock."

Ernest looked at me as if he finally saw me, and I felt as if I finally loved him. "Are you ready to leave Cuba with me tomorrow?" he asked.

"Yes."

"So we won't fight the FBI boys?"

I shook my head.

He said, "We can still get your manuscript to *Life*. Where is it?"

I told him how I'd hidden it for days in the locked drawer of the desk up in the tower. I patted the bulk of the carbon copy still under my blouse but he didn't notice. My prince had passed out.

The high tower had crumbled.

Sunday, July 25, 2010

We would be lying together . . . and it was lovely in the nights
and if we could only touch each other we were happy. . . . I
wanted us to be married really because I worried about having
a child if I thought about it.

"There's no way to be married except by church or state. We
are married privately. You see, darling . . . I haven't any religion. . . . You're my religion."

Ernest Hemingway, *A Farewell to Arms*, 1929

Morning

The phone woke us at 7 am. My fury morphed into fear. Only
someone very upset could call a young couple in a holiday
hotel so early on a Sunday morning.

"Alf?"

"Yes, Aunt Sylvia. Are you two okay?" I was half asleep but
managed to be concerned. Beth flopped over and buried her
head under the pillow.

"Oh, yes, dear. I'm so glad you made it home safe. We heard
there was a theft at the Finca, and we came over to your hotel
but you didn't come home. Finally Federico told us you were
both fine but presumably sound asleep."

That was a speech of more words than I usually heard from
her in the course of a year. "You mean you were sitting downstairs waiting for us?"

Guilt, guilt, guilt. I had watched the flamenco dancers and
musicians setting up, then packed it in as the show began.

"Well, we won the weekly tango competition," said Aunt Sylvia.

"The tango competition?" I had no idea what she was talking about.

"During the flamenco show. Your uncle has taken tango lessons. I just hold on and keep my feet out of the way."

"Well, uh, congratulations. Listen, Aunt Sylvia, have you heard anything from my dad lately?"

"No, but the people taking care of him agreed to contact us if there's a change in his condition."

"Okay, I know."

"Alf," she paused and I groaned silently, "did you find the papers you were looking for?"

"Yes, the rest of Mary's article."

"That's good, dear. I won't ask where you got it."

"Can I help you in any way?" I couldn't figure out what she wanted to say.

"I just want you to know that there's a lot of buzz going around the diplomatic community." She paused and I imagined she was bemoaning the necessity of having to explain so much to me. "We're leaving for home this afternoon, dear. Be more careful, okay?"

"Like you're saying someone might be listening? Or watching? I don't think I know what you really mean."

"It's a rough place, dear, especially for foreigners, especially

for foreigners who take the road less traveled, if you will."
Why was she so awkward, so obscure? Was she hampered by
the presence of her husband?

"Are you okay, Aunt Sylvia? Do you want me to come and get
you? You can spend the day with us and go back tomorrow if
you like."

"Goodness, dear! What are you imagining? Give me a call
when you reach home tomorrow." And she hung up.

Right, regroup. I resolved to speak with my dad about his confusing sister. And I was hungry!

Beth rolled over. "What was she on about?"

"I don't know. She seems to be worried about our getting
mugged, because there's a lot of diplomatic buzz around."

"I thought they flew home yesterday."

"Well, it's today. I guess they stayed an extra day because of
us."

"We thought they were going home the day before yesterday
as well."

We contemplated my erratic relatives and their concerns. Beth
pronounced, "A tour of churches shouldn't be unsafe. Alicia
knows what's what." She swung out of bed. "Speaking of
which, we need to get a move on." She squinted at the clock
and muttered, "We need to go back to sleep."

"Aren't you going to ask what was in Mary's article?"

"Yeah!" She paused. "Sure, that beats sleeping. What did old
Mary have to say?"

I felt an instant's irritation, and swallowed it. "Well, the FBI clearly harassed them. I wonder if we are being watched. Ed's been implying it all week. He should know, working for CSIS and all."

She sat in the middle of the bed, her head tilted to one side. "Why don't we just get started with the day? Alicia said she's aiming to wait for us this morning after keeping us waiting every other day." There was obviously a satisfactory logic involved in that plan.

"How about breakfast first, like right now?"

"Good call. Give me a second." And in the time it took me to put the article in my chest pack and to make sure our passports and wallets were in the right pockets and purse, Beth was at the door, room key in one hand and plane tickets in the other. "I woke up wondering where our tickets were."

"Getting ready to go home?"

"For sure." Beth put both tickets safely in her purse.

The sun was shining brightly down through the skylight and down through the stairwell to the café where Fede was setting our favorite table for us.

During breakfast, Beth asked again what I'd learned from Manuscript A. I told her about the great sufferings of Ernest and Mary in their last week in Cuba, how cruel and miserable they both were.

"How do we make sure that we stay in love?" Beth asked.

I stared at her for a few seconds, unable to find a simple an-swer to her question, the one I had been asking myself. "My mom, I remember her yelling at my dad that he didn't work at their marriage enough." It occurred to me that I hadn't mentioned her to Beth all week.

And she'd noticed. "You almost never talk about your mother, ever. When did they break up?"

I wished I hadn't quoted my mother. "She just left him, us. I think all the secrets he had in his job absorbed him. Still, she was the one who was all about herself."

"What did she mean about working at their marriage?"

"I don't know, but Dad yelled something about if he had to work at their marriage it wasn't a marriage. I've always thought that he meant they weren't in love anymore."

We were both silent, looking at our food.

Beth asked, "Are we still in love?"

"I hope. I've been thinking about nothing else since . . . ."

"Since our quarrel?"

I nodded.

"Me, too," she said. "And this morning we're doing the religions tour and we don't exactly see eye to eye on this subject. Maybe you'd like to take the morning off and I can take the tour with Alicia."

"But I want to learn about what you care about. And you've spent days and days helping me with my Hemingway research." I was not at all interested in our last scheduled tour but, with yesterday's quarrel still fresh in my mind, I felt it was the least I could do. Plus, I wanted to protect her.

"I'm interested in Hemingway because you are. So isn't that better than your parents?"

"Right. My mom was just interested in herself, not in Dad."

"Or in you?"

I just nodded and mumbled through my toast. "I haven't seen her in twenty years."

"We don't need to repeat our parents' mistakes." Beth leaned towards me and took my hand.

I glanced up and saw my love's familiar, warm smile. "Right, we can figure this marriage thing out because we want to."

"Just no working at it. It's got to be fun and profound."

"Soul mates?" We smiled at each other, and I sensed that this conversation was our marriage ceremony.

What came after was the celebration. I started the jokes. "We can always come down here for a vacation and look up Paulo, the great counselor."

"We've got to get him hitched up with someone: 'Paulo Landers in Love.'"

"Love to all the Chaps?"

"What are you implying?" Beth responded.

I shrugged and continued, "What I got from Mary's article is that she and Hemingway sure didn't seem to love each other, or anyone else for that matter. It's amazing how he had so many loyal friends. Maybe they were friends because he was rich. Mary's only friend seemed to be the bottle. Still, she showed loyalty, if not love, for him in some bits of her article. Regret, as well, that such a great idealist was hounded and intimidated by his own country's government agents."

"So your dad's theory is right about the FBI?"

"I wouldn't call it a theory. Dad talked to Julio, and Castro, and Trudeau who was friends with Castro. What impressed Castro, according to my Dad, was that Trudeau claimed to be 'under the protection of the Jesuits,' as was Hemingway. And Dad was one of the first Hemingway scholars to post links to the FBI documents when they entered the public domain."

"Sorry."

"It's okay, I know." I drained the last of my coffee.

"Mary must have been lonely," Beth said. "It's too bad she had no friends in Cuba."

"But he did. I don't see how she could be so loyal for so long. Her obituary said he once threw red wine in her face at a dinner party. If he did that in public, he must have been worse in private."

"You're always as good to me in private as you are in public." Beth blew me a kiss.

"But Richard wasn't?"

"Not really," she murmured. I moved to hug her but stopped.

We sat before the remains of our breakfast until my pity for her turned into a familiar anger. She was watching me. I spoke carefully, "I love you. I just wish you'd never met him so he wouldn't have hurt you."

"I'm sorry. I shouldn't have told you about him."

"No, no. You need to talk about the jerk, get it out."

"But then you get hurt."

"That's okay, if it helps you." I was trying to reassure her.

"It does help me."

"We'll get through with him before long, right?"

"Right." She smiled, and I thought that what I loved most about her was her smile.

Then I had to ask, "What did he do to hurt you?" She looked as if I had slapped her, and I gasped, "I'm sorry! I shouldn't have asked that."

"No, it's okay, Alf." We sat in silence until she finally said, "Not today, okay?"

"Okay, when you're ready."

Another silence. "Two things."

"One?" I prompted.

"I'm going to miss Fede's breakfasts."

"And?"

"I wish everyone had a lover like you."

Fede joined us just then for coffee, and he talked about his dreams of becoming a Cuban diplomat abroad. He told us that my aunt and uncle were going to sponsor him as a student in International Studies in Toronto.

Was this code for spy school? I didn't know or want to know. He looked over our heads, along the street. "Here's Alicia sauntering in." He paused as we turned around. "Actually, more like dragging herself. What is bothering her?"

I smiled and said, "Nothing serious. Tell your cook we've enjoyed his meals, okay?" Tomorrow was the day for tips.

The biggest gap between Beth and me is that I have no religious background. While loving her makes me want to understand what draws her to spirituality, I still don't get it.

Her religion, the Anglican variety of Christianity, seems cultish to me. The Choral Eucharist services we've attended back home strike me as a confusing babble of ancient rituals and postmodern theologies. No better or worse than any other religion.

The secular world, in contrast, feels empty. There's nothing to turn to, no non-human being to worship, no God to create us in the first place, no love beyond the human. My mind was not convinced. How could Beth buy into the words of the service? What exactly would I have to say I believed in order to marry her? Or baptize our baby? I assumed that she, too, was putting off talking about these questions until we got home. One thing at a time.

Ernest Hemingway, brought up in his mother's Congregational church in Oak Park, Illinois, lost his faith early. He probably became negative about the whole church thing as part of his rejection of her. That was a no-brainer.

We walked with Alicia to the Roman Catholic Catedral de La Habana, San Cristóbal. She explained, "You probably think that this cathedral is named after the European explorer, yes?"

"Well, yes," I answered.

"San Cristóbal was a third-century Christian martyr, now a patron saint of travellers. The ashes of the explorer were kept in this baroque building for a century, and everyone has heard about him, not the saint. Today the San Cristóbal medal is often found hanging from a car's rear-view mirror."

I wondered if Cristóbal offered a safer trip than a voodoo doll or an insurance policy.

Alicia, meanwhile, seemed preoccupied, distracted by Beth's knowledgeable and perhaps intimidating questions. She left us to tour the cathedral on our own as she chatted with a young woman who looked pregnant. Was this contagious or what?

As Beth and I meandered around the interior of the cathedral, the Sunday Mass was in progress. Worshippers moved slowly from the pews to the high altar. We couldn't take communion, she told me, because we aren't baptized Roman Catholics. "Great PR," I muttered. "Why don't we just do it? They'd never know."

Beth shook her head, and I felt a familiar irritation. How could she not see how power-hungry and just plain weird traditional religions are? Still, I felt a great relief that she was not offended by my observations and questions. The church's power structure seemed designed to keep the laity in line. It was simply undemocratic.

The "miserable sinner" label seemed to me to be used by all-too-human priests to intimidate, to keep people in line. Like

the American government judging Hemingway to be "unA-
merican" in order to intimidate him and anyone watching.

I felt baffled by a wave of questions washing around and over
me like the wet cold squalls of an autumn windstorm. For an
instant I saw how depression was the disease of our time, was
primarily spiritual and secondarily psychological, was another
way of saying Conrad's horror, Camus' absurdity, Hemingway's irony and pity. Believers must feel comforted by the
Words of the God who creates order out of chaos. A comfort,
but a cop-out. I remained convinced that I was unconvinced.

What did that leave me? A human clinging to scientific integrity? "You look," said Beth, linking her arm under mine, "like
a man who has lost his best friend."

"You happy, I happy," I answered with a grin. A rational adult
might disparage the immaturity of that line but, truth to be
told, I often felt quite childish. And panicked at the prospect of
becoming a parent.

Woody Allen is my favorite theologian: "Not only is there no
God. Try getting a plumber on the weekends."

Holding hands, Beth and I went out of the church, looking
around for Alicia. We heard a commotion behind us. There,
coming along the street was a loud gang of masked kids, some
on stilts, some on foot, wearing multicolored ribbons, beating
on drums or shaking large rattles about their heads. All were
singing, shouting, mocking tourists and church-goers with
tricks, while begging for change. One boy, on the run, tried
to disappear in the midst of the group, and jostled another on
stilts, and that one, in struggling to stay upright, lunged out,
into the crowd. Screaming. Yelling. Chaos.

It was a great moment for pickpockets, but our inner pockets held and I pushed away the loose stilt that almost toppled onto Beth's head.

Beth yelled something, but I couldn't make it out. We shoved our way out of the crowd that was quickly dispersing as other tourists fled from the children. Under a tree where we could see the door to the cathedral where Alicia would presumably emerge before long, we drank from our water bottles and shared our amazement that the kids with stilts and drums we had assumed all week were having fun actually were begging by bullying.

Beth was indignant. "Here we are, Sunday morning, showing a genuine interest in their culture, their religion, and they're threatening us, trying to steal!"

I thought of Hemingway's glasses and the papers in my chest pack. "What have we stolen from them?" I asked. I thought also of all the waiters who had, over the week, been surly when we attempted to order in Spanish. "They hate us, you know," I said softly. "Especially José. Paulo seems forgiving. I don't know about Alicia."

"Not all tourists are bad," Beth objected.

"We're from a rich society, and they've got to be mad they don't have all the stuff they see on their televisions. And the thing is we try to understand and help them, but when things get rough we retreat into our safe houses, our gated communities. They have no insurance, no safety standards, no court of appeal."

"I don't feel the danger you're talking about."

"Maybe since you're the one with religion you feel safety, spiritual as well as physical? If you pray, doesn't God provide?"

"That's the God that the football player prays to before the game, not thinking that the quarterback on the other team is praying for the opposite result from the same God. Craziness!"

"What is your new God? If you're going to be religious, don't you need a God?" I pulled her onto the sidewalk so that we could evade the kids who were gathering around us. We no longer had any loose pesos to give them.

"That is what the leaders of all the world's religions are meeting to intuit, to pray for." Beth's voice sounded more confident.

"You mean the World Council of Churches?"

"No, that's just some Protestant churches, no mosques, temples or Roman Catholics."

"Then they need a new name!"

"There are all kinds of groups trying to get the religions of the world to work together for world peace."

"But to get to that new way of thinking will be a huge change for the average person in western societies, and even a bigger change for indigenous believers, right? Some in both groups are still having trouble with Copernicus and Darwin."

"That's what I want to find out about, the indigenous religions," Beth answered. "Let's see if we can find Alicia. She told me she has friends who will welcome us into a Santeria service as long as we agree not to take pictures or interrupt."

"Well, without our iPhones we're not taking pictures."

"Maybe I could do my thesis on the theology of John Lennon, or a comparison of Martin Luther King, Jr. and the Occupy Wall Street movement."

"Have you noticed," I asked, "that I'm studying the past and you're studying the future?" She looked at me, and raised one eyebrow. I shrugged. "I'm just saying."

We both laughed.

Alicia appeared and apologized for disappearing on us. She was not suffering from nausea as we had deduced. A friend of hers had taken her aside to let her know that Luis and Rosalía had been released with another warning from the police.

"I wish we'd photocopied the manuscript," I said.

"Let's go see the Santeria worship centre closest to here," Beth suggested to Alicia.

Alicia said, "No theft on Sundays. I will pray for you. Come with me, please." She seemed energetic, professional. "What do you know about Santeria?"

Beth answered, "Colonialism forced the people of the native traditions to lose or rearticulate their West African gods. Science, especially space travel and evolution, forced the people of the Abrahamic traditions to lose or rearticulate their God. Both processes are wrenching to the human psyche."

Alicia replied, "You're the first tourist I've heard connecting these two experiences. Can you say what a synergist religion is?"

"Ancient tribal gods disguised as Roman Catholic saints. Santeria is the main religion in Cuba although most Christian priests don't acknowledge that the West African customs have just gone underground. When the natives and the slaves did their ceremonies, the whites thought they were converted. The whites were wrong. An exception was Ernest Hemingway."

"What? Hemingway was into voodoo?" I really had thought this was a joke. Beth said nothing.

"Didn't you tell us Mary asked him to paint protective symbols on the cover of her manuscript?" Alicia asked.

"Yeah, but that could have been, like, a decoration." In my mind's eye I could see the top piece of paper with Hemingway's strange painting pulsing out.

"Do you remember what Mary wrote about his painting?" Beth asked.

I shook my head at first, then answered, "He had said he'd paint some ancient images on her cover page. He did it quickly and she was happy, saying they would scare off anyone who might think to steal her story."

"Did they believe in voodoo? That's the same thing as black magic, right?" Beth sounded really interested in Hemingway for the first time.

"More or less," Alicia answered. "That's the negative, like curses. I think that most Westerners are intrigued by indigenous religions. Some just like to play pretend. Do you not have shamans in Canada? And religious people from a Christian church doing a sweat lodge on a First Nations reservation?"

I remembered an incident. "Mary wrote about how Hemingway had become totally drunk as he lost all his cash betting at a cockfight. He claimed it was a Santeria ritual but she wasn't at all convinced."

"I have heard it said," replied Alicia, "that Hemingway took this very seriously and was, in fact, an initiate."

"Do you think this is true?" Beth asked.

"I don't know, but I have not heard of him attending any Christian services. Somehow they're not so interesting."

"That's for sure! 'Hemingway, the Voodoo Tourist.' That would be a good magazine title for you," I said to Beth.

Alicia had stopped walking. "Are you ready to see the Santiera place of worship?" We were standing at a wooden door once painted white, part of the wall along the sidewalk, not marked by any sign or symbol. We nodded and she said, "You must agree to say nothing, to keep total silence once we cross this threshold. Can you do this, Alf?" We nodded again. "And no pictures, or even pointing."

"Is this safe?" I asked, remembering my Aunt who would not be pleased.

"Of course," replied Alicia, somewhat impatiently. "Come on."

We entered into a dark hallway and were met by a large black man wearing only shorts. Around his neck were strings of large animal teeth, feathers, shells. "Follow him," Alicia said, as he headed up a spiral staircase into what looked like total darkness. Alicia patted my shoulder and up we went.

The room upstairs had windows open to the light and breeze and was, basically, a museum telling the history of the Yoruba people of West Africa who had been taken in slavery and brought by sailboat to work in the cotton and sugar plantations of the Caribbean islands.

There were tables around the room, each with a figure or doll of a Santiera spirit. On the wall was a piece of paper describing, in several languages, the role of the spirit. San Cristobal, for instance, became the saint associated with Aggayu, deliverer from bondage. I wondered how many Christian priests over the centuries were fooled by the ingenuity of the slaves and their descendants.

We walked around in silence. I read all the notes about each spirit, but I was also entranced by the eyes of the dolls that seemed to stare at me, neither malevolent nor benevolent, just staring. I wanted to run.

Beth was totally intrigued, I could tell by her expression. Alicia looked at me and smiled. What did that mean? I couldn't tell but I found a chair and sat down to wait for Beth. I was totally out of my depth in this place.

Afternoon

The second time we were robbed that week was just as scary as the first.

Beth was having a blast, jumping in the small waves, splashing around in the knee-deep water, exclaiming about the taste of salt and the miles of sandy beach stretching in both directions. I sounded like my grandfather, insisting that she put on more sunscreen and actually wear her light-weight, long-sleeved clothes and her hat and sit in the shade of the palm tree. After an hour of trying, I gave up and followed her example. I'd always wanted an island tan.

We'd come by taxi from Havana. Alicia had walked us back to the hotel, answering Beth's many questions, leaving us on our own to pick up our swimming gear, assuring us that we could buy hot dogs and pop or beer on the beach. We must have given the driver the wrong directions. This was a beautiful beach, for sure, but there was no concession stand in sight.

No problem, we could do without another meal. Beth was swimming again, laughing. "Come on, Alf," she shouted. The waves grew a little stronger and I thought of Mary being

grasped by the undertow, then by her husband. I put my chest
pack under our pile of clothes, leaned our backpack against
it and joined her. The only people in sight were some distant
soldiers patrolling the beach with their mammoth guns.

We had fun. She was more buoyant than I, and we played with
the baby, pretending to teach it to swim in its amniotic saline
sac.

"Let's visit my dad as soon as we can, okay?" I was eager to
tell him all about our adventures.

"What time do we land in Toronto?" Beth asked.

"I think it's 8:15 pm. We can go to my place and call him."

"Or you can do that. I've got to get home and get ready to
write a few essays." She sounded tired at the prospect.

"How about you just move in with me?"

"Yes, maybe. Who are those people?"

At first glance, I thought they were José and Alicia. I thought
they were taking off their shirts and pants and leaving them in
our pile of clothes.

"What are they doing?" Beth spoke quietly.

"Changing." But as I spoke I realized they were moving on,
still fully dressed and carrying a backpack. "That's José and
Alicia, right?" I blurted.

"Those are their clothes."

"What the hell!" I exploded. "Get out of our stuff!" It was my
backpack in the man's hand. He dropped it as I was pounding

out of the water, trying to run. We'd drifted east without noticing. I looked over my shoulder. Beth was not far behind me. "Stay in the water!" I yelled, already out of breath. "Where are the police guys?" A quick glance up and down the beach told me they'd disappeared.

Had they stolen the chest pack from the bag? They were running inland faster than I could, and other people were approaching. I couldn't leave Beth. A policeman materialized from behind a dune, his gun pointing at me.

I stopped running and put my hands up. Beth was walking slowly, both hands up, towards me.

"What are you after?" the soldier demanded, and it occurred to me that either he was in cahoots with the thieves or he thought I was somehow molesting Beth. I stood there, wordless, breathless.

Beth stood beside me. "We have been robbed by those two people." She pointed in the direction they had run.

"What people?"

Beth and I looked at each other. We couldn't get our friends in trouble. Alicia wouldn't do such a thing. I turned back to the soldier. "Maybe it was a joke by our friends."

"What kind of joke?" He gestured with his gun towards our belongings, and we headed over. This was one grumpy soldier.

I reached the pile of clothing and felt in my pockets. Passport and wallet were there. Beth stood close to me, watching as I dug under all the clothes and pulled out her backpack. She took it and found her passport, wallet and our plane tickets untouched.

"I think the only theft was from my backpack that they dropped under that tree."

"Okay, let's have a look. Señora, will you stay with your belongings here? I will watch you." He seemed to be relaxing, perhaps as he realized that this incident would not involve shooting.

A few strangers were passing along the beach, between the water and us. They looked like ordinary Cuban families. My shoulders were burning as I walked with the soldier to my backpack. As I knelt and picked it up, I swore silently. It was too light. I opened the bag and looked in. No chest pack.

The soldier was not interested in hearing about the theft. Beth tried to persuade him to organize the other soldiers to follow the suspects. She explained about Mary's manuscript, but he didn't understand, or he just didn't care. Perhaps he knew the robbers were now well out of the area, and perhaps he had other tourists and families to protect. For myself, I just felt discouraged.

José had told me I should give Mary's manuscript to him for safe-keeping, saying it was dangerous to leave it lying around on a beach. That's why we had taken turns swimming.

Beth flopped down beside me when the soldier moved on. We watched him meet two other soldiers and tell them something. They looked at us with minimal interest.

"Come on," I nudged Beth. "We need to get out of the sun. Let's get dressed and back to the city. We can get Alicia and José to help us."

"Alicia and José were the thieves," she muttered.

Evening

Our taxi ride back to town was glum. I wondered, were my
aunt and uncle right about our Cuban guides? Had it been
hopelessly naïve to assume that the third or fourth generation
of Hemingway's friends would instantly become our friends?
I had been thinking that Beth was easily fooled by religious
stories, but it wasn't that. Both of us had naively believed we
could find trustworthy friends so quickly.

I had actually thought I could get away with stealing from
Hemingway's island.

I looked out the taxi window, holding on to the sight of ordinary people enjoying their ordinary Sunday evening activities.
I would never achieve that level of social accomplishment at
this rate. I started to wish I had never come on this trip. Beth
was looking out her window as if determined not to throw up
or pass out. Her face was an odd shade of deep pink.

I got out of the taxi and paid the driver, then faced her. "Hey,
Beth, are you okay?" She nodded as the taxi pulled away. We
began to walk the last few blocks to our hotel up cobblestoned
streets too narrow for cars.

I reached to take her arm but we both flinched at the contact
because our skins were burning. "Listen, Beth, can you hear
me?"

"You're shouting in my face."

"Can you make it to the hotel?"

"Yes." Suddenly I knew what she needed. I swung my backpack down onto the street and pulled out a bottle, unscrewed it

and handed it to her. She needed help to drink. I looked around and spotted a bench under a tree in a little park, then gingerly helped her to it. The shade revived us, as did the water. I kept urging her to drink more, and more, and I did the same. I couldn't believe how nasty my thoughts had been just minutes before.

"I'm sorry, Beth."

"For what?" She actually looked puzzled.

I decided to tell her. "Being such a loser."

"As long as you don't lose me." She smiled, and I was flooded with gratitude.

"The theft doesn't matter." I could see our hotel. "We're almost there."

"I've got the worst headache ever!"

"You've got sun stroke or something. Let's see what Fede says. You've got to keep walking."

She staggered on, afraid to let me touch her to help her along. Fede was off duty, and his replacement, Max, handed me a sheet of instructions for the treatment of sunburn and sunstroke, then called a doctor. Max handed me the phone and I described Beth's condition. He explained to me that I was to keep her awake and that he would drop by in about an hour.

I coaxed her up the stairs, and we each took a cool shower from which we emerged a bright red. "We'll have to explain this to a dermatologist some day," Beth said.

She lay on our bed in her lightest nightgown, drinking bottles of water and peeing frequently. The doctor came by and checked her out, and I told him about how Beth had almost lost consciousness when we were walking up the street and how we were flying home to Canada in less than 24 hours. He said that shouldn't be a problem, and instead of giving me a prescription he handed me some pills to give her over the night.

He stood up and asked me, "So, you are fine?"

"Yes, and I'm the redhead. But she was out in the ocean longer."

"And she's pregnant."

Beth exclaimed, "I didn't know that it's showing already!"

"The baby won't be hurt from too much sun?" I blurted.

"No problem," he replied. "How about I listen to the heartbeat and see if he or she is excited?" He put his stethoscope in place, listened, moved it to another spot on Beth's belly, listened, and straightened up. "The baby has a strong heartbeat," he said.

"That's good to hear," she said.

"Your first pregnancy?" he asked Beth.

"Yes," we both answered.

"You'll be fine. The two of you look like you will be great parents."

I had to check. "These pills, they're okay for the baby?"

The doctor smiled and nodded, then hustled off as doctors hustle off in Canada, and soon the pills took effect and I watched as Beth slept. Every hour I woke her up and checked how she was doing.

Just as I was starting to nod off, she woke up hungry. We had not eaten anything at the beach.

We searched through our laundry to find clothes loose enough to avoid irritating our sunburns, and not too smelly. It was late and we hoped the kitchen would still serve us. Descending the staircase, we looked around. Yes, people were still eating. The flamenco musicians were leaving.

Our table was taken. The massive back of the man was what I saw first. He looked like Uncle Ed. I turned to flee back upstairs. Aunt Sylvia was leaning sideways in order to be seen by us. Beth was already waving back. I swore under my breath. Beth whispered, "They're waiting for us. Be nice." What choice did I have?

"Hi, Sylvia! Hi, Ed!" As we reached the table, I told myself that we needed to encourage them to see us as competent adults. "Don't get up." I put my hand on his shoulder as Ed started to rise. He gratefully sank back. The chair creaked. "You had tickets to fly home yesterday. Aunt Sylvia said you were going home today. What's going on?" That was a mistake, asking a question.

Ed stared at me. He looked irritated. I felt like a ten-year-old. One who has just thrown a baseball through a large window.

Aunt Sylvia whispered, "Dear, your Uncle Ed's quick action saved your friend's life this afternoon. You should feel grateful."

"What friend? What happened?" They both made shushing gestures. How annoying!

Uncle Ed looked like I was his migraine. "As you know, I work for CSIS. One of my fields is Cuba, and my agent, who shall remain nameless, has been watching one of your friends, Luis Ventura. We were able to follow the movements of Luis and his wife today."

"Luis is not my friend," I said. Uncle Ed winced. I whispered, "Is Fede your spy?"

Ed looked at the wall behind my head, then faced me, painfully embarrassed. "Can you keep this information quiet?"

"Do Beth and I need to know it?" I wanted him to know my priority was her.

"Not really, but the FBI is trailing you. If you want to get Mary's manuscript back, you need to know who has it."

"You mean the FBI has been following us?" I spluttered. "I thought you were warning us all week about pickpockets and thieves."

I nodded to Beth, and she nodded as well, her eyes huge. Surely he was stringing me a line. I whispered, "Luis stole the manuscript from my bag when we were swimming, you think?"

He nodded.

I continued, "Because the FBI doesn't want the truth of their mistreatment of Hemingway to get out?"

He nodded again.

"How did Luis know I had it?"

Beth whispered defiantly, "Jose and Alicia wouldn't betray us!"

"Probably not."

I demanded, "Then who did?"

Ed looked at his wife, and back at us. "Do not trust anyone except Fede. We'll see that you get safely onto the plane."

"What about Mary's manuscript?"

"We're working on it."

I thought for a minute. "All these years, you've been a spy runner?" I had never got control of this conversation. It was all I could do to keep my voice down. He nodded, and a wisp of suspicion lingered in my mind.

"How did you save Luis and Rosalía?" put in Beth.

"They got a bit greedy," he said. "They failed to hand over the manuscript to the FBI as agreed. They are in great danger, so they're probably in hiding." His eyes kept flicking around the room. His voice was so low I wasn't sure I got what he was saying. "That's all I will tell you. Hopefully we can keep this quiet."

Aunt Sylvia, as Beth says, tends to fly in from left field. "Did you know that the RCMP has a file on Northrop Frye?"

"No!" I was astounded. "Professor Frye?"

This conversation was bewildering me, but the pattern was familiar. Aunt Sylvia distracted us to take the heat off Uncle Ed.

"What for?" Beth sounded equally shocked. "He was an ordained minister from New Brunswick, the shyest intellectual, the greatest intellectual, in Canadian history! I've heard so many stories about him at Vic, but nothing about anything remotely illegal."

Aunt Sylvia said, "I know what you mean. He was the gentlest introvert I've ever met. I had the honor of hosting him at a grad dinner once."

"You did? Was my dad there?"

"No, it was in the Vic women's residences and I was the Annesley Hall student rep."

"Was Mrs. Frye there?"

"Yes, chatting away at the other end of the long table. But he, well, I realized that the most useful thing I could do for the universe at that moment was to shut up and leave him to his great thoughts."

"Wow, cool!" I sighed, amazed to realize that Aunt Sylvia had a life.

Beth said, "I haven't thought about college in a week, but now I can't wait to get home."

"So the FBI is not the only police that spies on its people," said Uncle Ed, determined to make his point. "Frye was an anti-Vietnam protester, nothing spectacular, but for a leading egghead to take a stance against American foreign policy was risky back then."

"I took several of his courses, and not once did he mention current politics," said Aunt Sylvia.

Finally they stood to leave, probably having waited until Beth looked tired enough that we wouldn't be likely to go out and get into any more danger or mischief for the night.

"What are you planning to do tomorrow?" Uncle Ed glared at me as he pushed in his chair and drew his critical mass to its most ponderous posture.

"Nothing, just get ourselves to the airport in lots of time."

I lied.

Monday, July 25, 1960

"You are rated as politically unreliable," said the President. [J. F. Kennedy]

"You haven't checked M.I.5," said I.

Mary Hemingway, *How It Was*, 1976

I woke up sometime before dawn and listened: the house was quiet, except for Ernest's snoring. I had to pack my manuscript. I hadn't written most of what happened Sunday, but I was too tired, too worried, to sit down at the typewriter. So much for Mary Hemingway, intrepid reporter.

I dragged myself to my room in the tower and wondered how my life had led me here and how it would take me back to the States that day. I'd lost all my energy. Ernest, it finally occurred to me, had never cared what I'd written. I shoved the typewriter away, folded my arms on the desk, lowered my head and fell asleep.

When Valerie called up to ask if I would join them for a drink, I almost threw something at her, so cheerily messing up our lives. Self-restraint worked. I had no reason to blame her. I put on a capable face, but couldn't stop my stomach from growling. Alcohol in the morning makes me feel wretched.

I folded the top copy of what I'd written into the chest pack for Ernest to wear, and I stuffed the carbon copy that no-one else knew existed into the bottom of my carryall.

Bloody Mary, the drink he named in my honor, or to belittle me. Equal parts nutrition, violence and ironic religion. Off

I went to see if a bloody Mary would make Mary feel any
bloody better.

I longed to be having breakfast on the trail in Idaho. The
horses would be resting after a one-hour ride into the foot-
hills, and our friends, Lloyd and Tillie, would be building a
small fire and stirring buttermilk and eggs into my home-
made pancake mix. I would be warming the maple syrup.
We'd soon eat and mount up again, Ernest always pushing
on to the next place, his rifle always loaded.

As I descended the tower, I felt calm for the first time in
months. What was going to happen would happen. And I'd
type it up in Key West. The storm had passed; our ferry ride
would be smooth.

A few hours later, we were cleaned up, moving, thanks to
coffee, squinting in the sunshine as we watched our suitcases go into Juan's trunk. We patted the ceiba's trunk
and walked around it silently and then got into the car. I
watched the Finca Vigía until it was out of sight. Ernest was
staring straight ahead. Valerie was squashed in the front
seat between Julio and Juan.

"You have the manuscript?" I asked, and he nodded, patting the old chest pack that he'd dragged around the world.
"Here is your passport," I said before he could ask for it.
Still, he didn't know about the carbon copy in the bottom of
my purse.

"Did you get your papers validated?" He was talking to
Valerie.

She turned her head, and sighed. "I forgot to."

"What's this about?" I had a bad feeling.

Ernest panicked, within an instant. "But you told me you would! How are you going to get off the island?"

And here I'd thought keeping legal papers in order was my job. Julio obviously thought that taking care of Valerie was his territory, since he spoke to her quietly, and she turned away from us.

I shrugged at Ernest, indicating that she was an adult and that we were cut out of the problem. He sat, head shaking back and forth, muttering to himself.

At the ferry dock, José Luis was waiting for us, and as he opened the back door of our car for me, I realized the value of his selfless and courtly presence that had reassured and challenged me all those years when we both put so much energy into caring for Ernest. And now we were saying goodbye.

I had to trust that, if we were unable to take my story through customs, René, always faithful, unlike Ernest or me, would keep the top copy hidden in the agreed-upon place, the hollowed-out interior of the fourth volume of that ancient series. Hopefully no one will toss those musty tomes!

"They'll kill him."

"I guess they will."

I had been silently repeating these words all morning. Now they clicked into my consciousness. I seemed to be watching the group of us in slow motion. Events unfolded in awkward silence.

Usually, when the great Hemingway leaves a country there's at least a small crowd. Today, there was no one except our people, Thacker and his two back-up thugs, and Castro's men another perimeter beyond them. Valerie stayed close to me, suddenly distraught. I disengaged myself enough from her clinging to see that Ernest had removed the chest pack from under his shirt. Why? I was furious.

It was lying on his lap as he did up his shirt buttons. The two American agents swarmed René as he opened our suitcases for their inspection. Julio went over to Ernest and knelt in front of him, apparently asking if he were feeling alright while he received the manuscript, rolled it so that it looked for all the world like a newspaper still folded in a waterproof pouch. With this beneath his arm, he stood up and smiled at Valerie as one of her nightgowns nearly fell off the inspection table. I grabbed her arm to stop her from charging at the FBI men. My heart was pounding. Ernest, still showing no interest in the activities around him, sat staring at his empty hands.

The spooks were soon finished with our suitcases. As they stepped aside for a low-voiced consultation with Thacker, Julio turned his back to them and nodded at René whose backpack was now open. They both approached Ernest who heavily pulled himself up to shake hands and say goodbye. He embraced them, both at once, and for an instant I witnessed once again the powerful Hemingway bear hug. René, his face wet with tears, his backpack no longer empty, nodded to me, then Valerie, and shook hands with Julio.

José Luis who had stood quietly beside Ernest since our arrival, next spoke to him and they embraced like brothers. Polite to the end, he smiled at René and then left us. Meanwhile Julio drew everyone's attention to his embrace of the now-sobbing Valerie. Without having once spoken to us, his mission accomplished, Thacker turned and led his men out, and the Cubans followed. Julio alone watched us board the ferry, and I felt that he was the only one whose tears were not true.

Crossing to Key West, I sat on the open deck at the back of the ferry, by myself, clinging to my purse. Valerie, whose papers had not been checked, cheered herself up by trying to engage Ernest in conversation. He sat motionless, unresponsive. I felt impatient: why did he have to suffer so much over everything?

On the dock in Key West, I almost gave my carbon copy to the *Life* editor who turned up there. I had seen him talking on the dock with a man I thought was one of the spooks. What if giving it to him would be giving it to the FBI? I had thought that *Life* was on our side. I paused. Unsure, exhausted, I said and did nothing. I couldn't talk with Ernest because he was in his own world, and he had betrayed me. Valerie was busy with our suitcases and her loss of Julio.

My husband and I parted company without saying goodbye, he going to Spain and I to our Key West home.

I decided that no one would see the carbon copy, for a while, at least. I am the only person who knows of the existence of the carbon and of the pages that belong at the end of the manuscript put in the tower by René.

I will travel to New York, settle into my apartment, and enjoy my old friends. *Life* will pressure me to give them whatever Ernest or I wrote during our last week in Cuba, but I have decided that it is too blunt to be good for my business as Mrs. Hemingway. As well, I have agreed to rejoin him in Idaho, and I need all my strength for that.

When we arrived at the waiting room of the Havana ferry I was still hoping that Ernest cared about what I had written. By the time I reached Key West I could see that Ernest wanted my story left unpublished. Writing was his territory. Had he read any of my manuscript? Had he bothered? Whether he had or had not, he did not import my story into the States.

If leaving the original manuscript in Cuba was Ernest's rejection of me, keeping the carbon copy was my revenge.

How I regret that parting.

Monday, July 26, 2010

It is silly not to hope, he thought. Besides I believe it is a sin.
Do not think about sin, he thought. There are enough problems
now without sin. Also I have no understanding of it.

Ernest Hemingway, The Old Man and the Sea, 1952

Morning

I was in a funk, awake and grumpy. All my schemes had led
to this, my chest pack empty, folded neatly in my still-empty
carry-on. As a Hemingway researcher, I had discovered nothing meaningful. I had no document to show my dad.

A better story starred Beth and our baby, priority one, where
happiness lives. We'd been happy together for most of the
week. That was success. Plus we'd survived morning sickness,
arguments, adventures and misunderstandings. My dad, no
word from him, so that was good. Maybe his heart would beat
long enough to gladden at the sight of our baby. Maybe his
heart would be strong enough that he could dance at our wedding. Probably not.

I lugged my large suitcase and my carry-on down the stairs.
My plan had been that the latter would contain Hemingway
treasures, in particular, Mary's manuscript. All I had was a lot
of sweaty laundry in the large one.

Once these non-treasures were parked in Fede's storage area,
I went to talk with him. He wasn't in sight. Gingerly I opened
the front door of the hotel and stepped out into the predawn
empty street. The air, still and warm, smelled only of the sea.

I pictured the harbor just a few blocks away, the natural wonder we had barely glanced at in our hectic seven days. It was

so close by but we had ignored it in our fevered search for a
document of crazy people long dead. My search.

I wanted to see the harbor with its fishermen probably coming
in already, but I couldn't just leave the hotel open, couldn't
just leave Beth alone, with no explanation for my disappear-
ance if she chanced to wake up.

A man walked by me, a construction worker by the look of
him. He seemed half asleep, content with where he was going.
So was I. With Beth, I could hope. I shook off my morning fog
and went inside to awaken her.

As she showered and dressed I took her luggage down and
paid our bill, 70% mine and the rest hers as we had agreed seeing that it was my thesis we were researching. I longed to be
a family sharing one bank account, and for a minute I imagined the house we would buy in Bloor Village or the Annex,
or further out from the university, whatever we could afford.
Probably way out. My knowledge of real estate was minimal,
but that too would change.

I reached the breakfast table at the same time as Beth. She had
been thanking the cook for all the meals we had enjoyed over
the week and joking that he had our taste buds totally figured
out.

"Let's eat," I said, lifting my glass of orange juice. "Cheers!"

"Blessings!" Beth responded. "Our last breakfast here."

"'The Last Breakfast.' That would be a good title for a painting, not a magazine article. Maybe we'll come back some day
when you won't have morning sickness for most of the week."

"I'll remember how our breakfasts here were cooked and

served and maybe every Saturday morning we can pretend we are here and have orange juice, eggs, bacon, toast and coffee, like these." She paused. "Then Sunday mornings would be Canadian, with maple syrup and pancakes, frozen blueberries and yogurt."

This fantasy was uncharacteristically detailed for Beth. Was she wishing we could stay a few more days? I could relate to that, but I was also eager to see my dad and tell him all about the Finca. He would be interested, even if I had only the copies of a few pages.

Right then and there the best idea ever popped into my head. I put on an imitation of Beth's zine headline voice: "Talented Journalist takes on Religion Column."

"Who's the journalist?" Beth asked, intrigued.

"You are." I was so excited. "Listen, you know how you've talked about a whole range of thesis topics, and how none of them grabs you, really?"

"Yes?"

"And what game have you been playing at least as long as I have known you?"

Beth looked at me, puzzled. "What game?"

"Making up headlines for magazine articles."

"What's that got to do with my choosing a thesis topic?"

"Well, it tells me that you should stay with world religions as your field but also take some journalism courses to help you become a freelance magazine writer on the topic of world religions or a weekly columnist for a newspaper. Or both.

Book reviews, interviews, that sort of thing."

She was staring over my head, thinking. I waited for what felt like ages, then added, "Remember the speaker you dragged me out to see at your church, just before Christmas? You could have written a great article on that guy."

"I think so," she began tentatively. "Thanks." She scratched her jawline and winced at the sunburn.

"What?" I was trying not to show my impatience.

"I don't know. Thanks, thanks. You've just caught me by surprise."

"Doesn't the Saturday *Globe* have a regular Religions article?"

"I know it used to."

"But now I bet it's just waiting for you to come along. Young people are getting curious about religion now, don't you think?"

"Okay, okay, I hear you. Why don't we get going over to Alicia's place? We can talk on the plane?"

That was a bit weird. Probably one of her dumb former boyfriends was a journalist or something.

We cleaned off our table and stacked our dishes on the shelf by the entrance to the kitchen. Max said that Fede had called him in because of family business, but Fede had asked him to tell us that he would see us before we left Cuba. Beth and I looked at each other, puzzled, then shrugged.

The morning so far had the enchanted sense of enough time. We decided that we would walk over to the harbor, and that was a good decision because we enjoyed the sight if not the smell of the sea and of the fishermen's catches. Over the squawking of the seagulls we played with the idea of buying a whole fish and mailing it to Uncle Ed in Ottawa.

We meandered back through the market and spent our last spare cash buying Beth a purse made of woven sea grass and me a white shirt like all the men wore. At the hotel, I changed into my new *guayabera*, and we said goodbye to Max.

It crossed my mind that our suitcases weren't locked and that we should probably check them for drugs. Since that dreary thought had apparently not occurred to Beth, I decided to trust the situation and move on. For once, Paulo would have approved of me. We began pulling our luggage, bumping over the uneven paving stones, to Alicia's where we'd agreed to say goodbye to our friends at mid-morning.

As we knocked at her family's door I was conscious of a huge feeling of regret that we were leaving this third and fourth generation Hemingway community. Alicia opened the door, laughing at our surprised expressions—from behind her came a roar of people partying.

Alicia reached to help Beth with her suitcase, nodding to show me where to put mine. When she opened her arms to hug me, since I was closest to her, Beth and I stepped back. Both talking at once, we explained about our sunburns.

"So at least you had a fun time at the beach!" Alicia exclaimed. "What happened with your manuscript? José has not been home all night. He just came in the door with a whole lot of people."

Beth interrupted her, and I could see that this is what she had been thinking of all morning. "Our, well, Alf's, actually, Mary Hemingway's manuscript was stolen, when we were both in the ocean, by two people." She stopped, and Alicia, puzzled, turned to me.

"The two people," I slowly said, "looked like . ...."

"Like Luis and Rosalía?" asked Alicia. "You are thinking I will be insulted that our friends would steal from our friends?" I nodded. I could not just come out and say the thieves had looked like her and her husband. She continued, "That must be why José has been out overnight. Come in! You must listen."

She turned and we followed, sharing a worried shrug with each other and stopping in the doorway to the kitchen to greet her mother. In the dining room, squeezed around the table, were José, Julio, Aunt Sylvia and Uncle Edmond, Paulo and Fede. What were they all doing here? They looked triumphant but disheveled as they all talked at once and Alicia's father served them coffee and pastries.

When we came through the door the group cheered and applauded. Aunt Sylvia called for them to be quiet. Uncle Edmond got to his feet, and I could tell he was about to take command of the situation when she motioned to him to sit down. He actually sat down.

Aunt Sylvia gestured to Julio, and he nodded to her as he stood. José found seats for Alicia and her mother as well as for Beth and me.

Finally, there was silence and Julio spoke up. "Beth and Alf, you have no idea what's been happening around you this past week. It does not concern you directly. Indeed, it involves half a century of Cuban rivalries and Cuban politics. You have been the match that lit the fuse, if you will, of an explosion of espionage activities." He paused, as if to make sure we appreciated his extended metaphor.

I gave him a thumb's up and he continued. "The sale of Hemingway artifacts on the black market, controlled by Luis Ventura and his wife, Rosalía, has become quite lucrative. Some Americans interests were using the Venturas to further their own agenda. Now the people of Cuba have taken over, and Hemingway's belongings will be kept, guarded, in the museum we know as the Finca Vigía."

I tried to interject, but Julio smiled. "I will explain, though, about yesterday's theft. Luis and Rosalía, wearing clothes like José's red agency shirt and Alicia's long red scarf, stole Mary Hemingway's complete manuscript. We caught them in a trap that had another, more important, purpose."

José stood up quickly. Julio looked at him in surprise, but sat down without objection. I was so frustrated! José had interrupted just at the wrong time. Where was the manuscript, and what was the spy maneuver about?

José began, "My grandfather asked me to say that we, the Fuentes family, rightfully deserve to run the business of the Hemingway estate in Cuba. Alicia and I, along with my grandfather, have been meeting this past week with representatives of the government, including Julio. We have committed to maintaining the Finca property in a modern, scientific and legal manner. Alicia will be the curator of the library."

He gestured to the pile on the table. I could see the Vatican medical book and the Nobel Prize. "We are beginning by returning numerous items. Paulo, the picture, please."

Paulo opened a paper bag on the table before him, and there was the photo he had taken from Mary's dresser. He added it to the pile.

José continued, "Alf?"

"Yes?"

"Hemingway's glasses, please." Damn. Fair enough.

I pulled them out of the front pocket of my carry-on and put them on my nose. "What Hemingway glasses?" Everyone laughed, and I removed them and put them beside Paulo's picture. At that moment I noticed an iPhone and a Blackberry on the table. "Are those ours?" I asked José.

"Yes, they were returned to us," said José, but he did not elaborate.

I decided it was best not to comment further about the phones. Beth looked at me, and I shrugged. She picked them both up and checked that they were ours and still functional.

I asked, "Doesn't the Nobel Prize belong at el Cobre?" José nodded and sighed.

I blurted, "Do you have Mary's manuscript?"

"This gringo is always in a rush!" said José.

José nodded at Julio and sat down. So did I. Beth asked, "Why is it that so many people have kept saying they were leaving the island but have yet to do so?" Good old Change-the-topic-at-the-wrong-moment-Beth!

Paulo waved at her. "I made up a story about being in jail because I wanted to start a new life in Canada. Then I realized that I could not run to sanctuary without a legitimate story. I needed the truth to tell officials of the Canadian government's refugee agency, and Beth's parents. I did not have a true story, so I came back."

Uncle Ed said, "We stayed because we felt the need to take

care of our feckless nephew and his beautiful but equally careless fiancée."

Beth interrupted, "We only pretend to be clueless."

Aunt Sylvia exclaimed, "That's what I've been saying all
along!" Once again I was puzzled. Why had she married him?

Uncle Ed ignored them both. "The other reason we stayed on a
few more days is that there has been a lot of espionage activity
stirred up by the discovery of Mary's manuscript. The FBI file
on Hemingway was active until her death. Now it's hot again.
There are those in the States who would do anything to derail
negotiations to remove the American embargo that has been so
harmful to Cuba for so long."

"The FBI is behind the theft on the beach?" I spluttered. "Do
they now have Mary's manuscript? Are you saying Luis and
Rosalía were stealing it for the FBI, not just the black market?"

Ed glared at me again. "I have already explained to you that
these two no-goods double-crossed the FBI by keeping the
manuscript. We had the Cuban police toss them in jail to save
their butts. This, in turn, gave the FBI the impression that
CSIS was not totally on side. Canada has always irritated the
US by maintaining diplomatic and trade relationships with
Cuba. Now, we are assisting the arrival in September of a
delegation of high-level international negotiators led, in ac-
cordance with the Castro brothers' request, by former American President Jimmy Carter. Carter had, by the way, asked for
your father to be translator as he had been for Fidel Castro and
Carter at Trudeau's funeral."

"I wish I could translate!" I burst out.

"Well, your friend Alicia will have the honor," Julio replied.

"Now, before our esteemed Canadian diplomats, Sylvia and Edmond, leave to catch their flight to Ottawa, I want to thank them, especially for stopping the FBI infiltration of our preparations for the Carter visit. The FBI has been very busy, this last month or two, using Luis, Rosalía, and their gang to disrupt our talks with the Americans. The Venturas have been funded by the far-right groups in both Cuba and Florida who have always thought Hemingway was a Communist and who certainly did not want Hemingway's problems with the FBI to come to light. So," he nodded at my aunt and uncle, "thank you for helping the people of Cuba and the reputation of our great author."

Before Ed could pull himself to his feet, José was on his, again uncharacteristically interrupting his guest. "Alicia and I will always be grateful to Mr. Edmond and Ms. Sylvia for changing our lives for the better. I am sorry, I do not even know your last name, sir."

Ed smiled smugly. He and his wife simultaneously opened their mouths to speak, but José and Alicia stopped them by shaking their hands. This evolved into hugs during which José removed a cylinder of wrapped-up papers from Ed's jacket pocket. I saw José swing his arm around his back, for Julio to slip the newspaper-like rolls into the inside pocket of his jacket.

Uncle Ed shouted, "Goodbye, everyone! We're now really going home. We're getting too old to be rescuing you youngsters from your underhanded heroics."

"Speak for yourself!" laughed Aunt Sylvia. She turned to Julio as if he had asked her a question. "José is driving us to the airport. Otherwise we will miss yet another flight." Julio gave her a hug that she obviously enjoyed. Go, girl!

I followed them to the front door to wave them off. Did Luis know that his taxi had become José's car? The crowded room to which I wanted to return was way too hot for a jacket so I removed mine and folded it into my carry-on. What a relief!

Everyone was chatting at full volume when I re-entered the living room and sat down again beside Beth. I whispered in her ear, "The manuscript is in Julio's pocket!"

"We're getting closer," she said, and handed me the iPhone.

"Do you want to know what happened last night?" asked Paulo.

Paulo told us how, the night before, he, Fede and José had watched until the Cuban security forces had arrested Luis and Rosalía in their home, charging them with theft and black marketeering. When this drama had moved to the police station, our friends had entered the house and easily discovered, on the floor of the bedroom closet, the red scarf and shirt. The manuscript was nowhere to be found.

"Why did my uncle have the papers?" I asked.

"Early this morning he met with the Cuban security police and talked them into giving the papers to him," Julio said. "He can be very persuasive. And he insisted on keeping them, saying that Mary's manuscript was more important to various government agencies than to your thesis."

Alicia looked indignant. "Ed is the thief, stealing the manuscript from Alf who did all the work of finding it!"

I said, "Thanks for your support, Alicia, but I guess I stole the papers in the first place."

Paulo said, "Everyone has been stealing from Hemingway."

I said to Julio, "I would, nevertheless, like to take the original manuscript home to show my father." I looked around and everyone was nodding.

"Yes," said Julio, "Tomás and I agreed that you can take the original home, show it to your dad and colleagues, make copies, and return it to the Finca via the diplomatic pouch of your wonderful aunt and uncle." He took the papers out of his pocket and held them on his lap.

Beth was smiling at me. I said to Julio, "Excellent! Thank you. I'll make sure that it is returned to you." I started to reach towards the papers, and he raised his hand to stop me.

Julio said, "One more thing. There is some background information from sources you have not thought enough about, it seems to me."

I was more than a little irritated, but I managed the polite tone that José always uses to address older people. "What do you mean, sir?"

"I mean you have not yet asked for the observations of some participants. For example, I remember discussing this manuscript with Hemingway."

"What?" I exploded. "I mean, pardon?"

"Just listen," Julio answered. "On Monday, July 25, 1960, Hemingway gave me his last order as my employer. He called me over to where he was sitting in the ferry dock waiting room.

"He said, 'Take this manuscript to Tomás. I do not want it published by an American magazine, or hidden at the Finca.' He slowly but powerfully thrust the document into my hands. 'Tell him to bury it.'

"'Where?' I spluttered.

"'In Cuba--where the story took place. Tomás will do this. It is your job to tell Tomás to give it to someone you can trust to keep it from the FBI, someone who will publish it when the time is right.'

"'But Papa,' I replied. 'Señora Mary has written it. It is hers.'

"'No, it is about me.' He paused to catch his breath. 'I no longer consider her as my wife. Tell the publisher I wrote it, pretending to be Miss Mary.' He paused, then spoke sarcastically, 'Say I was experimenting with the feminine narrative voice.'

"'But Papa,' I insisted. 'Señora Mary worked so hard on it.'

"He looked at me as if from a great distance. 'That is why I do not ask you to burn it.' He dropped his head and stared at his empty hands."

Julio paused, and I stood beside him, not knowing how to react. He continued. "I will write down this conversation and any other information that might be relevant to your thesis. I will also collect the impressions of Valerie, René and Tomás for you."

For a few seconds Julio looked very old, unable to move, looking at the papers in his hands, then gently placing them in mine. "Here, take what Mary wrote."

"Thank you so much, sir!" I was almost in tears.

"You must realize, my friend, that this original document was lost and buried until you and your father undertook to find it. You must have the honor to publish it."

The room had become silent during that conversation and suddenly everyone was congratulating me. I made my way to the luggage and put Mary's papers and my iPhone into the carry-on.

Before long my friends were back into their conversation that seemed to be focused on trying to understand why the Americans had imposed their embargo of Cuba in the first place. Fede said he was delighted by the prospect of American tourists being free to travel to Cuba. "The word, 'American'," he told us, "translates into 'money' in the Cuban language."

"Cuba is the only place on the planet that Americans have been forbidden, by their own government, to travel to," said Paulo. "I have heard that rich Americans have for years got around the law by flying to Cuba through Montreal or Mexico."

"The land of the free," I thought out loud. "That's the myth."

"Silence, please," called Alicia. "I have a present for our newly-engaged friends." She gave me what felt like a wrapped book on top of a notebook.

It was my copy of *Hemingway en Cuba* by Yuri Paporov. Yeah, that was kind of funny. Underneath it was a notebook. "Open it," said Alicia. "This is the real present."

"Just imagine," laughed Beth, "a student given something to read."

I smiled at her and flipped through it. "You've translated the first chapter on the Finca. That's amazing! Thank you, Alicia!" Sunburn or no sunburn, I was happy to give her a big hug.

Julio spoke up. "It is now my turn for applause. I have almost finished negotiating with Paporov's original publishing company to put out the book in English, translated by our dear

Alicia. She has already started, as you see."

Beth said, "Alicia could subtitle the book, *I Spy*." Alicia and her Spanish-speaking friends looked puzzled. One thing I was looking forward to about getting back to our world was that people would get our jokes.

I paused, thinking that I'd never have as good a moment to ask one more pressing question. "Alicia, can you tell me—you've never come out and said—what happened?" She looked away from me. "Excuse me if this is a rude question."

Beth interrupted. "Maybe this isn't a good time."

I gave her what I hoped was a reassuring smile, swallowed one more time, and took the plunge. "Alicia, you have said, or at least hinted, that you know the location of the Hemingway manuscripts that Hadley is believed to have lost. Correct?"

"Oh, yes," Alicia answered, "but that does not mean I will tell you, my friend."

Fede nodded. "Well put, Alicia. This Canadian cannot know every Hemingway secret."

Alicia looked at me as if to dare me to discredit her "secret." I saw her, then, as a clever young beauty using her wits to make a living by intriguing tourists with Hemingway lore.

I stood up and smiled. "Can anyone give us a ride to the airport?"

"I will," spoke up Julio. I had been hoping for someone a little younger, in other words, faster, in other words, José. There he was, back from one run to the airport and now packing our suitcases and my carry-on into the trunk of the car. I thanked Julio for his offer. He looked relieved.

We stood around, chatting, reluctant to part, until suddenly there was little time. José herded Beth, Alicia and me into the car. Beth and I checked our passports, tickets and wallets. Too choked up to speak, we waved goodbye to the friends still standing at the front door. Off we went.

I was eager to show Beth the billboard that looked like Dr. T.J. Eckleburg, but it didn't appear. Perhaps it was visible only on the road from the airport towards Havana.

Our arrival at the airport was a blur of farewells, line-ups and tears. Inside, I was laughing.

Afternoon

By the time we approached the security check, our friends were out of sight. We put our shoes, belts, wallets, phones, boarding passes, and so on into the grey plastic bins. I put the carry-on with its precious papers onto the black conveyor belt. No problems.

Well, Beth's bra must have had some metal in it because she received a quick check with a bored-looking woman's magic wand. We chatted with relief as we collected our belongings.

Where was my carry-on?

"Keep moving, sir. Out of the way." A guard had a grip on one of my elbows. Beth was being propelled in the same direction.

"I don't have my carry-on yet!" I protested. I opened my mouth to yell the same complaint again when there it was, being handed from one guard to the next and finally to me.

I shook off the restraining hand and saw Beth unhindered coming to stand beside me. I did not hurry off, as they seemed to expect I would. Instead, I laid the leather bag on an empty table at the end of the conveyor belt and, slowly, unzipped it. I held my breath and opened it. There was the pile of pages. But the top cover was not a painting. Beth looked in and gasped. It was a blank. I ruffled down the pile. All the pages were blank.

I stood there, staring, breathless. I looked around, and there were no tourists in the security room any longer. Only a handful of intent-looking men, some speaking English, some Spanish, most in uniform, most wearing a handgun.

"Just take the bag, Alf!" Beth whispered. I could hear the fear in her voice. "We'll miss our plane."

I yelled, "Someone in this room has stolen my valuable papers! Right now I'm calling the Canadian Embassy." I pulled my iPhone from my pocket.

A security guard gave my wrist a chop and caught the phone as I dropped it. "Electronic devices must be turned off at this point, sir." He turned my iPhone off and tossed it into the open carry-on. "You need to catch your plane now." He gave me a shove. "Run!" I grabbed the handles of the carry-on.

"Which way?" demanded Beth.

He waved to a doorway, and we started walking. Behind us, he shouted again, "Run!"

We walked quickly. The doorway led to a corner which, when we turned it, led to a huge, empty hallway. All the walls were white and the floor grey. Silence. No one in sight.

Beth grabbed my arm. "Come on, Alf! There are some people down the corridor on the right."

She pulled me into a run. We sprinted to the two people. Above their heads, on the screen, I saw that the plane was scheduled to have left one minute before.

Beth held out her passport and boarding pass. "We are on this flight."

"I am sorry, ma'am, but we have given your seats to standby passengers." The woman speaking to us did not look sorry.

"Listen!" I didn't have a chance to unload all my anger on her. The airline rep picked up the phone, asked a question, then repeated her question.

Meanwhile, I was telling her assistant that our luggage was on the plane. She reassured me that we could find it waiting for us in Toronto. We could simply take the next flight.

I noticed two men stomping out of the gateway towards us. One of the women at the counter said to us, "Go! Those two men are the standbys. The pilot has bumped them off so you can have your original seats. He's not happy wasting all this time bringing the plane back to get you."

"Thank you!" Beth said to her. "Come on, Alf!" She took off running.

I resolutely and stupidly walked as she sprinted down the ramp and into the plane, carry-on still in one hand and passport and boarding pass in the other. By the time I stepped onto the plane, Beth was waving to me from halfway back. The passengers glared at us, as if the few minutes' delay was our fault. The airplane was already backing away from the terminal.

On the plane, I sat immobile and silent. Beth was staring out the innocent window. It struck me that if I could cheer up Beth I might cheer up myself. I feigned a casual tone. "We never made it to the fifth floor of the Ambos Mundos. And we didn't have a mojito at the Bodeguita del medio. We've got to come back some day soon."

Beth turned and glared at me. Her voice was low. "I can't believe all that hassle! Why did you argue with armed guards?"

"Getting and losing, we lay waste our powers."

"I don't want to hear another literary quotation that doesn't communicate what you mean for the rest of my life!"

I sighed. Over the past seven days I had discovered, through trial and error, that the best solution was to keep my mouth shut until Beth cooled down enough to hear the words, "I'm sorry." As if all her moods were my fault. I told myself not to fight. Besides, we were on a plane.

I waited as long as I could. "Beth, I'm sorry for all the hassles I got you into this week."

She half-smiled. "This week was more exciting than most people get at a resort."

"That's what I love about you!" I picked her hand off her knee and kissed her fingertips.

"Umm! You've learned some sophisticated moves." Actually, I had been wondering what Julio would have done in this situation.

I asked, "Remember what Julio said about Hemingway's instructions?"

"You mean his chauvinist garbage? How come you have chosen to spend your career studying such a person?"

What kind of insult was that? "I have an answer, but right now I can't explain it." I thought about what I wished I were doing--reading through the entire seven sections of Mary's manuscript again and writing my dissertation.

I had to make up with Beth. The question was, how?

"Beth, can you forgive me?"

"For what?" She looked calmer now.

"How about for a lifetime's mistakes, like an advance, because I never want to hurt you."

"Well, you don't hurt me, sweetheart. I get frustrated too quickly."

"Maybe we'll mellow with age."

We grinned at the thought.

Beth lifted my hand to kiss the inside of my wrist. "I love you."

"I love you, too."

Evening

When the plane came to a stop and the seatbelt sign went off at the Pearson Airport in Toronto, Beth switched on her Blackberry that promptly rang. My iPhone remained silent with the blank papers in the carry-on bag at my feet.

Beth laughed as she opened the text message. "It's from José!" She muttered to herself, "This is bizarre. He's the one who substituted the blank pages." She looked at me and read aloud. "u were so tense saying goodbye u missed what happened open attachments sorry to steal from u but fbi was closing in." Beth passed me the Blackberry and I saw the icons of seven documents, starting with "Tuesday."

Hoping, holding my breath, I clicked on the doc called "Tuesday" and there it was, a scan of the voodoo image on the cover page of Mary's manuscript. Still seated, I looked at Beth, and I read aloud the opening words of the story of two people who never learned how to love beyond selfish pretense and hopeless longing:

And if you ask how I regret that parting?
It is like the flowers falling at Spring's end,
confused, whirled in a tangle.
What is the use of talking! And there is no end of talking--
There is no end of things in the heart.

The End

Sources

A lifetime of reading Hemingway's works and works about Hemingway has contributed to the plot, characters, setting and themes of our story.

We must acknowledge many critical studies of Hemingway, too numerous to specify, and the supportive community of Hemingway scholars and aficionados to be found in the Hemingway Society, the Michigan Hemingway Society and the Hemingway Society of Oak Park, along with the enthusiastic participants checking in regularly to the Hemingway Listserve.

Particularly, the following biographical works inspired details and incidents for our novel:

Lloyd R. Arnold, *High on the Wild with Hemingway*; Carlos Baker, *Ernest Hemingway: A Life Story*; James D. Brasch, *That Other Hemingway*; James D. Brasch & Joseph Sigman, *Hemingway's Library*; Norberto Fuentes, *Hemingway in Cuba*; Gregory Hemingway, *Papa*; Hilary Hemingway, *Hemingway in Cuba*; John Hemingway, *Strange Tribe*; Mary Hemingway, *How It Was*; Valerie Hemingway, *Running with the Bulls*; Christopher Ondaatje, *Hemingway in Africa*; Yuri Paporov, *Hemingway en Cuba*; Michael Reynolds, *The Final Years*, René and Raúl Villarreal, *Hemingway's Cuban Son*.

Acknowledgements

For this book, Wayne provided the expertise of a Hemingway aficionado and Eleanor made up the story. It has been a labor of love on many levels, and the first major project of their retirement.

Thanks to Hilary Caters and Elizabeth Hibbert of Caters Design Group for their creative expertise in designing both the book and its website and for their professionalism in guiding the authors through the challenges of self-publication. Larry Williamson is both a friend and a passionate photographer whose work can be found online. Lulu.com is our practical printing company. Please visit:

     Catersdesigngroup.com

     LarryWilliamson.ca

     Lulu.com

So many family members and friends have given us their wholehearted support and devoted such great interest to the content and process of this book. They humored our probably incessant talk about Hemingway, read and discussed his novels, and eventually proofread and made suggestions for the story's characters and events. Some of these generous volunteers of time and talents were Katherine, John, Alexa, Kim, James, Fran, Sandy, Frances, Isabel, Eduardo, Terry and Rob K.

This book is a loving tribute to Hemingway scholar, Dr. James D. Brasch, Wayne's undergraduate mentor at McMaster University, Masters supervisor, doctoral inspiration and guide, and consistently our most challenging commentator. The story of his 1970's correspondence with Mary Hemingway that led to his adventurous trip to investigate the Finca Vigía library sparked questions that set this ultimately very different plot in motion.

Biographies

Dr. Eleanor Johnston and her husband, the Rev. Dr. Wayne
Fraser, have retired from teaching and administrative work in
private schools in the Niagara Region of Canada. Eleanor is
a committed chorister in the Anglican churches where Wayne
preaches the exciting new ideas of progressive theologians.
They share the joys of loving each other and their children and
grandchildren, reading and writing, dancing, bird-watching,
gardening and enjoying music and feasts of Niagara food and
wines with family and friends. Eleanor has published regular articles for *The Niagara Anglican*, self-published a birth
mystery and a self-help book for parents and teachers, created
a book for young children about death, and written a multi-
media dramatization about the 1945 East Prussian massacre
that she and Wayne produced and performed together.